LIVING ON THE EDGE

Amor Vincit Omnia

For my wife June

Without her this wouldn't have been possible.

I would like to thank my family for their support.

And my four kids, Sam, Katy, Jess and Holly,

And my two step kids Sam and Matt,

For generally being a pain in the arse.

ANDY KEYWORTH

2018

CHAPTER ONE

Through an alcoholic haze, I hear my phone ringing. Fumbling, I finally find it and glance at the screen. Donna! My brother's crazy ex-wife! I let it click onto voicemail, it's never good news on the rare occasions she rings me, so I need to be a little more compos mentis before I even listen to the voicemail. I throw on shorts and a t-shirt and wander downstairs for my morning caffeine and nicotine hits. While the machine is chugging away making my espresso, I glance at my watch, seven fifteen and the morning sun is shining on my Gloucestershire village, which has been my new home for the last week and the cause of my hangover. Last night I wandered into the Red Lion, my new local pub, and integrated myself by about five pints too many!

As the two pronged attack of caffeine and nicotine work their magic on my hangover I contemplate listening to my voicemail.

My brother, Rob and Donna split up two years ago, shortly before I got out of Sheffield to escape my old life. I have led a nomadic life since then and have spoken to neither of them since I left. Not that I spoke to that crazy bitch Donna much anyway. I dial voicemail and wait for it to connect.

"Dan no one has seen Rob in over two weeks….. since…. since they nearly caught up with you in Shropshire…… thought you ought to know."

Hmm not what I was expecting! Rob often disappears for a couple of weeks, usually re-appearing with a new woman in tow! So there is no need to panic yet.

'They' are the Steel Riders MC. A nasty bunch into everything that is illegal, I used to be part of them and Rob still is, well as far as I'm aware. I got out two years ago, when I decided to sort out my life. Hitting forty and still causing mayhem with a bike gang suddenly didn't seem so appealing. So I just took off. They've looked for me a few times, but I just keep moving. I sold the Harley and bought an old Jag, I'm now trying to settle into village life. I'm renting a tiny cottage in a place called Hanley, a small Gloucestershire village. It has two pubs, a newsagents and a post office, what more do you need? The only thing I'm missing from my old life is a motorbike, and not a bloody Harley! I spent far too many years rattling around on those piles of shite because they are what 'bad assed bikers' are supposed to ride! What utter bollocks, they are slow, ill handling, under braked tractors. Actually, that's probably a slur on tractors, better be nice to tractors as there are a lot of them around here.

Anyway the need for two wheels is calling, and what better way to find a bike locally than to wander over to the Red Lion for a few pints and ask around.

On my way over a couple of the youngsters shout and wave hello, I can't remember their names but they know mine. One downside to moving here is I'm the 'new bloke', so everyone knows my name, but I have a whole village of names to remember. I follow the two lads through the door and see someone whose name I do remember. Molly is behind the bar, I remember her from last night. She is tall, pretty and curvy, with a wicked sense of humour, just how I like them. Best of all she pulls a bloody good pint. "A pint of your finest Abbot please Molly, and I'm looking to buy a motorbike any suggestions on who I should ask to point me in the right direction?"

Molly puts my pint on the bar, obviously deep in thought, then she suddenly flashes me a smile "Allun the Welsh bloke you were having a laugh with last night, he's a biker, that's three pounds please," she puts my money in the till then turns back to me, "he'll be in soon, if you get one you'll have to take me out on it," she winks at me.

"Deal, is it the bloke in leather or the thought of something big, powerful and throbbing between your legs?" I flirt back and get a beer mat in my face for my trouble, as she wanders off to serve someone else, laughing loudly.

"Hello boyo," Allun has just walked in, I wouldn't have remembered his name but for Molly.

"Hi mate, just the man. I'm looking for a bike and I believe you're the man to talk to, do you want a pint?"

"Carling please Dan, tell me what you're after and we'll see if we can sort you out."

Three hours and several pints later we have a plan. Allun's mate runs a bike shop in Gloucester, so we are going there tomorrow to see what he's got in, with the promise of a discount, brilliant! It's time to head back to the bar and flirt with Molly some more.

"Has he sorted you out? Or do you need me to?" Molly asks, beating me to the flirting.

"I'm going to look tomorrow so you may get a ride then," I quip back, "In the meantime another pint please, it would be rude not to, especially as the scenery is so good around here."

CHAPTER TWO

The bloody phone wakes me again! This is getting to be like 'Groundhog Day'. I let it click onto voicemail and clamber out of bed. Sitting in the kitchen with my espresso and cigarette, my phone rings again, I glance at the screen, its Allun, so I answer it.
"Morning boyo, polish your helmet and I'll pick you up in an hour, OK?" he chuckles.
After promising I would be ready, I wonder how he can be so cheerful after the amount he drank last night. Remembering my wakeup call I dial my voicemail.
"Dan it's me Rob, I'm in the shit big time, we need to meet, I'll let you know where and when, OK bro take it easy."
Well at least my brother's running true to form, I wonder what it is this time. Money, pissed off husbands, or unwanted pregnancies are the usual causes. Oh well, at least he's still breathing so it can't be that bad.
I wander upstairs to get my leathers and helmet. I know we give women a hard time about matching shoes and handbags but when it comes to bike gear we are no better. After browsing my collection of leathers, I go for a classic black Alpinestars two piece with matching black Shoei helmet and black visor. It's like a woman's little black dress, it goes with anything, as I have no idea what colour bike I'm going to get.

Ten minutes later I'm climbing onto the back of Allun's Ducati Multistrada, and bracing as he wheelies it up the road.
He's been giving it some stick all the way, nipping in and out of traffic, and then thrashing it when the road clears, with me hanging on grimly, he certainly doesn't hang about. As we approach Gloucester, and the traffic starts to build, I start to relax and take in the scenery. A moment later I lurch backwards, scrabbling for a grip as Allun wheelies past a line of cars! I settle on hooking my feet under his armpits to stop myself being flung off the back. He holds the wheelie expertly, cackling loudly inside his helmet. Eventually he crashes the front wheel back to earth catapulting me forward so I

head-butt the back of his helmet, he pins the throttle again still cackling.

Pulling up outside Castle Motorcycles, in Gloucester, I climb off the bike and glare at Allun, lighting a cigarette to calm my frayed nerves.

"Bastard," I curse him.

"What," he tries to protest his innocence as he heads inside to find his mate, Gareth. I have a look through the window while I'm smoking and something immediately catches my eye. A gleaming black Triumph Speed Triple, up for £4,700, perfect. I wander inside, Allun introduces me to Gareth, telling me they were both at school together.

"Do you boys want a coffee?" Gareth asks.

"Go on then, white with one sugar," Allun answers.

"What about you Dan?"

"Cheers just black for me please."

Gareth returns with two mugs and asks me if there's anything I fancy. I wander over to the Speed Triple, "any chance of a spin on this?"

"I'll get you the keys, take it for a good thrash and I'll work out a good price for when you get back."

I watch as Gareth pushes the Triumph out of the showroom, "there you go enjoy."

I put on my helmet and gloves thumb the starter and ease it out of the car park. I'm gently getting a feel for it as I head out of town. I peel off onto a twisty B-road, drop it into second, line it up and fire it through the bend, snick up to third as the front wheel starts to come up and charge towards the next bend, hard on the brakes, back into second and tip it in. At the apex I nail the throttle, the back tyre scrabbles for grip, the front goes light and we rocket forward. This is why I love bikes I think to myself as I feel a grin spreading from ear to ear.

An hour later I'm parked outside Castle Motorcycles, with the Triumph pinging gently from the heat of a good thrashing. Gareth comes out, "any good?"

"Depends on the price" I answer, already knowing I'll pay the screen price if necessary.

"Four grand, as Allun says you're a good bloke."

"Card OK? Don't wrap it I'll take it with me," I break into a grin as I go inside to pay.

It's now six o'clock and we have just pulled up outside the Red Lion. We've had a mental afternoon thrashing around Welsh backroads at highly illegal speeds, and are now heading for a well-deserved pint. "Did you see the look on that blokes face as we both wheelied past?" Allun asks, "priceless."

"Carling darling?" I ask as I head off to the bar to order the beer and flirt with Molly. "An Abbot and a Carling please gorgeous and a ride if you're still up for it?" I'm feeling brave as the adrenaline is still coursing through my veins from the manic ride we've just had.

"Cheeky bugger, well it depends what you've got I'm not the kind of girl who'll just get on anything," retorts Molly.

"Come and have a look and see what you think its outside." I pick up the pints and go outside, with Molly following.

"If it's the black one you're on! I don't like the beak thing on the red one."

"Cheeky sod," retorts Allun before necking his pint, then turning to me, "I'm off, we'll have to do that again soon." I grin and nod as he puts on his helmet, fires up the Duke and shoots off up the road, leaving me with Molly.

"So when do you fancy it?" I smile.

"Tomorrow is good; I've got staff in all day."

"You own the place?" I ask.

"I do indeed, it's all mine," Molly winks at me.

"Tomorrow it is then, I'm gonna take my bike home and climb out of my leathers, then I'll be back for a few beers and your phone number." I put on my helmet and fire up my new bike and head home.

What a day, I've bought a cracking new bike and found out Molly owns a pub! She is fast becoming my perfect woman.

CHAPTER THREE

Groundhog Day again! After being woken by my phone and letting it go to voicemail I jump in the shower. It rings again while I'm sat in the kitchen with my coffee, this time it's Molly.

"What time today? I thought we could go for lunch somewhere, if you like? And I hope you've got some bike gear for me as I haven't got any," all without taking a breath.

"Yeah that's fine come over about eleven, and I'll sort some gear out for you, lunch is on me but you can choose where I don't really know my way around here yet," I reply.

"See you at eleven," she says with a twinkle in her voice and hangs up.

I drain my coffee and dial voicemail.

"Dan, its Rob, on Saturday I'll meet you in the café on Barmouth seafront where we used to go as kids, just text to let me know you're coming OK."

Well only three days till Rob's mystery problem is solved, time to get ready for a ride with the luscious Molly.

At bang on eleven the doorbell goes, I open it to be greeted by Molly in her finest bike gear, tight jeans, low cut top and high heeled boots. "I didn't know Sidi made them with heels!" I quip and smile at the confusion on her face, "come in and try on what I've got." After an entertaining half hour watching her wriggle in and out of various items of my bike clothing, we settle on a blue and white Alpinestars jacket and matching blue Shoei helmet.

"It'll have to do as you haven't got anything in pink," she laughs as I follow her out of the door, admiring her cheeky wiggle as we go.

We are sitting in the Old Coach House in Molden, having both polished off a steak, laughing and swapping ever more improbable stories. Molly suddenly stands up grabs my t-shirt and kisses me.

"Mmm good kisser as well, I've wanted to do that ever since you first walked into my pub." Bloody hell! This village life keeps getting better and better.

"Right then, don't piss me about or I'll punch you and have you chased out of town! Is that OK?"

I mull things over and ask, "What time do you have to be back?"
"Not till eight why?"
"Well I'd better fill you in on my life story, it could take a while!"
I sit back in my chair and begin. "It started when my brother and I were teenagers. We've both always been into bikes and always ridden together, but we both felt we needed to find other people to ride with, so we joined a bike club. The first couple of years were fine, we had ride outs and went to watch racing. We rode fast and had fun, it all changed when the decision was made to go to a few rallies, the first was the Bulldog Bash. We ended up spending the entire weekend with a gang of Hells Angels, generally getting drunk and behaving badly, a few of the older guys seemed to get on with the Angels really well.

Within a month our bike club had turned into the Steel Riders MC, and was closely affiliated to the Hells Angels. Two years and many battles later, we were a fully-fledged bike gang. We dealt drugs, extorted money, ran protection rackets and anything else that paid well for little or no effort. Our clubhouse was bought outright and became the centre of our operations and a no go area for anyone not invited.

Rob and I settled into the life easily, both giving up our jobs, and we all rode the ubiquitous Harley's. Although they were tuned I still found them slow and ill handling and hankered after the sports bikes we grew up with. Our gang tattoo, a devil slaying an angel became a thing of terror for anyone that crossed us. We fought battles with other gangs, each victory bringing more spoils. Our early affiliation with the Hells Angels paid dividends as they basically left us to it as long as we didn't step on their toes. Soon we ran the criminal activities across all of South Yorkshire from our Sheffield base.

By the time I was in my late thirties I had been living the life for fifteen years, and beginning to think there must be something better. I tried to talk to Rob about it but he was having none of it. So on my fortieth birthday, a snowy January day, I packed up my Harley and took off. I moved around quiet a lot then, as I often heard rumours that the gang was looking for me, because I had too much information about their activities and I'd helped myself to the petty cash when I left. I had my gang tattoo covered up and now have a leaping tiger on my back in its place. I sold the Harley and moved on; eventually I got my head straight and finally settled down here, the rest of which you know. I have a fair chunk of money saved but I will eventually have to get a job, at the moment though I have no idea what I want to do, I'll figure that part out when the time comes I suppose."

Finally, I look up at Molly, to see her with her chin resting on her hands gazing intently at me.

"Well I'd say your first worry would be not getting bored! It's hardly exciting round here!" Molly laughs.

"I think I can find enough to keep me entertained" I laugh. "Right if you've finished scoffing let's get back on the bike and you can show me some more of the local sights." I flash Molly a grin and wander off to the bar to pay, while she heads off to the toilets.

CHAPTER FOUR

The great thing about riding bikes is the sense of being in your surroundings rather than just passing through. Lush green fields blur past on both sides as I gun the bike forwards, then stroking the front brake tip it in for a long sweeping left hander, then hard on the brakes for a nadgery right- left- right, before I open it up on the straight. I glance in the mirrors to see Molly, her eyes are flashing and from the crinkles it looks like she's grinning. I reach back and stroke her leg affectionately. Life is good! I ease the throttle instead of pinning it enjoying the scenery and the closeness of Molly as she gently grips my hips.

We roll back into the village and I pull up outside the Red Lion. Molly hops off the bike and removes her helmet. I feel my heart flutter as she shakes out her hair, smiling softly.

"Are you coming in?" she asks.

"I'm gonna take the bike home first, I'll only be five minutes so pull me a pint of your finest beer which will taste even better when it's pulled by the best barmaid in the world," I quip cheesily. I pull away turn left and head home. After parking the bike and dropping off my helmet and jacket I head back to the pub whistling softly.

I wander into the pub and slide onto the stool by the bar next to Molly, my arm gently encircling her waist, as I reach for my pint, "What's a girl like you doing in a nice place like this?" I banter and receive an elbow in the ribs for my trouble.

"Watch it!"

I glance around the bar to see who else is in what is fast becoming my second home. I spot Allun coming in and shout a greeting. "Ey up how's it going?"

"Alright boyo what's new?"

"Just thinking, what you up to Saturday?"

"Nothing what you got planned?"

"A trip to Barmouth to meet my brother, you fancy it?"

"What time you leaving?" Another bloody question instead of an answer, what is it with these Welsh boys?

"About half eight" I answer.

"See you at your place then, I take it we aren't going to be hanging about, so leathers then?"

"Sounds good, we can fuel up at the petrol station up the road then crack on should be a good ride the forecast is good and you'll like my brother." So the date is made for three day's time and I've got company when I find out what shit Rob is in this time."

I turn my focus back to Molly, "Did you enjoy the bike then?"

"I did when can we do it again?"

"How about on Sunday after I get back from Barmouth?"

"Great, but does that mean you're staying in Barmouth overnight?"

"I don't know, it all depends what kind of shit my brother is in this time and how long it takes to sort out but hopefully not, now how about another pint?" Molly slides off her stool, and slinks behind the bar, while I admire her arse.

"Not a bad view is it?" grins Allun, "I've a feeling you like her a lot more than you're letting on."

"To be honest with you mate it was the last thing I was looking for but between you and me I'm hooked."

"Oooh shall I start looking for a hat for the wedding then?" he grins.

"Bugger off! Just get yourself a new helmet for that big fat ginger head of yours," we banter. Allun is fast becoming my new best mate, and to be honest you would be hard pushed to find one better. He's big, tough and honest, with a great line in banter, not bad for a Welsh bloke.

There's a stir at the door, its Russel. "Quick you lot come and have a look at this you'll never believe it." We all rush to the door to see what has amazed him. Allun barges past me, with Molly following closely behind. Allun stops outside then starts to laugh, "Russel, you twat." I crane my neck trying to look past Allun, eventually giving up and pushing past him to find out what is so amazing. And there it is the most amazing thing to happen in Hanley this year! There is a duck followed by five ducklings waddling down the street. They get to the door and stop.

"How sweet," proclaims Molly, as she bends down to pet the duck.

"You're supposed to be looking at the ducks not her arse you perv!" grins Allun.

"Fuck off!" I retort, "Russel, you really need to get out more, when was the last time you left Hanley?"

"1993, I got the bus to Bristol but I didn't like it, there were too many cars and too many people I didn't know so I haven't bothered since."

"Bumpkin," I mutter to myself under my breath.

"Right let's get back to our beer and put some tunes on the jukebox," exclaims Allun. So we all trudge inside to quench our thirsts.

"What do you want on?" shouts Allun from the jukebox in the back bar.

"Anything but bloody Tom Jones again," I shout back.

Allun comes back smiling as Gary Glitter 'Do you wanna be in my Gang' comes on the jukebox.

"Not funny," I retort huffily.

"Actually it is quite funny," laughs Molly.

"Well I suppose it's not bad for a Welshman," I say giving in with a grin.

"So how was your ride today Molly?"

"Ooh it was fantastic, he was very gentle at first then built up faster and faster," she enthuses.

"Was that before or after you went out on the bike?" he banters.

"Watch it, I'm not that kind of girl," she looks at me shyly, and then grins, "well maybe," we all laugh together.

"I'll leave you boys to it," Molly gets up and heads back behind the bar.

"So she likes the bike as well then it's all looking good."

"It definitely is mate I'll get some more beer same again?"

"Cheers mate."

After a couple more pints Allun announces, "I'm off mate I'll catch up with you soon."

"No worries see you later," I reply and head back to the corner of the bar, where I sit and watch Molly pulling pints. Eventually she calls time and the bar stars to empty, leaving just myself and Molly.

"Give me a hand to tidy up then, and I might let you stay over," Molly winks at me alluringly.

An hour later, after some passionate lovemaking, I'm laying cuddling Molly, musing over what trouble Rob could be in this time. Oh well I'll find out soon enough and at least I'll have Allun as back up. I start to drift gently off to sleep.

CHAPTER FIVE

Half past five Saturday morning brings daylight, as I open my eyes and spend a few moments looking at the gorgeous Molly. Lucky boy I think to myself, gorgeous, sexy, like's bikes and owns a pub! What's not to like. I kiss her neck as she gently stirs, "Morning babe do you fancy a cuppa?"

"I quite fancy a repeat of last night but I suppose a cuppa will do" says Molly wickedly.

"I'll make the drinks, and then I'll see what I can do," I reply as I slide out of bed.

Molly wolf whistles, and I realise I'm as naked as the day I was born! Not being the shy retiring type I go with it and wander off to the kitchen. Ten minutes later I'm back in bed with two mugs, tea for Molly and instant black coffee for me.

"If we're going to keep making a habit of this I'm gonna have to get you a decent coffee machine, I need my espresso hit in the mornings."

"Ooh you really know how to spoil a girl," laughs Molly, "next you'll be buying me an iron and a new hoover!"

"Not a bad idea," I retort.

"Don't even bloody think about it!"

"I'm gonna have to head home and get ready, Allun is coming in an hour," its seven thirty as I kiss Molly passionately.

"OK baby but please give me a ring when you get there so I know you're safe, and I'll be waiting when you get back."

After sorting myself out with a shower and several coffees, I hear Allun's Multistrada coming down the road so I grab my helmet and wander outside to meet him.

"Morning you tart, another good night then?"

"I don't know what you mean," I reply innocently.

"You forget I can see the pub door from my house and you never left last night, again," winks Allun impishly.

"OK fair cop, and yes it was a good night and again this morning," I grin.

"Too much information," he replies. "Right then what's the route? Or are we just following sat nav?"

"I've looked at the map, and was thinking, take the M5 up to Kidderminster, across to Shrewsbury, then the A458 through Welshpool and finish on the A470 through Dolgellou, what do you reckon?"

"Some cracking roads there boyo, let's get on it!"

We both go through the ritual of earplugs, helmet, check zips, gloves then sling a leg over the bikes and fire them up. We pull out and set off up the road in the morning sun. After fuelling up we pull onto the M5 for the first boring motorway stint, I'm not a fan of motorways but at least it's quiet this early on a Saturday morning. Before long we hit junction 8 and peel off towards Kidderminster. Allun has warned me about speed cameras around here so we take it easy as the Saturday morning traffic starts to build. We are soon out of urbanisation and cracking on down some decent country roads. Allun flashes his headlight and indicates showing he wants to stop. I spot a layby and we both pull in, I crack my visor and ask "What's up?"

"Fag break." So we climb off remove our helmets and light up. "What's the story with your brother then?"

I sigh, "You know we were both Hells Angels and I got out, well he's still in. He's often in trouble, usually for shagging someone else's missus but who knows this time."

"Right then I'm in front this time, let's see if you can keep up you tart."

We go through the ritual of earplugs, helmet, check zips, gloves, thumb the starter and roar off up the road.

Allun picks up the pace and we thrash along, only slowing to circumnavigate Shrewsbury. After another brief fag stop and refuel we are finally on the glorious Welsh roads, barrelling through the gorgeous scenery, taking none of it in. Scratching round bends, foot pegs scraping, then full throttle where the long sweepers allow. All too soon we are pottering along as we head into Barmouth. We take a left by the station and head for the car park on Marine Parade. We dismount and I glance at my watch, three hours! Not bad for a one hundred and sixty mile trip with two stops.

I pull out my phone and see a text from Rob, 'I'll be there at 12 grab a table and I'll meet you in the caff.'

I show Allun the text, "Where's the caff?"

"Mabel's, it's just the other side of those rides!"

"Right then," shoots Allun, "helmet back on we're going on that bloody roller coaster!" With that he strides off laughing.

'That bloody roller coaster' turns out to be about ten feet high and designed for kids. Still, the sight of two grown men dressed in leathers and crash helmets, laughing uproariously, soon draw a small crowd, clapping appreciatively. We eventually clamber off, take a bow to the crowd and stagger off towards Mabel's, still laughing loudly.

"What you having?" Allun asks as I slide onto a chair at a table by the window.

"Coffee, strong and black."

"Like my men!" We both quip quoting the old Airplane line.

Allun returns with two mugs. As he puts them on the table we hear a rumble, we both turn to admire an Aprilia RSV 4 as it grunts past. Allen whistles softly, "Mmm nice."

"It's not my cup of tea, too much plastic for me," I answer.

"When you grow up in Cardiff even the girls have too much plastic! But it certainly makes them easier on the eye." We both guffaw loudly, attracting disapproving looks from the old dear behind the counter.

A couple of minutes later I spot Rob coming up the road dressed in immaculate one-piece Dainese leathers and carrying a Shoei GT-air helmet. A definite change from his usual oily jeans, battered leather jacket, and cut. He slips a furtive glance over his shoulder and enters Mabel's.

"Ey up bruv, who's the company?" He glares at Allun.

"It's alright Rob this is Allun, a very good mate of mine, he's sound."

"I can leave if you want mate," Allun interrupts, "I'm just here to look out for my mucker."

"Nah stay, if Dan vouches for you there ain't no higher praise than that."

Allun gets up, "What you drinking?"

"Coffee strong and black,"

"Like my men!" We all chime. Rob slides onto a chair at the table as Allun heads for the counter to get more refreshments.

"Looking good Rob nice disguise." I look him up and down but he just answers with a grunt, as Allun returns with more mugs.

"I suppose you know what we got up to in the MC?" Rob eyes Allun.

"We've had a few conversations, I know some of it and all about Dan getting out," says Allun sternly.

"Well I'm out as well now, hence the new leathers and bike, but that's not all the problem," we both stare at Rob intently. "When you left and erm borrowed the petty cash, I took over the finances, so when I left I borrowed a bit more than the petty cash!" I stare at him open mouthed before I regain the ability to speak.

"How much more?" I glare at him.

"Hmm let me see, including the petty cash approximately five point four million quid!"

"Jesus boyo if I'd known that you could have paid for your own coffee," splutters Allen.

I sit quietly musing. I can see the problem and also why it involves me, I walked away with two point four million and now this! They will stop at nothing to hunt us down, and retribution won't be pretty.

"Great, you big prick!" I say eventually.

"Just copying my big brother," he replies.

"The way I see it we need to hole up somewhere," Allun smirks looking between the two of us, "and when they come we can have a big shootout like in the Magnificent Seven," he chuckles. "Then when we've kicked their arses we can ride off into the sunset with the girls!" He's now holding his belly as his chuckles get louder.

"In all seriousness It's not that bad a plan," I say, "except for the shootout bit, Allun you've got a spare room do you fancy putting this daft lad up for a bit?"

"No problem mucker," then turning to Rob "but if you snore and fart like him," nodding in my direction, "you're out!"

"Thanks fellers but where exactly are we holing up?" Rob smiles gratefully.

"A little village in the middle of nowhere," I smile at him, my little brother, "about a three hour thrash from here so I hope you've got rid of that bag 'o shite Harley and got something decent."

We head out of the door back towards the car park. The summer sun is dancing on the calm sea, belying the mayhem to come.

"There were only two bikes in the car park when I pulled in which I suspect are yours so I hope you two ladies are ready for a good thrashing," Rob grins from ear to ear.

As we round the roller coaster, there it is, the gleaming red and black RSV 4 we saw earlier, Allun whistles softly again.

"That's better than a Harley," smiles Rob.

This time the three of us go through the usual routine, mount up and head out on to the road, ready for a mad thrash back to sleepy Gloucestershire.

CHAPTER SIX

Three hours later, after leaving Rob to settle in at Allun's, I arrive home and park my bike. I'm just putting my key in the lock when my phone pings with a message, it's Molly. I'll wander over and surprise her as soon as I get out of these leathers I think to myself. Ten minutes later I push open the front door of the Red Lion, Molly squeals and runs round the bar to hug me tightly. "Thank god you're safe," she gasps.

I let her hold me a little longer, then cupping her face in my hands I ask, "What's all the fuss about I've only been gone a few hours."

"It's been all over the news hasn't it?" She casts around the bar looking for confirmation, the others nodding sagely. "A gang of Hells Angels have been running riot in Barmouth, that's where you went isn't it? Oh thank god you're safe! Oh my god where's Allun?" She starts to blub.

"Calm down we're all fine, my brother came back with us Allun's just settling him in, what time did this happen?"

"About an hour ago it was on the news, Oh god it was awful!" Molly sobbed.

"Well it had nothing to do with us it's a three hour ride back and I've been to Allun's then home to drop the bike off before coming here. get me a pint love and I'll just ring them to come over then I'll tell you all about it." I wander outside to make the call.

"Bollocks how the fuck did they find me?" Shouts Rob as I tell him of this afternoon's shenanigans.

"I don't know but get yourself over here in a bit and we'll try and work it out."

I slide onto my usual stool at the end of the bar, smiling as I watch Molly pulling my pint.

"There you go baby," she flashes me a smile, "Hang on I'm coming round, Jack take over for a bit love," she shouts to the young barman collecting glasses out the back. She settles on the stool beside me, "So tell me all about it."

"Everything?" I ask innocently.

"Yes everything, don't miss anything out, I want every last detail."

I take a slurp of my pint and settle back on my stool to begin, "Well Allun arrived just after eight, farted and started taking the piss," I got a slap on my shoulder, "What? You said every detail," I protest as I grin at her.

"Well maybe not that much."

I regale the tale of the day, others crowding round and laughing heartily, as I tell of the roller coaster, then drifting away as I finish my story.

"So those Hells Angels were nothing to do with you lot after all?"

"Maybe, maybe not, Rob is out now so they'll look for him, the same as they did me. We'll watch the news later and see if we recognise any of them."

The door swings open and Allun walks in, closely followed by Rob "And this is our salubrious local, the squeeze at the end of the bar is the landlady, Molly, she's with your Dan," he grins knowing he's winding Molly up.

"Oi less of your cheek!" She flashes, then returning behind the bar, "What'll it be boys?" She asks them as she gives her most flirtatious smile.

Rob winks at me, "I can see why you like her," then returning his attention to Molly, "Abbot for me, and Allun?"

"Carling please mate."

"Looks like you two have hit it off," I laugh.

"Yeah he's not bad for a ginger Welsh prick."

"And he's alright for a thick Yorkshire wanker!" Allun fires back and they giggle together like naughty schoolboys.

The chatter carries on around me as I idly look at my watch, wondering what time the news is on. Janet, of Janet and John, an older couple who sit in the corner at the opposite end of the bar every evening, shout "Put BBC News on, it'll be on there."

"Great idea" replies Molly, grabbing the TV remote and flicking through the channels until it reads 'BBC NEWS'.

Now while I am a bit of a whizz with computers, hence how I was able to fleece the MC without them knowing, although, they would have suspected but they could never prove it. I am at a loss with modern digital TV. I still remember the excitement about getting channel 4! After a brief article about the latest interest rate rise, the camera pans from the studio to a report on 'THE SHOCKING

SCENES IN BARMOUTH THIS AFTERNOON'. The reporter waffles on about the mayhem, carnage and downright disgusting disorder caused by a gang of Hells Angels in Barmouth this afternoon. It then cuts to mobile phone footage, at which point I zone out from the reporter to concentrate on the faces. There are several younger guys who I don't know, generally being badly behaved. Rob later told me they were Billy, Dodge, Boy, Chimp and Zach. Oh how imaginative they have become with names. Then a huge figure lumbers into view carrying a picnic table above his head, before launching it at a passing bus. He turns to face the camera grinning manically! Donk! Or Donkey, as we named him. He's six foot four of pure muscle but unfortunately with nothing between his ears. He had been a fantastic soldier; set him any task and he would complete it without question or fear, the more violent the better as far as he was concerned. Then on the corner of the screen I saw a figure in a cut entering Mabel's, coming out a few moments later, smiling. 'Hatch,' or Hatchet, he was a once trusted lieutenant and the answer to how they traced Rob. The old woman behind the counter, who had constantly glared at us, must be on the payroll. Bollocks! I notice the time on the corner of the screen flashing fifteen forty three, a good two hours after we had left. I wrack my brains trying to remember what I had told Rob about where we were going but could remember nothing. I nudge him and gesture towards the toilets, as the camera pans back to the reporter.

"How the fuck..." started Rob before I interrupted him.

"The old dear behind the counter in Mabel's, I bet she's on the payroll, timings about right,"

"What the fuck…?" Exclaims Rob and I interrupt him again.

"Think! This is important, what exactly did I tell you about where we were going?"

"Nowt, all you said was its three hours away and Allen would put me up!" He exclaims.

"Good, they've got nothing then, except about a two hundred mile radius from Barmouth and as this place has never been on either of our radars we should be fine for a while, thank fuck, come on your round."

We wander back into the bar to hear John, backed by Janet, holding court. "These biker types should be put in the stocks and we can throw rotten apples at them and then get the horses to piss on them, that'll teach the buggers!"

I chuckle to myself imagining Donk in the stocks being pissed on by a horse!

Allun interrupts, "Now then boyo, us three are bikers, do you want to put us in the stocks as well?" He is laughing as he rolls up his sleeves in mock indignation.

"No you lot are nice fellers, not like these bloody hooligans! National Service! That would sort the buggers out!"

Later, as the bar starts to thin out as closing time approaches, I lean over and whisper to Molly, "Need some company tonight?"

"Are you propositioning me?" She winks lasciviously, following with, "Help me get rid of this lot and tidy up then I'm all yours."

CHAPTER SEVEN

I gently stir, opening one eye then the other. I roll over to watch Molly sleeping and am surprised to find the bed next to me empty. I sit up and stretch to ease the remaining sleep from my body. I catch myself smiling as I can hear Molly singing softly in the kitchen and the smell of fresh coffee started to permeate into the bedroom. I throw on my boxers and wander into the kitchen asking "What happened to the instant shite?" She looks stunning wearing just a plain white t-shirt.

Smiling at me she says "Oh I thought I'd treat you, I got it while you were out yesterday, now get those off and get back into bed" she orders as she points at my boxers.

"I aim to please" I grin over my shoulder as I leave the kitchen. An hour later we are both in the kitchen again, this time fully dressed. "White or brown toast?" Molly asks as I fight with her new espresso machine.

"Mmm brown with butter if you have it."

"For you Sir anything," she winks at me.

I pour the coffee, light a cigarette and watch as she butters the toast. This is all going so well and so quickly, a few short weeks suddenly feels like years. We enjoy the comfortable silence as we sip our drinks and munch on our toast.

When we have finished I get up and start to wash the dishes, "I'm impressed" she mocks "and without even being asked, there's hope you are trainable yet."

I love her sharp wit, always keeping me on my toes but her next sentence surprises me.

"How long have you rented the cottage for?"

"I paid for a month in advance, which reminds me I need to go and see Pat and sort out staying as I don't plan on going anywhere soon," thinking how quickly my life has turned itself around.

"Well I was thinking now Rob's here and he needs somewhere to live and the cottage is too small for both of you." She hesitates and leaves me wondering what she has in mind for us both. Then she continues "you could er, let Rob have the cottage and you could move in here with me, that's if you want to?" She finishes hurriedly.

"Wow I wasn't expecting that," I am stunned for a moment, then standing up I grab her by the waist and kiss her passionately. "I would love to" I smile when I have finished kissing her. "That's settled then I've got loads to do getting this place ready for opening so why don't you go and tell Rob then bring your stuff over later." With that she turns on her heel and marches out of the kitchen singing softly.

An hour later I'm sat in Allun's kitchen recounting this morning's events.

"Whoa stud!" mocks Allun when I have finished.

"Does that mean I get to play with your car?" Asks Rob, "Allun told me you've got an old Jag but he hasn't seen it, is it one of those Inspector Morse types? I always fancied a go in one of those." I look at him sternly.

"I suppose you can if you behave in it and if you help me move my stuff over to the pub this afternoon."

"If I must, come on then what type is it?"

"It's a '98 XKR," I sigh resignedly, "four litre supercharged 370 bhp, in British Racing Green with a black mohair hood and cream leather interior, so be bloody careful with it!" Rob grins from ear to ear.

"Awesome, Sally will love coming for a spin in that."

I look at him quizzically, "Sally?"

"Oh the little blonde I was chatting to in the pub last night."

Allun interrupts, "Sally Thomas, she's a nice girl, I've heard about your reputation so don't go messing her about or you'll have me to deal with." Rob laughs.

"Blimey two big brothers, a nice cottage, a Jag and a cute blonde I'm starting to like this place already."

Allun glares at him, "I've warned you!"

Rob raises his hands backing away mockingly, "I'm joking, calm down big bruv." Allun throws an empty cigarette packet at him catching him squarely on the forehead and we all descend into fits of laughter.

Later, at the cottage we are packing up my stuff and working out what I can leave for Rob, as he had arrived wearing leathers with a few clothes in a rucksack. "I've got my wallet surely they must have shops around here?"

"Nope," retort Allun and I together.

"You can take the car down to Bristol this afternoon and do some shopping after you've finished helping me."

We carry on packing and Allun wanders up to me, "Seriously is this all you've got?" He looks concerned.

"Nah," I reply, "you know that truck stop on the A38 just past the petrol station?" he nods in answer. "Well I've got my Transit stashed there with most of my stuff in it, just in case I needed to make a quick getaway."

Rob shoots me a look, "You might still need to, shacking up with that Molly." I scowl at him, I know I haven't been the most decent human being in the past, but since getting out of the MC I have changed. I'm just hoping that change is permanent given the trouble that is following Rob.

"Right I'm going over to see Molly I won't be long so you two behave OK?"

"Yes dad!" They both descend into fits of giggles as I close the door behind me.

I wander into the pub and shout to Molly, "You decent?" She pops her head out of the back bar.

"Unfortunately yes, why what do you have in mind?" She flirts.

"Mmm later," I wink. "Just checking it's OK to bring my stuff over, there's not a lot in the cottage but I'm gonna pick up my van with the rest of my gear in it if that's OK?"

Molly grins at me, sticks out her tongue and retorts, "I'm sure there's an empty drawer in the bedroom you can have, the rest will have to go in the spare room till we get sorted. I'm going to sort out the barrels in the cellar so drop it off. Go get your van and I'll see you later baby."

An hour later I'm sat in the passenger seat of my Jag, giving Rob a lot of grief about driving my car.

"Did you ever pass your driving test?" I ask testily.

"I've got a license you cheeky sod!" He retorts huffily.

"That's not what I asked, I'm well aware the MC has an examiner on the payroll even Donk has a license for fuck's sake!" He shrugs resignedly.

"Fair cop but I can drive you know, now stop being a girl and point me in the right direction."

I gesture for him to drive and sit sulkily in the passenger seat. I'm not a good passenger at the best of times, and even worse when it's my own car. I direct him to the truck stop and he screeches to a halt beside my van, spraying gravel everywhere. As I get out of my car I glare at him and he laughs.

"See you later bruv, I'm going shopping, I've gotta impress Sally tonight." With that he slams the Jag into reverse, spraying gravel again and then screeches off up the A38 in the direction of Bristol.

I unlock the van and check the contents; all good, even my paintings are safe. I'll have to sweet talk Molly into letting me redecorate the flat above the pub. I ease the van into gear and set off back towards Hanley and the Red Lion, my new home.

CHAPTER EIGHT

I seem to have found my spot, a stool on the end of the bar, it's a good spot from which I can survey the whole of the front bar and see through to the back bar as well as the front door. It seems my instincts from my old life haven't quite left me yet. Molly wanders over smiling, "Pint babe, you all done?" I return her smile, admiring her dazzling blue eyes and pouty cherry red lips framed by her long wavy auburn hair.

"Sounds good and yeah it'll do for now but I was gonna ask, now I've got all my gear here, do you mind if I redecorate the flat? I've got loads of paintings I want to hang."

"Ooh look at you all domesticated, next thing you'll be cooking as well!"

"I can do a mean beans on toast if you're interested?" She laughs and wanders off to serve in the back bar.

The door opens and Allun walks in speaking Welsh to another guy I don't know. "Two Carling's please Molly when you're ready" he calls through, then turning to me, "This is Bryn, a mate of mine from back home, he's working down this way so I asked him over to meet you." I offer my hand and receive a firm grip and a handshake.

Molly puts their pints down in front of them with a hello and a smile, takes the money and wanders away.

"Alright boyo, Allun's told me all about you, he reckons you're alright for a Yorkshire boy."

"Well I've heard nowt about you, so pull up a stool and we'll have a chat." He plonks himself on the stool besides me and starts on his pint while Allun takes the stool at the other side of me.

"So are you a biker as well?"

"No chance" laughs Bryn "I leave that nonsense to the likes of this daft ginger twat, I do like a drink though," he drains his pint and puts the empty glass on the bar. He wasn't joking about liking a drink.

"It's Molly isn't it?" he asks and I nod in agreement, he returns his focus to Molly who has finished serving in the back bar and wanders back into the front to serve him.

"Two more Carlings please darling and a pint of whatever that muck is" he nods towards my pint.

"I can feel a good session coming on, what do you reckon Al?" Allun nods in agreement and sets about his next pint "You up for it Dan?" I look at Molly's exasperated face and turn back to Bryn.

"I'll have a few with you boys, but not too many, I've got plans later," Molly flashes me a look like a cat that's got the cream, and saunters off to carry on serving in the back bar.

I'm halfway down my Abbot when Bryn slams his empty glass on the bar, "Whose round next?"

"I'll get them, same again?" they both nod in agreement, with Allun putting his empty glass on the bar while I fumble for my wallet.

After a couple of hours of beer, banter and generally talking bollocks, I hear the door open while I'm trying to neck my pint in a desperate attempt to vaguely keep up. Allun nudges me, I put my empty glass on the bar and turn to see two girls walking in.

"The blonde one is Sally, who Rob's got his eye on, the brunette is Lucy, who is, err, quite nice."

I look round and see Allun blushing, "Who's smitten now boyo?" I quip.

Bryn joins the banter, "The last time I saw him go that red was when Mary flashed her knickers at him in primary school!" Allun's complexion reddens even further as Bryn guffaws, then saves him any further embarrassment by necking his pint and proclaiming, "Your round mucker."

The door opens again, another face I can't put a name to enters, closely followed by Rob, sporting new jeans, t-shirt and trainers. Allun stands up and salutes, "Two more bikers entering the building," he shakes Rob's hand, then nods at me. "This is Dan, who I told you about, this is Steve," nodding towards the newcomer.

"He's an ex-racer so he's a bit handy on a bike, we'll have to go out for a thrash!" I offer my hand and again I'm greeted with a firm handshake.

"Alright" I proffer.

"Allun tells me you're not too shabby on a bike yourself, we'll have to arrange a ride out and see if we can't teach this sheep shagger a thing or two," he grins showing perfect white teeth.

"Don't knock sheep shagging," I laugh, "I'm from Yorkshire, but at least we only shag the pretty ones." I look at Allun seeing him redden, I think I've scored a point, but quickly realise it's because Lucy is fast approaching him. I settle back on my stool nudging Bryn to see what unfolds.

"Hi Allun, Rob is chatting with Sally and just asked if we want to go to lunch tomorrow. I wasn't sure as I don't fancy playing gooseberry but then he mentioned you would probably come as well, soooo I'm up for it if you are, what do you say?"

Allun stutters and blushes again, then finally manages, "Great what time?"

"Ooh I don't know Rob will let you know; now I must get back to Sally." She turns and blows a kiss over her shoulder. Bryn and I cheer loudly, Allun turns a bright beetroot colour and mutters, "I'm off to the toilet."

At eight o'clock Jane arrives to take over from Molly behind the bar, after handing over she pours herself a drink and comes round to join us. I stand letting her have my stool and letting my arm encircle her waist. More beer, banter and laughter ensues, with Molly more than holding her own in the banter stakes. Around nine o'clock, Molly winks at me and yawns loudly, I take the hint, I say goodbye to my new friends, shout, "ey up bruv, I'm off" to Rob and let Molly take my hand and lead me to the flat upstairs

CHAPTER NINE

Molly and I lay in bed covered in a sheen of sweat after another energetic lovemaking session. I kiss her gently as I hear my phone ringing beside me, 'Riders on the Storm' my new ringtone for Rob. "What's up Rob, how's it hanging?"

"All good I had a cracking night last night but unfortunately woke up on my own. It turns out the girls want to go to lunch on the bikes so I was wondering if you and Molly fancy it?"

"I'll ask," covering the mouthpiece with my hand I explain to Molly. "Let me try and get some cover Sam's always looking for extra shifts at the weekend as her hubbies home let me ring her."

Five minutes later I ring Rob back to confirm that we'll both be going and we'll meet them in the pub car park at twelve o'clock. I head off for a shower promising to return with tea and toast.

I wander back into the bedroom as naked as the day I was born, with a mug of tea in one hand and a plate of toast in the other, nothing hiding my modesty.

"Ooh I could get used to being served breakfast like this" squeals Molly.

"Might as well get used to me being naked, after all I am from Sheffield the home of the Full Monty," I retort.

"Ooer I best be careful what I put on the jukebox then, I don't want anyone else copping an eyeful."

"Come on get your beautiful arse out of bed I've got to get sorted with what I'm wearing. I can't let my brother down with his quest to impress Sally or Allun with Lucy for that matter, what are the girls like?"

"Well I've already warned Rob to be careful with Sally; she's a sweet girl with a seven year old son called Callum. Her husband ran off with one of my barmaids so I sort of feel responsible for her and I don't want her getting hurt!"

"Me neither but unfortunately I know what Rob is like, I'll have a word later, and Lucy?"

"Well she's a bit different she's free and single and has always had a thing for Allun, I've told her many times to go for it but she never has, she didn't think he was interested."

"Ha! Sounds like they are both the same, a couple of nudges might be needed methinks, are you up for a bit of matchmaking?" Molly nods and smiles.

Twelve o'clock, three bikes are ticking over gently in the midday sun. The three girls are chatting and giggling secretively, casting furtive glances towards us three blokes who are smoking and laughing loudly.

"Come on then let's go I'm starving," shouts Allun.

We all give the girls a hand getting their helmets and gloves on. I smile and gesture to Molly to watch Rob, gently helping Sally but all the time gazing into her eyes with a stupid soppy grin. We do our usual routine earplugs, helmet, check zips, gloves then mount up, holding our bikes steady while the girls clamber aboard. I'm vaguely amused at the sight of Sally trying to adjust herself to the postage stamp size seat and jockeyesque pillion accommodation of the RSV 4, fortunately she's slight, so with a bit of shuffling she settles. We nod to each other and ease out onto the road, no mad thrashing or wheelies today. A gentle bimble up the A38 and a couple of B-roads sees us pulling in to the Millside Tavern, a once working mill, now a rather fetching steakhouse, as I was reliably informed by Allun this morning.

We remove our helmets and wander inside to find a table, the girls chatting excitedly about their motorcycle experience. A young girl bearing the name badge 'Anna' escorts us to a table by the window and asks if we would like drinks. A quick check around the group and I order five diet cokes and a tea, Molly drinks the stuff by the gallon, I can't stand it personally. We remove our jackets and drape them over chairs; menus are passed around while I precariously balance a line of helmets on the windowsill.

Anna returns with our drinks and asks if we are ready to order, after a few "Ooh's" and "I quite fancy that's," we settle on six steaks, ranging from rare, mine, to very well done in fact incinerated, Rob. How two brothers can have such differing taste in steaks I'll never know?

We all chat amiably as we wait for our food to arrive; my interest is suddenly piqued when I pick up on a conversation between Lucy and Molly.

"Are you letting Benny have his eighteenth birthday in the pub on Saturday?" enquires Lucy.

"I'm not sure," replies Molly, "I can't get a doorman and after the trouble we had with the lads from Wolston at Nadgers last year I'm not sure it's a good idea."

"Rubbish" I chime in, "you must make a few quid out of an eighteenth birthday me and Rob will make sure it goes off without any trouble won't we bruv?"

"Well unless I have to kick his stupid Welsh arse we will" laughs Rob as he nods at Allun.

I notice Lucy flashing daggers at Rob before returning to gaze dreamily to Allun, definitely something there I muse, a couple of nudges later and I'm sure they will make a great couple.

"Well if you're sure, that would be great I'll text him and let him know it's a go."

"After some of the Hells Angel meets we've policed in the past it'll be a bit like babysitting," smiles Rob obviously eager to impress Sally.

The food arrives and after much toing and froing of condiments, we all tuck into steaks, conversation stopping as we all eat hungrily. Once we have all finished we pay the bill and retire outside to enjoy a post meal cigarette. The girls all disappear to the toilet together. As we watch them go Allun asks, "Well what do you think?"

"I think you need to get off your fat Welsh arse and woo her a bit, she obviously adores you."

"Even I can tell that" chimes in Rob "and I've only been here four days, but what do you reckon Sally thinks of me? And before you start Dan I'm not the same these days watching you and Molly together I want a bit of that."

"You know she's got a son?" I enquire.

"Yeah Callum he's seven I'm thinking if I get with Sally I'll get him one of those mini moto's and teach him to ride. In fact I might even get one myself, you two should as well, then we can have races." Allun and I both shake our heads in despair.

The girls return and we clamber back onto the bikes and bimble back to the Red Lion, none of us wanting to risk upsetting our prize pillions by cracking the throttle.

We drop the girls off at the pub, arranging to come back after we've parked the bikes in our respective garages. I tell Sally and Lucy to leave their jackets and helmets in the bar, and I'll take them up to the spare room when I get back. As I fire up the bike I hear Molly singing my praises, telling them how thoughtful I am, and how great it is having a real man about the place. I try to listen a little longer but they go inside and their conversation is lost to my ears. I realise I'm grinning broadly as I set off to park the bike. We spend a pleasant afternoon drinking and chatting in the bar, eventually calling it a night around eight. I circle Molly's waist with my arm as we wave them off. We turn to each other smiling as both Allun and Lucy and Rob and Sally head for their respective homes, hand in hand, chatting as they go. Mission accomplished!

CHAPTER TEN

Saturday arrives soon enough and I spend a large part of the afternoon helping Molly prepare for the party. I am busy setting up a trestle table in the garden for the food Molly insisted on having. I had protested that no one will eat it as all any self-respecting eighteen year old birthday boy wants to do is get as pissed as possible and maybe pull! She insisted, so I acquiesced. I finish off by placing paper plates full of sandwiches, sausage rolls and pork pies on the table. Satisfied with my work I head upstairs to shower and change for the evening's festivities.

Molly looks stunning in black cropped jeans and a bright red low cut top, displaying her ample cleavage, as she sits applying her make up. I chose the classic combination of jeans, Adidas trainers and tight white Ralph Lauren t-shirt. I wander down towards the bar to get a pint as Molly applies the finishing touches to her beautiful face. While I know many of the youngsters by sight I know very few of their names so I intend to use the evening to get to know them a bit better. Molly joins me pointing people out as they approach. First in is the birthday boy Benny, accompanied by Ash, Luke and Charlie.

"The first drinks on me," I shout to Sam behind the bar, "can't have the birthday boy and his mates going thirsty."

"Cheers Dan" they all mutter, as I said they all know my name but now I have another four to remember.

Jack, James and Kev were next in, followed by Chelsea, Laura and Chloe, with Roxy and Chantelle closely behind. Bollocks there's no way I am going to remember all those names.

A couple of the older lads Matt, Sam and Josh wander in "Alright Dan" they all greet me.

I have chatted to these three before so their names aren't a problem.

Rob finally turns up with Sally on his arm, both looking good. "Ey up Bruv," he calls out and I nod as I watch Allun and Lucy crossing the road arm in arm giggling, both obviously smitten.

The pub fills up and gradually empties into the garden where the DJ is playing. With no-one else on the horizon I wander inside to get a pint and find Molly. She isn't inside and I eventually find her in the garden tapping her foot to the music and chatting to Jess another of the barmaids. I sidle up beside her, grab her waist, spin her round and start to dance, well someone has to get the party started.

As the music finishes she hugs and kisses me. "Mmm this just keeps getting better, you're a great dancer too I am a lucky girl." I pull her inside the bar to let the youngsters get on with enjoying themselves.

Around half nine with the party in full swing, Molly, Sam and Jess are busy pulling pints as fast as they can.

I am standing by the door having a chat with Steve about his racing days. He is just telling me about when he destroyed a ZX9R after high siding it at Castle Combe, when Kev comes haring through the back bar.

"Dan quick come outside the Wolston boys are here looking for trouble!"

I look round for Rob who's nowhere to be seen, typical! I'll just have to handle this on my own, so I set off outside like a scalded cat.

I survey the scene, there are a bunch of local lads at the top of the car park in front of the girls to protect them. At the other end about fifteen Wolston boys, some of them in their late twenties, are shouting and gesturing menacingly. I wander into the middle of the car park and turn to face the Wolston boys.

"Now then lads this isn't a good idea."

"What you gonna do about it old man?" A shout comes from the back.

"Hurt you, if I have to but I'd rather not my pints getting warm inside." I tell them as I try to diffuse the situation.

"Well fuck off inside while we sort these tossers out," comes another shout.

Suddenly two of them run towards me, I get on my toes ready for battle. As the first one approaches I step in and smash his nose all over his face with a vicious straight right and he goes down whimpering and clutching his face. The other tries to skip past me but I stick out a leg tripping him. He is on his feet in a flash throwing a punch at my head; I grab his fist and give him two sharp left jabs to his ribs followed by a right uppercut that finishes him off.

"Anyone else want a go? I can do this all night?" I sneer menacingly facing the rest of the Wolston boys.

"No, Mister you're all right" comes a trembling voice from the back. Just at that moment Rob comes running around the corner, surveys the scene and utters, "Bollocks, looks like I've missed all the fun!"

He then proceeds to slap all the remaining lads around the head, shouting a word with each slap until he has finished. "Pick – your – fucking – scummy – mates – up – and – fuck – off – don't – ever – come – round – here – again."

The terrified boys gather their fallen mates and backtrack as fast as humanly possible.

A loud cheer goes up, followed by much backslapping as the local boys all thank Rob and I.

Molly comes rushing out, grabs me and kisses me, "My hero!" Another cheer goes up from the gathered throng.

Once Molly has finally let me go my brother approaches, we bear hug and clap each other on the back.

"Just like old times," he whispers in my ear, before adding "except this time we are the good guy's feels good don't it?" I grin and nod at him, as the crowd starts to disperse I take Molly's hand and lead her back inside.

The bar erupts into more loud cheering and clapping, much handshaking and backslapping follows as we make our way to the bar.

"Did you see that uppercut?" I hear John saying to another new face, obviously local but unknown to me, "It was like watching Tyson in his prime." I wander over to them, while Molly returns behind the bar to serve the thirsty hordes.

"Nice work young fella," says John shaking my hand enthusiastically. "Course in my day I'd have taken all of them out with a pint in my hand and never have spilled a drop." He proclaims, "National Service you see never did me any harm."

I turn to his companion and offer my hand, "Dan, we've not met are you local?"

I felt my hand being enclosed by another the size of a shovel and work hardened, the grip vice like. "Mike or Badger as I'm known in 'ere. Yeah I live on the High Street but I like to do a bit of hunting and fishing so I've been camping up in the woods. Nice work out there, of course I would have sorted it myself but I was finishing my pint first."

I laugh, there is genuine warmth emanating towards me and for the first time in years I feel at home, maybe I have finally found my destination.

It's one in the morning and Molly and I are finally in bed, it has taken an age to get rid of the revellers and tidy the pub. Molly lies with her head on my chest, "You were awesome tonight and..." she hesitates before adding "and... I love you."

I swell with pride, "You know what, I think you are the most beautiful, sexy and funny woman I have ever met and I am madly in love with you too!" We snuggle tighter as we drift off to sleep, both smiling.

CHAPTER ELEVEN

I have spent a productive morning finishing painting the bedroom and living room in the flat while Molly has been busy with the beer delivery. Now waiting for it to dry I make a couple of drinks and wander down to the bar to look for Molly.

"How's it going babe?" I hand over her steaming mug of tea.

"I'm going to have to open up today Jess has let me down and I can't get anyone else to cover," she kisses me, "The colours look good but isn't the paint supposed to be on the wall?"

We both laugh, "I'm stuck waiting for it to dry so as you're busy I'm gonna pop over and see Rob for a while." I kiss her forehead trying not to cover her in paint.

"See you later darling," she smiles.

I push open the cottage door and see Rob sat in the kitchen, "Get that coffee machine on," I gesture to the Rocket espresso machine which cost me the best part of a grand, "Molly bought one for me but it's got nothing on this bad boy."

Rob busies himself making coffee, "What's up?"

I take a seat at the table.

"I need to have a chat about the MC; I've got a few things on my mind." He finishes the espresso's and brings them to the table, sitting down, he offers me a cigarette and looks at me expectantly, so I begin.

"You said you took over the finances after I left, what did you find, anything?"

"It was four months before I took it on, you know what it's like, meetings and votes before anything gets done. I was really pissed off with you so I decided to go through the accounts with a fine tooth comb to prove you had either cheated us or fucked something up!"

I interrupt nervously, "And?"

"It took me months, it all looked good but then I found it. A regular payment to HD Ltd, regular until you left, then it stopped. I presumed, as anyone would, that HD stood for Harley Davidson and it was for maintenance and purchase of the bikes. It bothered me that it had stopped so I dug into the company a bit more. I discovered that for the last four years the MC had been making substantial payments to a bank account that no longer existed and the company was called Happy Days Ltd. I knew it had to be you and was going to drop you in it but then I thought if you had got away with it why not me. So I set up a new company called Hardly Daredto Ltd and restarted the payments to HD Ltd but at a much higher rate. I told the guys you had tried to screw them over by stopping the payments to HD Ltd, they thought the obvious, cursed you and thanked me."

"And what did you do with it when you left?"

"Well I thought about how I found it, so I've left it running at a lower rate so the MC now gives me a pension of a grand a month into an untraceable account," he finishes.

"You genius," I stand up and grab his head and kiss his forehead.

"Get off you poof," he protests, "Now tell me what happened in Shropshire?"

"When I left I had no plans so I drifted around for a week or two. I knew I needed to get rid of the Harley, so I headed off to see Lentil in Much Wenlock. You know the tuning guy all the Hells Angels use?" Rob nods. "I spent a few days with him stripping the Harley and destroying the frame and engine numbers. He mentioned his sister had a place in Bomere Heath, a village just north of Shrewsbury, so I bought a transit van and moved in there."

Rob interrupts, "There's something I need to ask before I forget, where do you register your vehicles? The Aprilia is registered at Mum and Dad's but I don't want them getting dragged into this." I smile at him.

"I register everything at the MC and all my post is re-directed to a PO Box, I'll set you up later," I wink at him. "You're not the only genius in the family. Anyway back to Shropshire. All was well, the Devils run Shropshire and they are nasty fuckers, as you will remember from the battles we had with them. I managed to avoid them and live my life quietly. One evening I was sat in the local having a few pints chatting to Rick the Landlord when I heard a commotion in the car park, so I went out to have a look. There was a Devils prospect, obviously high on drugs, threatening the local youths. I was just about to put my head down and go back inside, when he punched one of them knocking him to the floor. I would still have left but he started to lay the boot in while he was on the ground. I ran over, pushed him and told him to back off. His eyes were wild with the drugs and he was drooling as he turned to face me, saying "you want some Grandad?" He charged at me arms flailing, I waited for my moment, then, bang, one punch and he was on his arse.

I turned back towards the pub thinking it was over, then, I heard a shout "watch out Mister." He was back on his feet brandishing a knife! He came at me slashing wildly, backing me up. I felt the pub wall at my back; I knew I had to act fast. I waited for him to lunge; side stepped and grabbed his arm. Dropping to one knee I smashed his arm over my thigh, rolled him on his side then grabbed his hand and forced his own knife into his thigh. I looked up and saw the horror on the faces of the youths as he lay writhing and squealing on the floor. So I jumped over the fence and headed home, packed up the van and left. As I was leaving the village I could hear the rumble of Harleys approaching as the Devils arrived, so I got my foot down and didn't look back.

You probably know more about the rest than I do." I finished.

"Nice move Ninja," Rob grins, "Yeah the devils rang us, one of the kids had filmed it and they recognised you. Hatch and a bunch of others rode down to look for you and I took that as my cue to leave."

"Anyway, back to the future how's things with Sally?" I ask as I get up to make more coffee.

"All good and Callum's great we're all going go-karting later."

"Ooh a proper little family," I jest.

"You know what bruv, maybe it's time I settle down and I can't think of anywhere better to do it," adds Rob seriously.

"Right I'm off, got decorating to finish."

"And you're taking the piss out of me?" He laughs as I head out of the door and back to the Red Lion.

CHAPTER TWELVE

Its early evening as I sit in the corner of the bar watching Molly work. She is gorgeous and flirtatious, making each customer feel special, it's no wonder this place is always full.

A distant noise approaches reaching its crescendo as the door bursts open, revealing Allun, Rob, Bryn and Steve, all the worse for wear. "Four darlings Carling and a monk for Dan," proclaims Bryn. "Wait maybe it's a bishop? Anyway it's some sort of cassocky beer."

"Good afternoon boys?" I look between them hoping to find a glimmer of sense, but there is none.

"Shmashing," replies Rob stumbling towards the bar, "We've got a shurprishe for you" he slurs.

"Ooh let me guess, it's a flower you've just nicked from someone's garden on the way past?"

"Bollocks!" mutters Steve.

"No, no, that's for Molly," answers Allun, "yours is even better, go on tell 'im."

Rob steps forward, "We decided us two need to absolve, no, absorb the local culture! So we've," pointing to everyone in turn, "all of us here have booked a bus for Saturday and these boys," pointing again, "are gonna show us the local pubs I mean sights shound good?"

"Awesome," I reply sarcastically, "just us?"

"No no no no no no, it's a twenty eight seater so that's at least six more." He tries to count around the bar on his fingers then grins, "Acshually make that fourteen, brill innit?"

In their drunken state it probably does sound 'brill' but I'm sober, and at the moment I can't think of anything worse. I look to Molly for help, "I think we've got something happening on Saturday, haven't we Moll?"

"No I'm having a day off and seeing the girls," she grins wickedly, "so it's perfect, you go and enjoy yourself."

"Shmashing, that's shorted then," grins Rob inanely, and then stumbles again, "Perhapsh I better go home now."

"I'll take you, I've had enough as well, see you boys Saturday," announces Allun.

"Oh well I may as well finish those," says Bryn, necking his pint and eyeing the two full ones left on the bar. He turns to me," Rob's been

telling us about the Hells Angels, now I'm no biker but I can drink and scrap, so if it comes down to a battle I'm right behind you."
"Same for me," Steve adds, "anything I can do."
"Cheers boys, that means a lot, I'm off, see you Saturday," I say finishing my pint, I head up to the flat to finish hanging my artwork.

When Saturday comes, I hear the coach pulling up in the car park.
"See you later babe," I kiss Molly.
"Have fun and try not to get too pissed," she giggles as I head out of the door.
There's a motley crew in the car park, some boarding the coach, others standing chatting and smoking. I walk over to Allun, Rob, Bryn and Steve, "Looks like your idea is popular."
"Yeah there's a good turnout, I'll introduce you two boys as we go along," Allun smiles, "Come on let's get going there's beer to be drunk."
"And lots of it," says Bryn, jostling to get on the coach.
As the coach pulls off a cheer goes up and an older guy gets up and starts handing out cans of beer! "These should keep us going till we get to the first boozer," he announces.
"How long will that take then?" someone asks.
"About ten minutes," shouts the driver.
When the older guy reaches us Allun introduces him, "PJ this is Dan and Rob the new boys in the village. Boys this is PJ the local hard man, now retired."
"Nice to meet you fellers," he shakes both our hands firmly. "I hear you did a good job sorting out the Wolton boys."
"It was the least we could do," I answer.
"Nice one fellers, now let's have a bloody good piss up," he turns and heads back down the coach to his seat.

Our first destination appears; it's the White Lion, right on the A38. We all disembark and head towards the pub. Once inside PJ announces, "Right boys get your wallets out, I'm starting a kitty, twenty quid each should start us off, put your money in the bag and order your drinks."
I put my twenty quid in and order a Hobgoblin, Rob follows suit. I look round the eclectic mix of faces in our rag-tag group.
"Come on let's go and absolve ourselves in the local culture," Rob looks at me quizzically, "Don't worry you were pissed and I'm just winding you up."

Our first port of call is Jack, a gnarly old farmer, who seems to be a cantankerous old bugger, with a mischievous glint in his eye. Next up is Bob, who's every other word is an expletive but we later find out he's got Tourette's. Then it's Matt, Sam and Josh who I recognise from the pub. Steve shouts us over, "Come and meet these boys they're bikers." We wander over and are introduced to Jake and Joe, "What do you ride boys?" queries Rob.

"I've got a Gixxer thou K5," returns Joe.

"A Gixxer 750 for me in blue and white, the best colours," replies Jake, as they both shake our hands.

"Steve is organising a ride out, are you boys gonna come and play?" I ask.

"Definitely," they reply together.

"These boys are a bit special so we might have to let them get on with it and catch up with them later." Steve says.

Next we are introduced to Bill, the local farmer, his weather beaten face cracks a toothless grin. "I've heard about you Yorkshire boys, you taught those Wolton boys a lesson. Now don't be coming down my farm and worrying my sheep I've got enough trouble with those Welsh boys," he grins nodding at Allun and Bryn.

"You're safe with us we only like pretty ones," laughs Rob.

"Come on girls drink up the next pub is calling," shouts PJ. We all finish our pints and troop out to board the coach.

The next pub comes into view, the Black Swan, in a village called Little Hampton. We head inside.

"Same deal again boys get your beer I've got the kitty." We grab our beers and wander outside to enjoy the sunshine.

Matt, Sam and Josh come over to join us. "We've been hearing you might be having a bit of trouble with the Hells Angels," says Matt.

"Well after the way you handled those boys at Benny's party you can probably look after yourselves but if you ever need us we'll be right behind you, won't we boys?" Sam and Josh nod in agreement.

"We all play rugby so we can look after ourselves," adds Josh.

"Cheers boys we appreciate that," then turning to me Rob adds," I need a piss, do you want another pint of Landlord while I'm in there?"

"Yeah go on then, but I'm coming for a pee too."

The toilets are packed and Rob takes the last urinal, so I go into a cubicle. I hear someone go into the cubicle next to me, then young Sam jokes, "God this water's cold!"

"Aye and it's bloody deep as well!" I quip back.

The next stop is the Snooty Fox in a place called Almsworth. We are milling about in the bar, when old Jack nudges me, "Watch this," he chuckles as he heads towards PJ.

"Do you remember quiet Dave? The bloke who worked with us down the power station."

"Yeah what about him?"

"Well that's him," he nods to an obvious transvestite sat at the bar.

"You are fucking joking," splutters PJ, "He looks just like a bird! He's got tits and everything!" He stomps off towards the bar.

"Oi! Dave how's it going mucker, you want a pint? You've er changed a bit since we worked together mate." The rest of us are transfixed, waiting to see what happens next.

"It's Theresa actually," She informs him snottily as she looks at him horrified.

"Great tits by the way, can I cop a feel?" He leers, grabbing a handful of breast. Theresa squeals, looking mortified, and rushes off into the ladies toilets, as the entire pub erupts with raucous laughter.

"What did I do wrong?" Protests PJ innocently, cue more hilarity. The landlady shouts," PJ you can't go around doing that you need to be a bit more sensitive."

"Fuck that, I was just having a laugh with quiet Dave," he mutters, "Come on boys it's time to move on to the next boozer." We all troop out behind him, still laughing loudly. Today is proving to be more fun than I imagined rural life could possibly be.

Our next stop is the Anchor in Charfield-on-Severn, a huge white pub overlooking the river Severn. Most of us stay outside while a few go in to get more beer for us all. Bryn returns carrying three pints and chuckling to himself. "I've got you both Speckled Hen, but you've got to come and see this. Rob and I take our pints and follow him towards the pub. As we approach the door a guy comes out wearing a battered leather jacket and carrying a crash helmet.

"Jeff come over here, these boys used to be Hells Angels," Bryn shouts stifling a grin. "Come and meet them Dan, Rob, this is Jeff a proper Hells Angel., Turn round and show them."

Jeff eyes us suspiciously, before tuning round to show us the back of his jacket. I gasp; I can hardly believe my eyes. In white gloss paint he has inscribed the legend, 'HELLS ANGLES' and underneath 'CHARFIELD CHAPTER'. Rob laughs out loud, "Is it tri or right that's missing from there feller?"

"You guys can't have been Hells Angels as they don't let you out and anyway, you don't look like tough bikers to me," Jeff retorts huffily.

"Fair cop it's just our friends little joke," I mock. With that Jeff stomps off.

"Jesus Christ is he for real?" Rob asks bursting into laughter again.

"He looks a bit square, if you ask me," Rob groans at my bad joke, and then we all crack up as we head back to the coach.

Just as we are leaving the car park, Bryn shouts, "What the fuck!" We all look out of the window to see Jeff putting on his helmet and climbing aboard a Honda C90 twist and go! That sparks another round of raucous laughter.

Our next stop is the Cross Keys in Dorrington, I spent a night here when I first arrived in Gloucestershire, before settling in Hanley. I go in with Rob to get the beers and see Maureen the landlady behind the bar.

"Long time no see Dan my love, how are you darling?"

"I'm good Maureen, how are you?" I enquire.

"Well the sciatica is still playing me up and Stan's still a pain in the arse but other than that all good, what have you been up to? And who's this handsome chap with you?" She asks without drawing a breath.

"This ugly bugger is my little brother Rob, he couldn't resist Gloucestershire's charms either so he's moved down as well. I'm living in Hanley in the Red Lion."

"With Molly? She's a great girl, if you had stayed here I would have introduced you to her but it sounds like fate has beaten me to it."

Rob stays at the bar chatting to Maureen, while I wander off and bump into another new face. "Pete," he introduces himself," ex-football hooligan."

"Yeah you've been mentioned, who did you run with?"

"CSF Bristol City, why do you ask?"

"I used to run with the BBC Sheffield United back in the eighties and you look vaguely familiar," I gesture for him to sit down.

We both take a seat and he continues, "I've never been to your place, Bramall Lane isn't it? I've been to Hillsborough and we kicked the OCF's arses."

"Nicely, I've been to your place, Ashton Gate midweek cup match, we had a decent ruck until your boys had it away."

"Wouldn't have happened if I'd been there," he says bristling with bravado.

"Anyway it doesn't matter, I moved on and ran with the Hells Angels and that's a whole new world of violence."

Pete nods, "I've heard, sounds like you boys might have some trouble following you, what you gonna do?"

"I'm gonna try and broker a deal with them, if not it'll be a head on battle, winner takes all and it won't be pretty!"

At that moment Rob walks up, "Alright bruv, alright feller?"

"Were you BBC as well?" asks Pete.

"Fuck that, footballs for girls, I do my fighting with real men not poofs!"

Pete starts forward bristling, I put my hand on his arm, "He's winding you up," I say, "It's his way of making friends."

Pete relaxes and smiles, "You boys have certainly made a name for yourselves In Hanley, I've been on holiday but social media even reached Tenerife." He shakes both our hands, "I've always fancied a crack at those greasy bikers and I still know a few CSF lads so if it comes on top I'll be bouncing in the middle of it!"

"Cheers feller," I add warmly, "I'll keep you in the loop."

PJ shouts out, "It's time to go boys the girls from Hanley need servicing!" With that we all troop out and head for the coach.

We arrive back in Hanley at six, with the coach pulling into the Ship car park, the other pub in our village. I feel uncomfortable drinking in a competitor's pub, so I say my goodbyes and head back to the Red Lion, while the others file inside.

I open the door to see Molly, Sally and Lucy sitting at the bar chatting, "Did you have a good time on your jolly boy's outing love?"

"Well the local sights have certainly been interesting," I smile then add, "If I tell you I doubt you'll believe half of it."

"Try me," answers Molly, "not much surprises me round here." So I order a pint, grab a stool and begin to recount the day.

CHAPTER THIRTEEN

Molly stayed up until two in the morning, spending time with her friends after the pub had closed.

It is now six thirty and the sun is streaming through the bedroom window, time for a solitary thrash I think to myself. I ease out of bed taking care not to wake the gorgeous sleeping Molly and head to the spare room for leathers and a helmet. After a couple of espresso's and cigarettes, I head off to the garage for the bike. I fire up the bike in the garage, to muffle the noise and ease it out onto the road barely above tick over. I head north towards Gloucester, intending to find the glorious roads towards Tintern Abbey, that Steve has waxed lyrical about. At this ungodly hour on a Saturday morning the roads around Gloucester are deserted. I soon leave the city behind, cracking the throttle on each short straight, before laying the bike on its side, foot pegs scraping, rear tyre scrabbling for grip, as I round each bend. My rhythm improves and I pick up speed, sliding the rear occasionally. Up ahead, in the distance, I spot a sports bike, so I start to hunt it down. It takes fifteen minutes before I'm close enough to make out the bike. It's a 2017 CBR 1000RR Fireblade, in Repsol colours. The rider, a lanky lad, is gently grazing his knee sliders on every bend. I stay behind him for a couple of miles, watching his technique, it looks impressive but it's not that fast. I choose my moment, a long sweeping left hander, which he enters with his knee down. I hit the apex and pass him on the exit, briefly raising my left hand in acknowledgement, before quickly returning it to the bar to snick into fourth. I barrel along the straight, before running it out wide for the next left hander. I glance in my mirror to see him closing rapidly on my inside. I brake letting the prick through before he takes us both out. At the apex I nail it, firing it up his inside; I pass him and disappear into the distance. A few bends later I check my mirrors, no sign of him. I take it he's admitted defeat, so I carry on my solo ride.

It's now eight o'clock, with the bike safely stashed in the garage, I'm in the kitchen cooking a fry up. I hear Molly stirring; probably the smell of bacon, no one can resist the smell of bacon or toast! She comes into the kitchen dressed in my discarded t-shirt, which is slightly too short.

"Morning baby you're up early, mmm I thought I smelled breakfast, coffee?" Molly makes the drinks while I finish the breakfast, and we both sit down together.

Molly is hungrily tucking in when I say, "I didn't ask last night, how was your girly day?"

"Mmm good," she mutters between mouthfuls, "It seems Rob's a chip off the old block he's been a real sweetie with Sally and Callum adores him Sally is definitely smitten,"

"And Lucy?" I ask.

"Well she's trying to come up with a plan to get Allun to propose to her as it's not a leap year until next year seems like everyone's loved up!"

"I was chatting with Rob yesterday and he's hooked too I've never seen him like this before as for Allun he's so in awe of the fact that Lucy is going out with him the chances of him proposing are nil. I'm afraid she'll have to wait until next year."

"And you?" She asks pointedly.

"Me? Well I'm the happiest I've ever been but I need to sort out this shit with the MC before I can move on and settle down, I do have a plan but I need to speak to Rob about it later." Molly smiles weakly.

"I don't want you getting hurt baby can't you just hide out here and pretend it never happened?"

"I wish, but sooner or later they will find us that's why I need to try and broker a deal."

Later I call Rob, "Are you alone?" I question, "I've got an idea and I need a chat."

"Of course I've just got back from Sally's give me ten minutes to have a shower then come round and I'll fire up the Rocket."

We sit in the kitchen sipping at espresso's and smoking cigarettes.

"What's on your mind?" Rob asks.

"We both seem to be making a good go at making normal lives for ourselves down here, the only problem is the MC, we need to broker some sort of deal with them. The only person I trust to do that is Lentil, so do you fancy a trip up to Shropshire to see him?"

"Good call, but do you reckon he'll see us without grassing us up?"

"I'm sure of it, I rented his sisters place remember and it was through my own stupidity they found me, not because of Lentil."

"OK what about taking Allun as back up?"

"Yeah Allun would be cool."

"When you planning it, I'll ask him?"

"How about next weekend? I'll ring Lentil and set it up."

"Great, I'll go and ask Allun and make sure we are both free."

CHAPTER FOURTEEN

I'm sitting at my favourite corner of the bar with my pint waiting for Rob and Allun to show up, so we can finalise the details of our Shropshire trip.

They walk in laughing and chatting, "An Abbot and a Carling please Molly," orders Rob, then he turns to me, "How's it going?"

"Not bad I've spoken to Lentil," I answer as I get off my stool. They collect their pints from the bar and we head for the table in the alcove by the window.

"So what did he say? Is he up for it?" Rob questions.

"Yeah, he's gonna help us out, but he reckons we need to go up Thursday not the weekend, is that a problem for either of you?"

"Fine by me," nods Rob.

"And me," Allun adds.

"I don't see why you have to go up at all," Molly is hovering, "I thought you were just going to make a deal with them then everything would be OK?"

"Come and sit down with us Molly, I'll go through all the details of the plan and as you're involved you might as well join us."

"What is it you need me to do?" stutters Molly.

"I don't mean involved with the plan, just involved with me. I would have told you all this later anyway."

She sighs with relief, "Ok but if anyone comes in I'll have to serve them."

"That's fine; I'll start with the date change then the plan OK?" They all nod in agreement.

"Firstly, it's the middle of August so all the new bikes have just come out. That means for the next month or so Lentil is going to be busy sorting out all the new Harley's and he reckons the weekends are busiest, so if we want to get in and out without being spotted the best day is Thursday."

"I don't see why you have to go up there at all," interrupts Molly, "can't you just tell him the offer, let him tell them and wait for an answer."

"I thought of that but I know the boys and for them to take us seriously we need to make a video with Lentil and put our case to them, do you agree Rob?"

"Yeah he's right," agrees Rob. "We've no chance without playing it Lentil's way, he's the judge and jury when any of the chapters fall out."

"So what exactly is the offer?" asks Allun.

"When I left the MC, I cleared out the petty cash, that's four hundred grand, and when Rob left he did the same so that's eight hundred grand in total that's all they know about, I want to offer to pay them back with interest, so my proposal is one million pounds in cash! We will also vow never to reveal any of the dealings, dodgy or otherwise, of the MC or any other Hells Angels and we will stay away from all Hells Angels wherever possible!"

"Wow! Why don't you just give them your pants and socks as well?" retorts Allun.

"To be fair mate given what we've done that's a fair offer," adds Rob.

"And in return?" Molly asks.

"And in return they vow to leave us and our families alone and to never enter Hanley," I say seriously.

"Do you think they'll agree?" Molly asks.

"Well given the amount of shit we know, not just about them but all the other chapters, and knowing we could drop them into the law's lap at any time, they would be stupid not to," smiles Rob, "Right bruv?"

"It is indeed, at any point we could walk into a police station, hand ourselves in and start singing like canaries then before you know it the entire of the Hells Angels, not just here but in America as well, would crumble, the police would give us new identities to live out our lives in peace."

"Wow! This is serious isn't it?" exclaims Molly.

"Yeah it is, that's why we have to do it right, now will you pour us all another pint please Molly?" She gets up and curtsies mockingly, "Of course Sir!" She says before going off to get the drinks.

"So where does Lentil live?" asks Allun.

"On a farm on the outskirts of Much Wenlock in Shropshire," answers Rob.

"It's about eighty miles away, shouldn't take much more than an hour and a half," I add, "I'm thinking maybe leave about nine to avoid the commuter traffic." Molly returns carrying a tray of drinks, and sits down.

"I want you to promise me you'll be careful, that means all of you," she warns looking round the table.

"I promise babe."

"Promise, " mutter Allun and Rob almost together.

"Right then cheer up you lot I'm going to put some tunes on the jukebox, let's see if we can liven this place up." She sashays out to the back bar, and moments later the music is blaring out.

Thursday dawns but it's not your usual sunny August morning, it's grey and cloudy, almost fitting for our sombre moods.

"You all ready?" I ask and they nod in agreement. "Rob, you know the way don't you?" he nods again, "Let's keep Allun in the middle then and for god's sake take it easy the last thing we need is getting nicked for speeding."

We all follow the routine, fire up the bikes and head off.

An uneventful journey sees us approaching Much Wenlock from the south, with me leading. As we roll into the village I get a tingling sense that something isn't quite right. Over the years I have learned to trust my instincts implicitly, so as we pass the Talbot Inn I make a decision. Instead of taking a right after the church I turn into it and pull round the back away from the road, the others follow behind.

We all park up and remove our helmets, "What's up bruv?" Asks Rob as he lights a cigarette. "Dunno, I've just got a bad feeling, maybe nothing." I'm interrupted by the distant sound of rolling thunder, which can only mean one thing! Harley's and lots of them. My senses have warned me just in time, if we had taken the lane past the priory to Lentil's place we would have been trapped. I gesture for the others to stay back, as the thunder gets louder. Eventually I peer round the edge of the church, staying low so I'm not spotted.

"Bollocks," I mutter diving back behind the wall. "It's the Devils! And the whole bloody crew by the looks of it."

"Shit," snaps Rob, "looks like we're gonna have to call this off, I don't fancy going up against those nasty bastards with just the three of us!" As the thunder recedes up the lane I pull out my phone and dial Lentil, "Its Dan mate, you've got Devils approaching."

"Well I'm not expecting them, you guys OK?"

"Yeah we got off the road when we heard them coming."

"They're here now; I'll text you to let you know the score, as soon as I know." I hang up and turn to the two concerned faces.

"He's gonna text and let me know the score." We all pace and smoke furiously like expectant fathers awaiting the birth. Fifteen minutes pass then my phone pings to life with a message, the others crowd round trying to read it.

'Looks like they're staying will have to re-arrange.'

"Shit all that effort for nowt," moans Rob.

"What's the plan chief?" Allun asks.

"We best head home, that's all we can do, I might be being paranoid but let's push the bikes onto the road before we fire them up, just in case they've left a spotter on the lane and he hears us." We all push our bikes around the church and onto the road, kick the side stands down and park them. Allun and I are putting our helmets on while Rob is finishing his cigarette, when we hear the sound of a car being thrashed, approaching rapidly. A bright red Honda Civic Type R passes, slowing as they go by, with the two lads in the rear pointing excitedly at Rob.

"Bollocks!" shouts Rob quickly jamming on his helmet, "We need to get the fuck out of here they're Devils!"

"What the f….," I almost respond before being cut off by Rob.

"Some of the youngsters have fast cars now," he shouts thumbing the starter, "so no hanging about this time," as he lets out the clutch and roars off up the road, with me and Allun quickly following suit. We thrash out of the village, terrifying an old man who is trying to cross the road. I know the car will be turning around behind us, and they will be phoning the MC to see what they should do. I pin the throttle to the stop, thinking, I know we can out run the Harley's, but I have no idea what that car can do. Up ahead Rob takes a right, obviously trying to get off the main road, Allun follows but I get stuck having to let a lorry pass in the other direction. As I start to turn I see a glimpse of red in my mirrors, 'shit!' I think, this is going to be close. I thrash along giving the poor Triumph everything I've got, foot pegs scraping, rear tyre squealing and sliding in protest. Up ahead Rob and Allun are gradually pulling away from me but each time I sneak a glance in the mirrors the little red Honda is closing. The road starts to carve a path through the Wye Forest, twisting and turning like a long black serpent. I hear a loud 'crack' from behind so I look in my mirrors to see a young lad hanging out of the passenger window of the Civic, with a gun in his hand, while the driver slides the car around the corners. "Shit," I shout to no one, I'm dead if I don't get away from these bastards. I pin the throttle to the stop and press on. A long sweeping left hander lies ahead of me, I feather the front brake slowing as late as I dare and tip it on its side until the foot pegs are scraping. The rear tyre is starting to slide as I approach the apex but I'm holding it on my knee, as I grind my slider into the tarmac. Only a few more yards, as I drift towards the white line, then I can start to pick it up.

Then it happens, everything starts to slow down then go into slow motion, that's when you know you're in trouble. I seem to have an age to decide what to do but in reality it's only milliseconds. I feather the clutch and strain to move my upper body to the inside, gently caressing the back brake, trying to calm the rear and tighten my line, all the while acutely aware of the unforgiving trees lining the road. I'm almost at the apex when the front tyre twitches, 'shit' I think, I've hit a cat's eye. The front lifts and I start to lose it, we start to slide. I kick the bike away and flatten myself, looking for any sort of gap. Somehow the still spinning rear tyre grips the tarmac and the bike launches itself into the air. It smashes into a large oak tree, immediately exploding, as it bursts into a ball of flames. I curl myself into a ball and await impact.

Moments later I'm hurtling head over heels down a steep hill, clipping tree trunks and roots as I go. Thank god I've got decent leathers on I think to myself as I start to slow. I eventually come to a stop, half of me in a large bush, just behind a huge sycamore tree. I lay still for a moment trying to get my breathing under control. As my racing heart slows I start to check myself over, extremities first, fingers, fine, toes all working, I work my way up, arms, legs, all good. I gingerly try to sit up, "ouch," I curse silently. I seem to have broken a couple of ribs. I quietly ease myself out of the bush and move behind the large tree and peer up the massive hill I've just descended at speed. At the top I can make out the cars headlights illuminating the four lads trying to peer into the dimness of the forest. I stay still as I hear the sound of rolling thunder approaching, the rest of the Devils are arriving. I ease out my phone, keeping it hidden inside my jacket so the light doesn't give away my whereabouts; I dim the screen further before typing out a message. 'I've crashed I'm OK Devils are looking for me don't come back I'll call later.'

As I slide the phone into my inside pocket I hear voices from above, "If he's survived that drop he won't be alive for long, get a fire extinguisher and put that wreck out then tip it over the edge, the cops are out with the helicopter and we don't need to get caught up in this, move it!"

I hear the noise of the fire extinguisher, and then a few grunts, followed by metallic clanking as the remains of my bike are tipped over the edge. I can hear the sound of a distant helicopter approaching as I hear a shout, "Come on move out! Any direction will do just meet back at Lentil's!"

Many engines fire up and set off in both directions, as the sound of the approaching helicopter gets louder. I sit rigidly still as the helicopter passes overhead, hardly daring to breathe as it turns and sweeps by again. The sound starts to fade as it heads off in the direction from which it came, eventually descending into silence. I stay still for fifteen minutes longer, before gingerly getting to my feet and surveying my surroundings. The tree line ends about thirty feet away, opening out into fields, on the edge of which I can make out some houses, with smoke curling out of one of the chimneys. I carefully pick my way through the trees and head across the field in the direction of the distant houses.

CHAPTER FIFTEEN

I hop over the fence, wincing from the pain in my ribs, and follow the road into the village, noticing the sign which reads Far Forest. Up ahead I can see my saviour, a pub with the sign 'Plough Inn' blowing gently to and fro in the breeze. I walk in, place my helmet on the bar and look along the pumps in search of a decent pint.

"What'll it be love?" The barmaid asks, eyeing me suspiciously.

"I'll have a pint of Fuggles please," as I look down at my leathers to see them looking very battered and covered in mud. "I fell off the back of my mate's bike," I offer in explanation, "and he didn't stop, so I've been walking and trying to ring him, then I came across this place, so I figure I might as well have a few pints while I wait for him to answer his phone."

"Who needs enemies with a mate like that," she laughs and she turns to serve someone else. I pick up my pint and head for a table by the door. I pull out my phone and can hardly see the screen, so I turn the brightness back up. Two messages, one from Rob the other from Allun. I read Rob's first.

'No worries glad you're safe I'm waiting for Allun to catch up give me a shout when you need picking up'.

Then from Allun, 'With Rob god that was hairy see you soon'.

I flip to my phone book and dial Rob, it takes a few moments then starts to ring, after two rings he answers it, "You alright bruv?"

"Yeah just about and you guys?"

"We're both cool, where are you?"

"I'm sat in the Plough Inn in a place called Far Forest." I hear him relaying the information to Allun, who I presume is looking at a map on his phone as he almost immediately comes back with, "Ten minutes and we'll be with you, hold tight and hang in there," the phone clicks off.

I finish my pint and wander back to the bar to refresh it, "Can I have another one please love?"

"You managed to get hold of him then?" She asks as she pulls me a fresh pint.

"Yeah he'll be about ten minutes," I answer and I return to my seat by the door. I'm halfway down my pint when I hear the drone of two bikes approaching, moments later Rob and Allun come into view and park outside the front of the pub.

"Jesus boyo, look at the state of you!" Allun looks stunned as he enters the pub.

"That's what happens when you slide down the road at one hundred and thirty, followed by a trip down a steep hill through the trees," I grimace.

"You OK?" Rob looks worried.

"Apart from a few broken ribs, yeah fine, gonna be sore tomorrow though and by the way if she says anything, I told the barmaid I fell off the back of your bike," I nod towards Rob, "I don't want word getting around of a random biker who's crashed walking in here, the Angels think I'm dead."

"You probably should be," smiles Allun affectionately.

"Always said you had nine lives, just like a cat, you must be running low now though," laughs Rob as I grimace at them both.

"Come on let's get out of here before the pain really kicks in, and Allun I'm on the back of you so no bloody wheelies this time!" We get up to leave and the barmaid shouts over, "You're brave getting back on his bike."

"It's OK I'm going on the other one this time I'll just give him a good kicking when we get home," she joins us in laughter as we head for the door and walk out of the pub.

"Don't make me laugh," I clutch my ribs, "It bloody hurts."

We all mount up, with Allun asking for the third time if I'm OK, then we set off in the direction of Hanley, at a much more sedate speed than the one which saw us leave Much Wenlock.

"Oh my god! What's happened?" Exclaims Molly rushing around the bar to hug and kiss me.

"Ouch! Careful babe," I wince.

"Oh God, you're hurt, where does it hurt baby?"

"I'm OK, honestly it's just a couple of broken ribs, help me off with my jacket and get me a pint and I'll tell you all about it."

"Poor baby," says Molly worriedly, as she helps me off with my jacket, then, "Oh God! Look at that" as my t-shirt pulls up, revealing a mass of angry bruises all down my left hand side.

"It's just a scratch," I try to laugh, but end up wincing at the pain from my ribs.

"I've got some codeine in my bag," pronounces Janet, wandering over while rummaging in her oversized handbag. "Some of these and a few pints and you'll be right as rain," she says still rummaging.

"It's like Mary bloody Poppins," laughs Allun, "Oh look there they are on the bookshelf next to the elephant!"

"Here we go," Janet triumphantly produces a packet of tablets.

"Get them down you," says Molly handing me a pint of Abbot, "and tell me who's done this to you. "

We all sit around the table by the window and I start to tell Molly what happened, I get to the point where they are chasing us out of Much Wenlock and turn to Rob, "What was that car? It's fucking quick, I was flat out and I still couldn't shake it."

"I told you some of the younger ones have got fast cars, they call themselves the 'Fast Response Team', the one chasing us was a Honda Civic Type R, one hundred and seventy flat out, it handles too."

"Tell me about it, I was pulling one fifty and they were catching me they took a pot shot at me so I decided to go balls out to lose them, then I crashed." Molly clasps her hands over her mouth to stifle a scream as both Rob and Allun look concerned.

"What happened mucker?" Allun asks.

"Pushed a bit too hard and lost the front end, the bike flipped up and hit a tree and exploded, while I shot down a steep hill through the trees and landed in a bush about thirty yards down."

They all look at me shocked, holding their breath, waiting for me to continue.

"The rest of the Angels arrived and decided I was dead, or at best nearly dead so they tipped what was left of my bike over the edge and disappeared as the police helicopter was on its way."

Molly gets up and kisses my forehead then sits back down transfixed.

"Go on," mutters Rob.

"I text you two, dusted myself down and set off walking through the fields to a village I could see in the distance. I found the pub and rang you guys," turning to Molly "and we came home carefully."

"If you weren't so bruised I would punch you," Molly retorts kissing me again.

"Punch him anyway," laughs Rob, "a few more bruises won't show." The tension relieved we all start to chuckle.

"How long will it take your ribs heal?" Allun asks.

"Two weeks and they'll be fine I've broken plenty before."

"Great we need a shopping trip then, you need a new bike, leathers and helmet and I fancy a new bike after daft lad here left me for dead."

Molly helps me up, I say my goodnights, and she leads me upstairs with the promise of a hot bath. As we head out of the bar I hear Rob and Allun bickering about whether it is their respective bikes or riding skills, which shows who's the quickest.

I climb into the bath, easing my aching bones, Molly walks in and kisses me, handing me a glass.

"Brandy for medicinal purposes," she says biting her upper lip, "If they think you're dead then it's all over isn't it?"

"No babe, they'll still come after Rob, I'll speak to Lentil and try and sort something out." I drain my glass and hold it up, "Any chance of another? It seems to be helping." She scowls at me as she goes off to get more brandy.

CHAPTER SIXTEEN

I awake the next morning feeling like I've been hit by a double decker bus, twice! I carefully reach out, feeling for the packet of codeine, I pop a couple out, then gingerly pick up the glass of water to wash them down. Molly stirs and reaches out to cuddle me, "Ouch," I wince as her hand rests on my badly bruised muscles. "Sorry baby I forgot," she quickly withdraws her arm, "Silly question, but how are you feeling?"

"To be honest, like death warmed up," I manage a weak smile.

"Stay in bed then and I'll make you some breakfast," she says lovingly as she puts on a t-shirt and slides out of bed.

"Nah, I'll get up in a minute once the pain killers have kicked in otherwise I'll just stiffen up."

"Might not be a bad thing," giggles Molly as she heads for the kitchen, and then looking back over her shoulder, "Poached eggs on toast OK?"

"Great," I answer as I swing my legs out of bed and sit on the edge. I ease myself to my feet and walk over to the full length mirror to inspect the result of yesterdays off road excursion. The left side of my chest, where my ribs are broken, is covered with angry bruises. The outside of my left leg is bruised from my hip to my ankle, and there's bruising on both of my forearms.

Molly pops her head around the door, "God you look a mess," she looks concerned, "are you sure you don't need to go to a hospital?"

"Nah, I'm all good, do me a favour though, grab my black holdall from the spare room will you please, it's got my first aid kit in it."

"Sure thing darling," she disappears around the door, returning a few minutes later with my bag, "This one?"

"Thanks," I take it and put it on the bed, rummaging through it until I find what I'm looking for. A tube of arnica cream, a roll of wide Elastoplast tape and a full box of codeine. I gently apply the arnica to my bruised body, my old man used to swear by the stuff when he played football and it certainly helps with the bruising. Next I cut three strips of Elastoplast, "Give me a hand with this tape will you please?" I raise my arm as Molly helps me to apply the tape over my broken ribs. "Pull that one a little tighter," I instruct. When she's finished I take a deep breath and smile, "Ready to face the world now.

"I hope you're going to get dressed first," she grins wickedly.

We are sitting in the kitchen eating breakfast when Molly turns to me looking nervous, "This is only the beginning, it's going to get worse isn't it?"

"Maybe," I muse pensively, "if I can get Lentil to pull through, everything will be fine," I pause before adding, "The worst case scenario is they find us before Lentil can do the deal."

"What will happen then?"

"To be honest I don't want to think about it," I pause before adding, "I don't want to keep any secrets from you so here goes, you saw what happened on the news in Barmouth, well those boys would arrive first with the intention of tearing the place apart then half an hour later Cecil and Mother or Hatch and Zeb would turn up to direct the end game."

"Cecil and Mother? What kind of Hells Angels names are those?" She laughs.

"I never dared to ask they are two of the most evil bastards on this earth, I've seen them torture other Angels for taking the piss out of their names."

"Oh God and they will be coming to Hanley?"

"Hopefully not, but if it does come to that I now know enough boys locally to take the first lot down then I'll deal with Cecil and Mother."

"I don't want you getting hurt darling, will you ring Lentil to see what's happening?"

"Chill babe the Devils will be there until at least Monday he'll call me when it's quiet."

"I trust you darling, I just can't stand the thought of you getting hurt again, I'm going to open up, you stay here and take it easy OK?"

I smile and nod, trying to reassure her, knowing her fears will abate, but also knowing that the battle may well descend on us.

Later that afternoon, I'm in my usual position at the corner of the bar, when Jess comes in. She goes behind the bar; Molly quickly hands over to her, pours herself a drink and comes round to join me.

"I thought we could have a bit of fun tonight, I've got karaoke coming and I've invited everyone round is that OK baby?"

"As long as you don't expect me to sing, that's great."

"Spoilsport," Molly glares at me.

"OK I will but when you realise how bad it is you won't ever ask me again."

"It can't be that bad everyone can sing."

"Not me, you'll find out for yourself later."

She flashes me a smile over her shoulder as she heads upstairs to get herself ready for this evening's entertainment.

An hour later two young lads arrive, lugging in equipment and start to set up the karaoke in the opposite corner of the bar. After twenty minutes of fiddling around and plugging various leads in I hear the classic, "One two, testing, one two" a few adjustments on the control panel, then again, "One two, testing, one two." Satisfied they wander over to the bar to order drinks. "I'll get those lads what are you having?"

"Two pints of Thatcher's please," then turning to me, "Cheers mate where's Molly?"

"Upstairs making herself look pretty, I'm Dan her other half," I offer my hand.

They introduce themselves, the taller one speaking, "I'm Nick and this is Dave, I heard Molly had found herself a bloke, so you're the lucky one?"

"I am indeed," I answer as the gorgeous Molly makes an appearance, resplendent in a long red dress, which accentuates her curves.

"I don't scrub up too bad do I?" She flashes them a smile then follows with, "I see you boys have met then and yes he is lucky, but so am I."

The bar starts to fill up; this karaoke lark is certainly popular around here. Allun and Lucy come in holding hands and chatting, followed by Rob and Sally, Rob slips his arm from around Sally's waist and heads for the bar, the others come over to me.

"How are you doing mucker?" Asks Allun.

"Not too bad mate I've got my ribs taped up I've broken plenty before so I know that after two weeks they stop hurting, until then just keep taking the painkillers and get on with it."

"You all right?" Asks Rob as he hands the girls their drinks.

"Yeah, I'll survive."

There's a stir in the bar and I hear Molly's voice over the PA system.

"Welcome to the Red Lion karaoke evening, there are slips here and some over on the bar so put your name and songs on them then hand them in to Nick or Dave," she looks round at the two smiling lads.

"Right then I'm going to get things started, OK hit it boys." With that she belts out her rendition of 'Only You' by Yazoo, all the time gazing directly at me, making me feel like the only person in the room. God I love this woman. Once she's finished singing she smiles at the crowd and asks, "Come on then whose next?"

She hands the microphone back to Nick who announces, "Janet and John come on up here."

"How are you feeling darling?" She asks as I encircle her waist with my arm and kiss her.

"Like I lost a fight with a double decker bus!"

"Poor baby," then turning to the others, "Have you all put your songs in?"

"We've got two in," giggle Sally and Lucy together.

"I will do one, but later," mumbles Allun mysteriously.

"And you?" She asks Rob.

"Not my thing I'm afraid Molly, I can't sing."

"That's what he says," she laughs nodding at me, "surely you two can't be that bad?"

"We tried it once in Spain after a load of beer it seemed like a good idea but after the first thirty seconds they turned us off and shut the whole thing down so we wouldn't try again, remember Rob," I chuckle to myself as I recall the experience.

"I do indeed and that's why I won't subject anyone else to that horror."

"You two are no fun," she laughs as she wanders off to collect some slips from the bar and take them over to Nick and Dave.

The evening proves to be a roaring success with most of the people there singing two or three songs. Eventually Allun gets up, straightens his shirt and says, "Wish me luck boys." We both slap him on the back and cheer as he makes his way through the throng. He whispers in Dave's ear, who nods then Nick announces, "Allun with 'The only Girl in the World', take it away," he hands the microphone to Allun. He belts out his rendition of the classic Dean Martin song. He works his way through the crowd singing as he goes. He approaches us and stops in front of Lucy, finishing the song, singing only to her. As the final bars come he slips his hand into his pocket, and then drops to one knee still gazing up at Lucy.

"Will you make me the happiest man alive?" He says opening the box to reveal a huge diamond ring, "and become my wife?"

Lucy bends to kiss him, "Yes, oh yes." As he gets up and hugs her, the whole pub cheers. Everyone comes over to congratulate the happy couple. When it eventually calms down I wander over to Rob, "Shall we get this over with then or we'll never hear the last of it."

"We might as well it's nearly closing time anyway," Rob grins.

"Go on boys," cheers Molly.

As we approach the karaoke I whisper to Rob and he bursts out laughing. I speak to Dave, he nods at Nick who announces, "A big hand for Dan and Rob, they reckon they can't sing so don't be alarmed."

We take a microphone each, and I announce, "This is for Allun," we begin singing, very badly, 'Another one Bites the Dust' by Queen. Molly shaking her head at how bad we actually are comes over and joins us singing. Soon the entire pub is serenading Allun.

CHAPTER SEVENTEEN

August rolls into September as we lay in bed cuddling. Molly asks, "How's my wounded soldier?"

"Not too bad considering," I answer as I slide out of bed to go to the toilet we both look at my now yellowing bruises.

"Jeez it still looks bad."

"A few more days and I'll look a lot better, I'm a quick healer."

"I've been thinking, we need to throw a party for Lucy and Allun, maybe Saturday what do you think?"

"Great idea, do you think Nick and Dave will do a disco?"

"I'm sure they will, I'll ask, ooh it's exciting I love a party. Will you make breakfast while I start making some calls to get it organised."

"Sure babe let me just take some painkillers, scrambled eggs on toast OK?"

"Mmm sounds good," she mutters distractedly, "I'm just going to make a list so I don't forget to tell anyone."

I clear the dishes after breakfast, while Molly is still on the phone. She pauses in between phone calls, "I'm gonna pop over and see Rob, see you later babe."

"See you later," she mutters as she dials again, ticking another name off the list.

I sit at the kitchen table in the cottage, "Get the coffee on. How's things?"

"All good," answers Rob as he fires up the Rocket espresso maker, "It was a good night last night wasn't it?"

"Yeah Allun's a dark horse I wasn't expecting that."

"Actually I knew, I was with him when he bought the ring."

"And you didn't bother to tell me."

"He swore me to secrecy I told no one; it's not a bad idea though is it?"

"What Allun and Lucy getting engaged? I think it's awesome they are great together."

"Not that, I meant engagement in general," he delves into his pocket and brings out a ring box, I stare at him bemused.

Eventually I regain my composure, "You as well? Let's have a look then," as I reach for the box. I open it to be greeted by a large diamond solitaire ring, "Wow I bet that wasn't cheap?"

"Hmm six grand, but she's worth every penny and Callum's a great kid, we'll make a great family."

"Wow, I never thought I'd see the day a woman tamed my brother!"
"We've all got to grow up and settle down at some point, isn't it about time you did the decent thing?"
"Maybe when this is all over, so when are you going to ask her?"
"Hmm I dunno, I'm not into public displays like Allun, we're going out for the day on Friday, having a picnic down by the river just the three of us I'm thinking of asking her then, I'd like Callum to be there, what do you think?"
"Go for it she obviously makes you happy," I get up and give him a big hug. "Molly is throwing an engagement party in the pub for Allun and Lucy on Saturday, might as well make it a joint one."
"Don't say anything yet. Not even to Molly she might say no."
"OK your call just let me know how it goes OK."
"Will do."

Friday early evening and I'm sat at my usual corner of the bar, when Molly comes down.
"All sorted, everything is ready for tomorrow I've even had a banner made up, exciting isn't it?"
I nod as I notice my Jag pass the window with Rob in the driver's seat beaming. I smile to myself thinking it looks like it's all gone well then.
"Come and sit down babe, Rob and Lucy have just pulled up." She wriggles onto the stool next to me, and we both stare expectantly at the door. They enter arms entwined and Rob holding Callum's hand, all wearing beaming smiles.
"I'm having a new dad!" Callum blurts out.
"Well done Rob," I get up to congratulate them but Molly pushes past me squealing.
"Oh my god does this mean…?" She falters as Sally holds out her left hand to display the ring.
"Wow it's gorgeous," she hugs Sally excitedly, and they both jump around. I hug Rob and clap him on the back.
"Open a couple of bottles of champagne Jack." He rushes off to the cellar to find some.
"I'd rather have a pint thanks all the same," says Rob still beaming.
"I'll get beer as well the champagne is for a toast to my little brother and his new fiancé."
Jack returns with two bottles, I open one as he opens the other, both letting the corks fly across the room. He lines up glasses on the bar and we slowly start to fill them. Once everyone is holding a glass of bubbly I announce, "A toast, to Rob and Sally."

"Rob and Sally," comes the reply from everyone in the bar.

"To your future happiness, may every day be as happy as this one."

"Hear, hear," shouts John from the corner. We all drink a toast and a cheer goes up. I put my champagne down and order two pints of Abbot and then Callum leaps into Rob's arms, putting his own around Rob's neck.

"Do I have to wait until you are married before I can call you dad?" He beams.

"No you can start now, son." Rob beams back.

"Cool I can't wait to tell them at school, hey everybody this is my dad!" And so a priceless memory is made. Sally comes over and slips her arm around them both. I pull out my phone and capture their first family portrait.

Molly grabs me and squeals, "We can make it a joint engagement party tomorrow, oh God I need to get another banner, I can't just have one for Lucy and Allun," she gasps, panicking.

"Calm down I've got one, I ordered it after I went to Rob's the other day."

"You knew he was going to propose and you didn't tell me?" She glares at me.

"I asked him not to," interrupts Rob, "I was worried Sally might say no."

"Not a chance," beams Sally.

"Right then when you've finished your champagne the next rounds on me," I announce.

"Cheers Dan," Rob looks adoringly at Sally, "what do you want to drink love?"

"Mmm I'm quite liking this champagne."

"Bring another bottle up from the cellar please Jack."

After everyone has gone Molly and I are tidying up. "Another happy couple," she smirks at me wickedly, "I don't suppose it will ever happen to me?"

I sigh, "I have every intention of making an honest woman of you, I just need to get the problem with the MC sorted first."

She kisses me, "well don't hang around too long or someone else might snap me up, oh and my ring has got to be better than either of theirs!" With that she flounces upstairs leaving me to turn off the lights and follow behind.

CHAPTER EIGHTEEN

Molly is already getting stressed about making tonight's party perfect. I find her in the back bar rearranging tables.
"I'm going out to the garage to get the ladders so I can hang the banners, OK babe."
She kisses me distractedly, "OK baby, humph I think they were better before" and sets about rearranging the furniture again.
I find myself gazing at the space where my bike used to stand, and start thinking to myself it's about time I start looking for a replacement. My phone rings stirring me from my thoughts, "Hello."
"Dan its Lentil sorry it's taken so long."
"No worries how's things?"
"All good but I'm flat out with bikes and there are always at least half a dozen Angels around the place. So I was thinking, I'm doing a parts run to Brum on Thursday, if it's any good I can arrange to meet you somewhere."
"That sounds great I suppose it goes without saying don't get followed."
"Where abouts do you want to meet, say twelve o'clock?"
"Hopwood services on the M42, is that any good for you?"
"Sounds perfect."
"I'm thinking bring your helmet leave your van there and I'll have you picked up, I don't want to be doing this in the middle of a service station."
"That's ideal I'll be in touch on Wednesday to confirm everything OK?"
"Sure speak soon mate."
Well it looks like everything is finally falling into place. As I move the ladders from the back of the garage a box falls from the shelf. As I start to pick it up it falls open, revealing Christmas lights. I have an idea, so I sort through the box, eight sets in total. I head back inside to find Molly rearranging furniture again, this time in the front bar.
"Are you OK babe?"
"Yes what do you think of the tables in the back bar?"
"They look great," I lie having not even noticed.

"Listen, I've just found a box of Christmas lights in the garage how about I hang them they will be great for the party."

"Fantastic idea," she comes over and kisses me, "Now that's why I love you."

Two hours later I stand back to admire my handiwork, the two banners are hung either side of the bar. I flick the switch and the criss-cross of Christmas lights hanging from the ceiling twinkle into life.

"That's awesome," Molly has sneaked in, "everyone will love it." She kisses me, "I'm going up to get ready, will you sort out Nick and Dave before you come up please darling?"

"No worries, I might as well have a pint or two while I'm waiting." Molly glares at me in exasperation, before heading up to the flat to make herself look beautiful.

"It should be a good night," says Jess as she's pulling my pint, "Who else is on the bar tonight?"

"Jack and Sam are both in so there should be enough of you."

"We'll be fine," smiles Jess, "Two engagements together, I wonder if they are planning weddings yet?"

"I doubt it, I suspect it will be a year or two before either of them get married, excuse me Jess."

I get up as Nick and Dave walk in. "Alright boys," I greet them, "Molly wants you to set up in the corner over there is that OK?"

"Yeah great Dan, give us half an hour and we'll be ready."

"I'm off upstairs to get changed, I'll get Jess to pull you both a pint, Thatcher's isn't it?"

"Cheers Dan that's great."

Molly and I are waiting at the bar when the guests of honour all arrive together. Molly kisses and hugs Sally and Lucy, while I shake the two boy's hands.

"Alright boys, I still can't believe you both did it in the same week."

"You next Dan," grins Allun.

"I need to sort out the shite with the MC first, on which note I spoke to Lentil earlier."

"What's happening then," interrupts Rob.

"His place is constantly full of Angels but he's doing a parts run to Brum on Thursday, I told him one of us would meet him at Hopwood services and bring him down here OK."

"I'm happy to go," offers Allun.

"It's alright mate I'll do it, Lentil doesn't know you and vice versa so it'll be much easier if I go."

Molly interrupts, "Right then I think if Allun and Lucy stand here," she says excitedly showing them a spot by the door, "and Rob and Sally stand here." She moves to the opposite side of the doorway. "Then you can all greet the guests as they arrive and thank them for coming," we all smile at her enthusiasm, "Come on then get in your positions."

"Chop, chop people do as she says," I laugh, "I'll get you guys some drinks the usual for you two I take it and girls?"

"Vodka and diet coke please," answers Sally.

"Ooh me too please," says Lucy.

"Right, on their way." I wander off to the bar to get the drinks as I hear the thanks and introductions as Janet and John arrive for their usual early evening drinks. A few more arrivals and then Nick and Dave start playing the music. Soon the party is in full swing with everyone laughing, chatting and dancing. I leave Molly chatting to Lucy and head to the bar where Allun and PJ are deep in conversation. "Another pint please Jack do you two boys want one?"

"Carling for me please mucker," answers Allun.

PJ turns and shakes my hand, "Alright Dan me old mate, I'll have a Carling with you if that's OK?"

"And two Carlings please Jack."

PJ continues, "I was just telling Allun here what a lucky feller he is and you as well, I mean you're a lovely bloke and all that but you two have got yourselves a pair of cracking women there."

"I know mate, so it looks like I'm staying here forever!"

"That's good, you and your brother are both nice fellers and if there's any trouble with those Hells Angels I'll be right in the middle of it, can't be letting you fellers have a fight without me now can I?"

At that moment some younger lads, who no one seems to know, barge into PJ's back making him spill his pint, I can see the red mist rising within him as he turns to them.

"Alright boys I take it you're gonna apologise and buy me another pint then we can get on with enjoying the party."

"Fuck off grandad you spilled it cause you're pissed."

"I'll say it again you can apologise and buy me another pint and we'll forget all about it," he leans in towards the lad, "Or I can beat the shit out of you."

I'm on my toes ready for it to kick off and I can see Rob hovering behind them, obviously picking up on the situation.

The lad laughs, turning to his mates in a show of bravado, "This old fucker reckons he's gonna do me what do you think boys?" I see him making a fist as he starts to turn back towards PJ; I'm ready for anything if he tries to throw a punch.

He grins at PJ then starts to unleash a punch, PJ's reactions are like lightening and before the lads hand has passed his own body PJ has unleashed a fierce right hand to the end of his chin. His knees buckle and he falls to the floor. There are a few moments of stunned silence, then one of the lads picks up a stool to attack us with.

Before I have a chance to react Rob has wrenched the stool from his grasp, with his hands full he head-butts him in the face sending him sprawling to the floor. Giving the other two no time to react I hit the closest to me putting him on his arse; I'm just about to go after the last one when Allun charges past. He grabs the lad by the throat and lifts him off the floor, squeezing his throat until his face starts to redden.

"Don't you little fuckers ever come in my pub again, abusing my mates, thinking you're hard when you're just a bunch of pussies," Allun shouts angrily.

The other three lads start to get to their feet nursing their injuries, Rob ushers them towards the door, with Allun still holding the lad in the air following. I open the door and Rob pushes then down the steps so they stumble and end up in a heap at the bottom.

Allun launches the hapless Lad he's holding on top of them.

"Now fuck off," I shout "and don't bother coming back you're barred!"

I let the door slam shut and head back to the bar.

"Nice one boys," says PJ grinning.

"You didn't do too bad yourself," replies Rob.

"I know and like I said to Dan earlier any trouble with those Hells Angels and I'm right with you."

Molly arrives at my shoulder, "Are you alright PJ? I've not seen you do that in years."

"Cheeky little buggers thought they were clever but they picked on the wrong ones tonight and no damage done well except to their faces!"

"Thank god," she kisses me, "it seems like I have my own posse of bouncers."

We all laugh and order another round of drinks. A little while later Molly comes back, "I've asked around the younger ones and no one seems to know who they are, so thanks boys."

"That's OK darling," grins PJ," and any time you need sorting out when Dan's not around just give me a shout."

"Watch it," she retorts slapping him on the shoulder.

"Ouch, that hurt," cries PJ recoiling in mock horror.

"Oh it does does it well think yourself lucky it was only those young lads you were fighting with and not me because I will kick your arse."

We all fall about laughing, including PJ. When the laughter eventually subsides, Molly whisks me off to dance with her.

As the last dance plays out there are only three couples left on the dance floor, Molly nuzzles my neck," You know these last few months have been amazing," she murmurs.

"I love you Molly," I murmur back, kissing her as we sway on the dance floor with the music coming to a close.

"Thanks for an awesome party," smiles Sally clinging to Rob.

"Do me a favour and look after him will you, there aren't many like him thank god!"

"I know we've only known each other a month and everyone thinks it's all too quick, but I really do love him and we are planning on a long engagement." We all smile in unison, six close friends brought together in this small village.

Lucy hugs Molly, while Allun claps me on the back, "Cheers mucker." Rob joins us, rests his hand on my shoulder and says, "Come Thursday bruv we can get this MC stuff all over and get on with enjoying the rest of our lives."

"Let's hope so, because I love mine at the moment."

We all say our goodnights and after locking up I lead Molly upstairs to continue the passion.

CHAPTER NINETEEN

Thursday finally arrives as a cool crisp September morning. I'm wide awake and fretting about how today will go. Molly is still sleeping, so I slip quietly out of bed, throw on shorts and a t-shirt and head out to the kitchen. I'm on my second espresso and cigarette when I hear Molly starting to stir. I make her a large mug of tea and take it to her in bed, "Mmm thanks baby you're up early."

"Yeah I couldn't sleep I guess I'm worrying about today with Lentil."

"Why what's wrong?"

"Nothing I'll just be glad when it's all over so we can put this thing to rest and get on with our lives." I kiss her and smile, realising how much I love this woman, "I'm going over to see Rob, just to check everything is on track."

"OK darling and Dan, try not to worry, I love you." I walk out of the bedroom feeling taller, my chest puffed out, as I head over to the cottage to visit my brother.

"Bloody hell you're up early what's up?"

"Nothing, I guess I just want to make sure that today goes off without a problem, I'll get the coffee on while you cover up that scrawny body."

"At least I haven't got a beer belly," he jests.

"That's the problem with living in a pub."

We sit in the kitchen drinking coffee and going over the plan for today. Rob will meet Lentil and bring him back to the cottage, we'll shoot the video, then he'll take Lentil back to his van. The film will be delivered to the MC by Lentil, who will call us when they give him their answer. He will draw up a binding contract and organise getting it signed and finalised.

Satisfied we move on.

"How are things going with Sally?"

"Great we were chatting yesterday and I'm gonna move in with her."

"You're certainly not hanging about bruv."

"I know everyone thinks it's all a bit too quick but sod them, we both feel the same and chances like these don't come along very often, so I'm just grabbing it with both hands."

"Fair play, I must admit I've never seen you so happy and dare I say it, almost like a normal bloke."

"Steady on bruv! I don't think I will ever be classed as normal but yeah I'm enjoying being part of a family and having a proper life."

"So it's still going well with Callum?"

"God yeah, he's a great kid, I never wanted kids but now I've inherited one I wouldn't be without the little sod. That reminds me when are you going to look at bikes?"

"I'm thinking of going on Saturday, why do you want to come?"

"Yeah I'll drive us up in your van I want to take Callum, I'm looking at getting him a PW 50 start him on two wheels young."

"OK Allun wants to go as well he wants another bike so he can keep up with you. I've no idea what he's after though."

"Just wondering, what are you fancying?"

"Well after seeing yours in action I like the idea of it but there's too much plastic, Castle motorcycles have got a brand new Tuono V4 Factory in for fourteen grand."

"Nice."

"I've spoken to Gareth and they've got a demo I can take out so that's probably what I'm thinking of, although I do like the look of the Yamaha MT-10."

"Proper nutters bike the Tuono you'll love it, they reckon the throttle on the MT-10's a bit snatchy."

"Right I'm off to see Molly give me a shout when you get back."

I'm sitting at our kitchen table with Molly and twelve twenty three is showing on the clock on the oven, when my phone rings, it's Rob.

"All right Dan we're back at the cottage I'll get the coffee on, you get your arse over here and let's get this done."

"On my way," I stand up and kiss Molly, "See you later babe."

"OK darling," she kisses me back, "I hope it all goes well."

I let myself into the cottage to find Rob and Lentil sitting at the kitchen table chatting and laughing, both dressed in shorts and t-shirts. I look confused as the plan had been for Rob to take the bike.

"Coffee's ready in the machine help yourself," then seeing the look of confusion on my face Rob adds laughing, "I didn't think it was fair to subject someone of Lentil's erm stature to the RSV's tiny pillion seat, so I thought I'd give the Jag a blast."

"He's as much of a nutter in a car as he is on a bike," Lentil laughs, "I've left fingernail marks in your passenger seat from gripping so tightly!"

He stands up and we hug and slap each other on the back, "Good to see you bro."

"You too it's been too long, Rob filled me in with all the gory details of your run in with the Devil's, you had a lucky escape man."

"Born lucky I guess," as I sit down with my coffee. "Right let's sort out the details of what we need to get in this video before we start."

"OK I've planned a running order but the first thing I need to know is have you both had your gang tattoos covered?"

We both remove our t-shirts, I turn around to reveal the tiger on my back, and meanwhile Rob raises his arm to show his Celtic tattoo down his left ribcage.

Lentil inspects both tattoo's, "Nice ink boys, right first thing is to apologise for leaving. Explain you both needed to start leading normal lives then we'll reveal the cover up tattoo's, with me so far?"

"Sort of," nods Rob "but do we do it together or one then the other?"

"In this situation as your brothers we'll do it together, next we'll go through your offer, a million isn't it?" He asks.

"Yeah I think that's a figure they'll go for," I add.

"If you're sure and you've got it, I think you're right, then you add your terms, don't push the bit about dropping them in it with the law, we'll save that in case they want to negotiate further."

"That's a good plan," interjects Rob.

"I'll film it all then we can have a look through the footage, when we're all happy I'll bugger off, I can add my bit about the binding contract when I edit it, any questions?" Rob and I both shake our heads.

An hour later, after more than a few mistakes and much hilarity, we sit at the table to review the footage we have just shot.

"Yeah I'm happy with that," I nod.

"Me too," adds Rob.

"Right then," says Lentil as he drains his coffee, "I'll be a couple of days editing this, then I'll send the final version through for approval before I send it to the MC."

Rob grabs the car keys, "Come on then, I'll try and keep it under a hundred and forty on the way back."

"God help me," laughs Lentil, then he hugs me as we clap each other on the back again, "Take it easy bro."

"You too bro," I answer as we leave the cottage together. Rob and Lentil get in my Jag and roar off up the road. I walk back over to the pub to see Molly, feeling a lot more positive than I have in a while.

CHAPTER TWENTY

Molly and I are sitting in the kitchen having breakfast. "I'm going up to Gloucester to look for a new bike today do you want to come?" "No darling I don't know what I'm looking at and I've got loads to do here, just make sure you get a pretty one."
My phone rings, I glance at the screen, it's Allun. "Ey up mate what's up?"
"Just wondering what time we are going today?"
"Anytime you like mate have you heard from Rob?"
"Yeah he's just rung me him and Callum are ready at the cottage."
"OK I'll meet you over there, are you taking your bike to trade it in?"
"That's the plan, give me ten minutes and I'll be there," he hangs up.
I let myself into the cottage, Rob is sitting at the kitchen table with Callum jumping around excitedly, and when he sees me he yelps.
"Daddy Rob is going to buy me a motorbike, I'm going to be a proper biker just like you lot," his grin spreads across his entire face.
"That's brilliant," I hear Allun's Ducati approaching, "Come on grab your coats let's go."
Callum squeezes into the back seat and Rob pushes back the seat and gets into the passenger side. I lower my window so I can speak to Allun, "OK mate we'll see you there," he nods and pulls out onto the road and I pull out and follow him.
As I pull into the car park and find a space Allun is already inside talking to Gareth. We all clamber out of the Jag and head inside chatting excitedly. Callum's eyes are like saucers as he takes in the vast array of machines on display, "Wow look at all these!" Rob takes his hand and leads him towards the off road section.
I head over to join Allun and Gareth, who are deep in conversation.
"So have you got a demo then?" Allun asks as I approach.
"Yes I'll get you the keys take it for a spin and I'll see what kind of deal I can do for you," he heads off towards the office.
"What are you fancying," I ask.
"BMW S1000 RR," Allun grins as he points to the gleaming machine next to us "and you?"
"Don't know yet I'm going to wander round and have a look I'll see you when you get back mate."
Gareth returns with the keys for the demonstrator, he wheels it outside then turns to Allun, "Go and enjoy it mate it'll feel completely

different to your Duke." Allun puts on his gear then climbs aboard and heads off up the road.

Gareth comes back inside, "Do you need any help?"

"Nah I'm just gonna have a mooch around and sit on a few bikes is that OK?"

"Sure give me a shout when you find something you like," he heads off to find Rob and try and make another sale.

I'm not sure what I want but I don't like bikes with too much fairing. I have a look at the new Speed Triple, but decide against it as the last one didn't end well. My interest is piqued by the Yamaha MT-10, so I get on to test it for size. It's a nice machine it feels light and flickable; it goes on my list to test. I wander past the Kawasaki's and Ducati's, and then I spot it! A brand new Aprilia Tuono V4 Factory, it's basically the same as Rob's but with no fairing and high bars. I catch myself smiling as I sit astride it, I put my left foot on the foot peg and immediately feel at home, the riding position feels like attack mode. It looks like I've found the one so I set off to the office to look for Gareth and ask if he has a demonstrator.

Rob is in the office with him as I get there his card in hand ready to pay for something.

"Dan, Dan come and see my motorbike come on," Callum enthuses. He drags me over to look at a brand new Yamaha PW 50, he clambers on it already looking at home on a bike, "What do you think?"

"I think it's perfect you're a proper little biker now have you chosen a helmet as well?" I ask.

"Yes I've got a blue one to match my bike I can't wait until I can ride it."

Rob and Gareth come over to join us, "Have you seen anything you like bruv?"

"Actually I have," I turn to Gareth, "I like the new Tuono have you got a demo?"

"I certainly have I'll get you the keys you're going to love it, proper nutter's bike," he grins and heads for the office.

"Copying me then," laughs Rob, "One thing though they don't come with a pillion seat it's an optional extra I had to buy one for mine." I spot Gareth wheeling a Tuono towards the door so I head over to join him.

"Rob has been telling me these things don't come with a pillion seat that can't be right it's got pillion pegs!"

"Unfortunately he's right, did you say you were looking at a new one?"

"Yeah at fourteen grand its fine so how much is the pillion seat then? Molly will kill me if I buy a bike and she can't go on it."

"I presume you're paying cash again if you are I'll throw it in free. I'll also throw in a paddock stand and I can do you an Akropovic full system which retails at two thousand four hundred for a grand if you're interested."

"Sounds good mate let me have a play and I'll let you know, I'm also interested in the MT-10."

I'm just putting my gloves on when Allun arrives back in the car park, so I go over to see him. He removes his helmet revealing a huge grin, "I'll definitely be kicking Rob's arse with one of these," then turning to Gareth, "Do me a good deal and I'll have a brand new one."

"I thought you might its fourteen and a half grand list your Ducati books at nine grand but if you give me four and a half grand you can have the Motoradd one I've got in stock."

"Perfect when can I pick it up?"

"I don't normally work Sundays but Rob has already asked to pick up the PW 50 tomorrow so I could PDI it and you can pick it up then and if Dan wants the Tuono I can do all three for tomorrow."

"Right then, I grin, "Let's try this bad boy out and I'll let you know, have you got a pillion seat and exhaust in stock?"

"I'm sure I have but I'll check and let you know when you get back."

I climb aboard and ease out onto the road, taking it easy until I clear the city boundaries but even at sedate speeds it feels like a naughty puppy straining at the leash. I give it some gas and the front wheel comes up so quickly it almost smacks me in the face! I hook it into third and wind it on again, same result! I quickly hook up into fourth and I'm greeted by a gentle foot high wheelie. I land it and drop two gears while braking hard then tip it into the sharp left hander, it sails round with nothing touching down daring me to go faster!! I'm completely hooked.

Half an hour later I return to the car park to be greeted by Gareth pacing like an expectant father, "Well what do you think of it?" He demands.

"It's absolutely awesome I'll have one," I grin like a Cheshire cat.

"I thought you might, I've promised Allun and Rob I'll open tomorrow so they can have their bikes if you want yours as well I'll get the lads in the workshop to get cracking on with the PDI and fitting the exhaust."

"Fantastic," I shake his hand, "Do you have the pillion seat in stock?"

"Yeah no worries Rob says he's coming in a van for the PW 50 so you can throw all the standard bits in there shall we say one o'clock?"

All three of us smile and nod in agreement. Allun pipes up, "I'll leave the Ducati with you and my helmet and jacket, sods law I'll crash it on the way home otherwise, I'll squeeze in the back of Dan's car and come up in the van with them tomorrow.

"I'm just going inside to take a few pictures to show Molly then we can get off, I won't be long."

We all walk into the Red Lion chatting and laughing, with Callum bouncing around like Tigger. We are greeted by Molly, Sally and Lucy all sat at the bar, "Good shopping trip boys," asks Molly.

"I've got a motorbike its blue and it's really cool," shouts out Callum before any of us can answer. Sally looks nervously at Rob, "Has he really?"

"Yeah it's a little 50cc twist and go we'll teach him to ride it properly so by the time he's old enough to ride on the road he'll be safer than any other kid on the planet," Rob answers.

"It's OK darling I trust you," Sally kisses Rob then Callum.

"So what did you get then?" asks Molly.

"Here I'll show you," I pull out my phone and scroll through the pictures of my new pride and joy.

"Ooh baby that's pretty I like that," then her face drops, "There's nowhere for me to sit," she announces grumpily.

"Ah I knew that was coming I had to buy the pillion seat separately here let me show you," I reclaim my phone and show her google pictures.

"Oh that's OK then it's very sexy isn't it?"

"So what have you bought?" Lucy probes Allun.

"You'll like it let me show you," Allun produces his phone to show off the pictures of his new toy.

"Mmm now that's much sexier than your Ducati," she smiles lovingly.

"We are all going to pick them up tomorrow Mum, here look at my new crash helmet," Callum proudly produces his new Caberg crash helmet.

"So can we all go for a ride when you get back then?" Molly asks

"Great idea," adds Lucy.

"Hmm maybe not us," Rob answers, "I think this one will be too excited to try out his own bike," he ruffles Callum's hair.

"That's fine bruv twelve o'clock round here the three of us can go up in the van then you can bring it back and drop it off whenever." We all shake hands and agree we are all looking forward to getting our new toys tomorrow. The only difference between us and Callum is our toys are bigger, faster and more expensive.

Gareth is as good as his word; we arrive in the afternoon sun, to find three gleaming bikes sitting outside. Callum's little blue Yamaha PW 50 flanked by Allun's glistening white, red and blue BMW S1000RR, and my absolutely stunning silver, red and black Aprilia Tuono V4 factory, resplendent with a pillion seat and full Akrapovic exhaust system.

"Nice work mucker," Allun grins.

"No worries boys glad to be of service, Rob paid yesterday so why don't you two come inside and pay while he loads the van then you can all go off and play."

Allun and I grin at each other and follow him inside wallets at the ready.

An hour later we are parked outside the Red Lion. Sally waves her goodbyes as she climbs in the transit, they are heading down to the farm to give Callum his first lesson.

Molly grabs my waist and kisses me, "Wow it's even sexier in real life!"

Lucy squeezes Allun's bum, "Take me for a ride on that beauty my big stud!" The girls go upstairs to collect their bike gear from our spare room. Allun grins at me, well I'm shocked at how good it is mate, how's yours?"

"Absolutely stunning I won't be getting left behind ever again!"

The girls return in their gear and we all mount up and head out for a gentle Sunday afternoon ride in the warm September sun.

Later, as we are sitting at the bar chatting, Steve walks in, "How's it going boys? I hear you've been and got yourselves new bikes."

"Yeah," both Allun and I grin and nod.

"Well I'm organising a track day at Castle Combe if you fancy it?"

"Sounds good when?" I ask.

"A week on Wednesday shall I put you both down for it?"

"Yeah make it three I'm sure Rob will be up for it," and so the date is set, we just have to make sure our bikes are run in and serviced before the day.

"If you like we can take the bikes out tomorrow and get some miles on them, we should be able to get the first service next week," says Allun, "in fact we could ride down to Castle Combe so you can have a look at the circuit."

"Great idea what about ten o'clock in the car park outside?" I ask and Allun nods in agreement.

CHAPTER TWENTY ONE

The morning of the track day dawns brightly, Rob and I are loading the bikes into my van and Molly and Sally are loading the car with a picnic while Callum is running around excitedly.

Lucy arrives pulling into the car park, "Hey guys Allun has got some last minute work stuff to sort out so he said to go without him and he'll take his bike and meet you there."

"That's fine as long as he's not chickening out," smirks Rob.

"Not a chance he's been like a little kid at Christmas waiting for this."

"Leave your car here and come with us," adds Sally, "there's no point in taking two cars."

"That'll be great," she says searching her bag for her phone, she fishes it out then adds, "I'll just ring Allun and let him know."

I double check the straps holding the bikes down, when I'm happy I jump down and close the door, "Right then are we ready for off?"

An hour later we are parking up in the paddock at Castle Combe. Rob and I carefully unload our bikes, while the girls busy themselves with camping chairs and picnic baskets.

Jake and Joe the two lads from the Jolly Boys outing come over, "Alright boys Steve said you were coming," we exchange handshakes.

"I've never even seen this track before looks like it's going to be fun," Rob answers.

"Damn right it is I can't wait to get out there," then as a bike approaches I add, "Look out, here comes the gay Welshman." We all fall about laughing.

I've been on many race tracks in my time and the paddocks are usually testosterone fuelled with everyone trying to psyche each other out but today it's just a mass of friendly bikers.

A call goes out and we all head off for the briefing. There are three groups, fast, intermediate and novice. Steve, Jake and Joe opt for the fast group, while Allun, Rob and I go for the intermediate. The novice group is going out first so we all head back to the girls for some refreshments.

"So do you reckon you can stay with me on that?" Rob mocks Allun grinning. "And you might have the same engine as me but you'll still get left behind," he laughs at me."

"Big talk little man," I smile and wink at him, "I'll do my talking on the track."

"Well I'll do both boyo," snarls Allun, "I know my way around this place and my bikes faster."

The word goes out ten minutes for the intermediate group. Molly comes over and hugs me, "Ride safely darling OK." I kiss her and then go through my routine of earplugs, helmet, check zips and gloves. Once I'm happy I fire up the bike and let it burble away as it warms up.

A queue starts to form so Allun heads off to join it, Rob quickly follows and I tag on to the back. The Marshalls wander along the line checking bikes and gear as they go. The novice group leaves the track and starts to filter back into the paddock. The rider at the front of the queue is waved off then each subsequent one in turn, I plan on using the first couple of laps as sighting laps to learn the track, then get my head down and reel in the other two. Rob is quick but a bit wild so I know I can catch him, Allun knows the track but even so he's on a new bike. A Marshall taps my helmet stirring me from my reverie and ushers me to the front. The next Marshall raises his arm and waves me out onto the track. Game on!

I accelerate away keeping the throttle wide open through the gentle right hander and over a small rise. A right hander looms so I move over to the left hand side of the track and haul on the brakes before I tip it in. At the apex I feed the throttle back in until I start to exit the turn then I nail it, feeling the back squat as the front end goes light. I brake hard for a chicane which is quickly followed by a right hander, as I wind on the gas it turns into a long sweeping left hander before braking hard for yet another right hand turn. A bit of a kink follows then a straightish section where I accelerate hard, then haul on the brakes for another right which leads onto the start-finish straight. It's not a bad little circuit I think to myself as I up the pace slightly. I can see Rob not too far ahead so I set my sights on hunting him down. Each passing lap sees me edging closer and closer to the back of Rob's bike. He passes someone on the brakes going into the first corner; I close the gap and pass the rider on the exit I'm determined not to let Rob get away.

Accelerating towards the final corner I have already decided to try and pass him on the exit, when I spot Allun just tipping into the bend. I grin, a chance to catch them both. I tuck in behind Rob on the left hand side of the track, he starts to turn in but I leave it and turn in slightly later. As we hit the apex Rob is still on full lean and starting to drift out wide, my later turn in means I'm already starting to lift the bike, enabling me to get on the throttle harder and earlier. My front wheel comes up eighteen inches or so as I pass him accelerating hard now starting to hunt down Allun. We circulate in the same order for another four laps passing quite a few other riders along the way. Eventually I'm in Allun's wheel tracks I decide to sit behind him for a lap to work out where I'm going to pass him. After half a lap I've noticed his lines are very similar to Rob's so I decide to pass him in the same place. As we head up towards the last bend Allun sneaks a glance backwards, he's obviously spotted me as he over cooks it braking slightly too late. I change tactics and squeeze the brakes harder and turn in a little earlier, at the apex I start to drift out slightly. I let it run knowing I'll block Allun's line and he will have to ease off giving me the chance to accelerate away from him, all the while grinning inside my helmet.

All too soon the flags are out signalling the end of our session, as I'm slowing down I glance back to see Rob and Allun exiting the last corner side by side. I laugh as I pull into the paddock, I gave them both a head start and still beat them, let the banter commence. I park the bike and kill the ignition, I remove my gloves and helmet revealing a grin from ear to ear.

Molly rushes over and hugs and kisses me. "Wow I saw you pass both Rob and Allun did you do it at that corner because you knew I could see you?" She squeals excitedly.

"Of course babe," I smile, "I couldn't have you missing me spank these two girls now could I?"

"Oh baby," she kisses me again before eventually letting me go.

"Boys," I nod as I approach the other two, "is that the best you've got?"

They both start to bluster, so I laugh, "Next time I might even take it out of third gear!"

I wander back to collect Molly and walk up to watch the fast group, leaving them behind still bickering.

By the time we arrive at the track side they are already a few laps in, Jake and Joe are out in front swapping positions with Steve pulling away from the rest of the pack. "He's right they are a bit special," I mutter, then turning to Molly, "Come on let's go and get something to eat." She slips her arm through mine and smiling leads me back to the picnic.

While we are eating and drinking I try to learn the names of all the corners but by the end of it I can only remember a few. The first bend is Quarry corner, one three quarters of the way round is Tower corner, I remember this as it follows a section called Hammerdown and the last bend is Camp corner, the site of my two great overtakes.

We line up for the second session this time I'm in front of Allun and Rob. I work my way to the front of the queue and wait to be waved out onto the track. No sighting laps this time I get on it from the outset. Within two laps I'm at the front of the field slowly pulling away. I concentrate hard on trying to perfect my lines and gain a few tenths here and there. Before too long I'm having to ease off as I catch up with slower riders in awkward places, eventually the flags signal the session end and I pull off the track. The fast group are waiting to go out and Jake and Joe at the back of the line gesture for me to go over. "You should be riding in the fast group your lap times are faster than Steve's and he's not slow mate."

"Thanks boys," I grin as they close their visors and catch up with the back of their queue. Allun and Rob are just getting off their bikes as I pull up next to them.

"Bloody hell boyo you weren't hanging about!" Allun exclaims.

"Fair play you haven't lost it," adds Rob.

We compare stories of our daring deeds as we pack up the van, it turns out that this session, after passing each other a few times, Allun tried to get up the inside of Rob at Camp and they both crossed the line together again.

We pull out of the circuit and head in the direction of Hanley, after a few miles of sitting in silence Callum pipes up, "How big do I have to be before I can have a go at that?" Then before either of us can answer, "I think I'm going to need a bigger bike aren't I?"

"Aw it's gonna be a while yet son you're only seven and you have to be sixteen," smiles Rob affectionately "but don't lose the dream and I'll make it happen." He ruffles his hair and we all drive home happy.

CHAPTER TWENTY TWO

Saturday afternoon, I'm sat at my corner of the bar watching Molly work. She's covering the bar until Jess comes in at six o'clock.

Steve, Jake and Joe all walk in together, "Three pints please Molly," then turning to me, "How is it Dan?"

"All good, it was a cracking day out at Castle Combe it's a nice little track," I answer.

They gather their pints from the bar as Molly pours them, Jake takes a swig and smacks his lips, "Mmm, next time you need to come out in the fast group with us your lap times were only a few tenths down on ours."

"Allun and Rob aren't too shabby either you all need to come and play with the quick boys," adds Joe.

At that moment my phone starts to ring, I glance at the screen, it's Lentil. "Excuse me boys I need to take this call it's important," I say, getting up and heading into the back bar where it's quiet, "What's up bro?"

"I've heard back from the MC," he pauses and I hold my breath.

"Yeah they agree in principle but they want to meet in person."

"OK where?"

"They've left that for me to decide, I've told them somewhere neutral what do you think?"

"I think it's going to be like walking into the lion's den."

"My thoughts exactly but I have a cunning plan."

Over the next half hour Lentil outlines his plan. I interrupt in places, and eventually it comes together.

"Alright bro I'll go over it with Rob tomorrow and get back to you."

"Cool bro, I think it's the best plan given what we have to work with, we'll speak tomorrow."

I head back into the front bar and take my usual seat.

"Everything OK?" Steve asks.

"Yeah mate just some stuff I've got to sort out with my brother that's all." Molly looks at me quizzically from behind the bar, "It's OK babe no drama, I'll fill you in later."

"So do you fancy another track day then?" Steve asks.

"Definitely and I should be a bit quicker next time, it was the first time I'd ever seen that track and I've only had the bike a couple of weeks."

"Fair play that's even more impressive then, you should be mixing it with us next time." They head off out to the back for a game of pool. Molly comes over looking worried, "Who was on the phone? What is it about Rob?"

"Its OK babe it was Lentil, the MC have agreed the deal in principle. I just need to speak to Rob tomorrow to sort out the plan then Lentil will set up the meeting."

"What meeting?"

"They want to meet us in person but don't worry we have a plan come with me to Rob's tomorrow and you'll hear all about it."

"OK darling but it's not going to stop me worrying." Jess arrives to take over from Molly; once she's handed over we have a couple of drinks together then head upstairs to relax.

The next morning both Molly and I are up early, sitting in the kitchen, bathed in the autumnal sun. "What time are we going to see Rob?"

"He's going to ring me when he's up, I don't expect it will be too early." And with that my phone rings, belying my expectations, It's Rob, "Ey up. Sure we'll be over in ten minutes."

"Looks like he didn't sleep well either, come on finish your tea and we'll go over to the cottage."

I knock then open the door and walk in; Rob is sitting at the kitchen table surrounded by boxes.

"Are you going somewhere?" I ask.

"Yeah I'm moving into Sally's this afternoon so can I borrow your van?"

"Yup no problem is the coffee on?"

Molly sits down while I flick the kettle on for her tea; while I'm waiting for it to boil I pour myself a very large espresso. With the drinks made I sit down and begin.

"Lentil rang yesterday, the MC have agreed the deal in principle and they want Lentil to set up a meeting with the two of us in a neutral place."

"Jesus that's going to be like walking into the lion's den," exclaims Rob.

"That's exactly what I said."

"We need a plan for a quick getaway then."

"Ah now Lentil and I have a plan!" Half an hour later and the plan's laid out. Both Molly and Rob have made a few suggestions, so we have made a few alterations along the way. We finally have our plan agreed for the meeting; the neutral place will be Hanley! The MC won't know any better but it will be our home turf with plenty of help to call on should they try something on.

"Come on then let's go and get the van," I say to Rob, "and I'll give you a hand loading it up."

"Thanks bruv."

"I'm going to stay here and clean this place," says Molly wiping a finger across the kitchen surface, "No offence, but you boys are rubbish at cleaning." We both laugh and head over to the Red Lion to collect my van.

As soon as we are out of earshot Rob asks, "Do you think they'll try something?"

"Yeah I do, think back to when we were in, what would happen?"

"We'd send in the foot soldiers to cause mayhem then half an hour later we would follow and up the ante."

"That's exactly what they will try so we need to speak to all the boys we know so we can be ready for them."

"Is Lentil on board with this?"

"Yeah in fact a lot of it was his idea."

We jump in the van and drive it around the corner. It doesn't take long to load up Rob's meagre possessions. Once we are finished I kiss Molly and say, "I'm going to help him unload at the other end then I'll bring the van back, do you want to jump in or are you walking home?"

"Leave me the keys," she says to Rob, "I'll finish cleaning here now it's empty then I'll take the keys back to Pat," she kisses me, "I'll see you at home darling."

As we get out of the van at Sally's, Callum comes rushing up to Rob and hugs his leg, "I can ride around the garden without putting my feet down," he beams.

"Well done son let me unload the van and I'll come and watch you."

"Can I help?"

"Of course," Rob opens the side door of the van, "Grab that small box there." Callum picks up the box and skips towards the house as happy as a sand boy. Rob and I unload the rest and start to carry it inside.

"Leave the boxes in the living room," Sally suggests, "then we can sort through everything before we put it away" and then eyeing my Rocket espresso machine "and you can take that thing away I haven't got room for that monstrosity!"

Rob starts to protest but I interrupt, "Its mine anyway Sally I'll take it with me," then turning to Rob, "you can have the small one Molly got for me."

"Are you ready to watch me now?" Asks Callum impatiently. Sally gestures for us to follow him, so we all troop outside. Callum puts on his helmet, fastening it with practised ease, then pulls on his gloves and thumbs the starter button making the little bike crackle into life. He sets off, immediately lifting both feet onto the foot pegs; he navigates the garden grinning as he goes, after three laps of the garden he stops in front of us.

"Well done mate," I give him a thumbs up.

He takes off his gloves and helmet, Rob ruffles his hair and gives him a big hug, "That's fantastic son we'll have to take you out so you can ride further, in fact I might get a small dirt bike so we can ride together."

I pat Rob on the back and kiss Sally on the cheek, "See you later guys I'm off." They wave goodbye as I climb into the van and head back to the Red Lion.

I carry the Rocket upstairs, Molly is in the kitchen. "I did wonder how long it would be before you brought that here."

"Sally refused to have it and we've got space."

"It's OK baby it's fine and you might as well let Rob have the one I got you as I know how much you both love your coffee," she kisses me.

"You're amazing," I put the Rocket on the worktop, move the old one aside and then manoeuvre it into its new home.

"It looks good there," smiles Molly, "Now turn it on and I might even have a coffee." I set the machine chugging away, when it's finished its magic we both settle down to enjoy our coffee and watch a film.

CHAPTER TWENTY THREE

I get out of the shower and start to get dressed as Molly walks into the bedroom holding my phone, "It's Rob he either wants to borrow your van or will you go with him to pick up a bike?"

"Tell him I'll ring him back in five minutes."

"He'll ring you back in five," she says into my phone then hangs up. She comes over and slides her arms around my waist and kisses me, "I thought he was happy with his bike?"

"He is," I kiss her back, "he's after a dirt bike so he can go out riding with Callum."

"Ooh that's good I'm glad they're getting along he needs a man in his life, go with him darling, in fact why don't you get one and you can all go out riding with him."

"I love you babe," I kiss her again, "I think I will, I can always teach you to ride it as well."

"Mmm maybe but I prefer sitting on the back with you between my legs," she winks flirtatiously and tosses her hair as she leaves the bedroom; I admire her wiggle as she goes.

I finish dressing and follow her into the Kitchen dialling Rob's number as I go. "Coffee baby?" she mouths.

I nod as the call connects, "Ey up bruv what's the deal?"

"You know I've been thinking about getting a dirt bike, well Gareth's got a couple of XT 250's in, he only wants two and a half grand for one so I was going to take the van up with me so that if I decide to get one I can bring it back with me, do you want to come?"

"Sure at that price I might get one myself I'll pick you up in half an hour."

"See you soon."

Half an hour later I pull up outside Sally's house or as it is now Rob and Sally's home. Rob comes out and climbs in the passenger side of the van.

"No Callum?" I ask.

"No he's got homework to do and until he's done it he's not going out."

"Is that Sally being strict?"

"It's not Sally she would let him go, I want him to work hard and get a decent job so he doesn't end up like me."

"Blimey parenting skills as well you are a dark horse," he punches me on the arm.

"Just drive."

I pull into the car park and wave to Gareth as I park the van. He is just showing someone the controls on Allun's old Multistrada, he shakes the customers hand and watches as he mounts up and rides off smiling. Another happy customer, for Gareth.
"That didn't hang around long," Rob states.
"Low mileage one owner, it was never going to and he doesn't know Allun has a habit of not running things in properly," we all laugh.
"Have you come to have a look at those XT's?" He asks Rob who nods in reply.
"I've got two in, a yellow and black one and a red and white one, both are road registered come inside and have a look," we follow him to the off road section. "There you go do you want the keys?"
"Bring them for both," I say, "I might have one as well." He goes off to the office to get the keys.
"Does Molly know about this?" Rob quizzes.
"It was her idea," I reply, "and I might teach her to ride it."
"Fair play there's a motocross track in Westonbirt we can go to."
"OK but if we have them I'm having the red and white one, the other one looks like a bloody wasp," I laugh.
Gareth comes back with the keys and puts them into each bikes ignition, "Take them out boys and let me know what you think."
We wheel the bikes out of the showroom, grab our helmets from the van and set off. As soon as he's on the road Rob pulls a huge wheelie. Not wanting to be outdone I follow suit. Half an hour later we are back in the car park both giggling like schoolchildren.
"Any good?" Gareth comes over.
"Yeah they are a right laugh," I manage through my laughter.
"Too right I won't get nicked for speeding but I'll probably get done for pulling wheelies everywhere," laughs Rob.
""Well at least you won't be wearing the front tyres out," Gareth joins in, "I'll sort out the paperwork come on." He leads us into the office.
"I'll get yours call it a present for my brother it's the least I can do after everything you've done for me recently."
"Cheers Rob," I put my arm around his shoulder affectionately.

Once we are back at the pub we start to unload the bikes from my van, Rob is going to keep his here as I've got a double garage and he only has a shed.
Molly comes to see the new bikes, "I hope you haven't bought that bloody wasp thing," she grins at me.

"Of course not this one's mine, come and sit on it."

"OK," she climbs on and sits astride it.

"Start it up," I show her the starter button which she thumbs and it bursts into life.

"Now that's the clutch," I point to the left hand lever, then pointing to the right "and that's the brake."

"I had a moped for a year when I was sixteen," she retorts, "I used to go everywhere on that little machine."

"OK babe, try riding it up the car park." She sets off expertly, turns in a wide arc at the top of the car park then rides it back down stopping in front of us.

"You want to watch out bruv," Rob laughs, "or you'll get up one day and she'll have buggered off out on your Tuono!"

"To be honest I'd love it if she learned to ride," then turning to Molly, "Do you fancy learning then babe?"

"Yeah why not I'll have a look where the nearest training school is" and with that she goes back inside to search on google.

"Do you want a lift home?" I ask Rob after we've put the bikes away in the garage.

"Nah you're OK I thought I might come in for a couple of pints." So we head inside to order ourselves some beer.

PJ is at the bar regaling a crowd with a farfetched tale about a dwarf and a pig. I leave Rob to order the drinks and wander over, as he is finishing the story the whole group descends into raucous laughter.

"Alright Dan me old mucker," he says eventually getting his laughter under control.

"All good mate, although I do need to ask you something," I look round the group, "All of you." Their attention piqued they all gather round.

"You all know about the MC we used to be in?" Nods all round in affirmation, "Well it looks like they are going to pay us a visit soon." Faces harden all round as I continue, "If my instincts are correct and they usually are, they will be coming here looking for trouble, so I was wondering if any of you boys fancy a bit of a ruck?"

"Bring it on, we're with you, they've got no chance," is the general chatter.

PJ starts shadow boxing, "What the fuck are you doing?" Steve asks.

"Just practicing for when I knock out those knobhead Hells Angels," raucous laughter descends again.

Rob comes over to join in the fun, "What's happening boys?"

PJ is just showing us his best fighting moves for when he knocks out a few Hells Angels?" laughs Joe.

"You've asked them then?" He says to me then adds, "Are you boys up for it then?"

There is a general consensus of agreement throughout the group, then from the corner Janet pipes up, "Ooh I love a good scrap are you all going to be taking your shirts off like they do in the films?"

"Shut up you daft cow," chimes in John, "although if your gonna take your shirt off and join in I'd pay to watch that!"

I leave them discussing their various fighting skills and recounting tales of fights from bygone schooldays, and head to my corner of the bar to chat to Molly.

"Well they're all up for it I reckon we can pull this thing off."

"They all like you Dan and Rob too, there aren't many people that come here and settle in like you two have and I think it's a great idea of Janet's about taking off your shirts," she grins.

"Now who's the pervert?" I shoot back.

CHAPTER TWENTY FOUR

I'm sitting in my usual spot at the corner of the bar, half listening to John and Janet having a bit of a domestic, while I'm waiting for Rob and Allun to arrive.

"No you dozy cow," John shouts loudly.

"Oh fuck off you fat prick," returns Janet as she climbs off her stool and marches towards the door barging past a couple of blokes trying to get into the pub.

"Aren't you going after her?" I ask John.

"Nah Dan, she'll be back she loves me and besides I've got the car keys in my pocket," he smirks.

The two blokes head for the bar then two more come in to the pub, one of whom I recognise, I'm just struggling to remember his name.

"Alright Dan how is it?" He enquires.

I remember his name in the nick of time, "All good Pete how's things with you?"

"Well I was having a few pints with PJ in the Ship last night and he mentioned there might be some trouble heading this way."

"Go on," I press him to finish.

"Well I'm always up for a bit of a ruck and these boys used to run with me, so if you'll have them they enjoy a bit of fisty cuffs if you know what I mean."

"Sounds good, the more the merrier, as long as you're all aware these Hells Angels are no walk over."

Pete grins at me, "We've been to both Millwall and Leeds away and come out on top haven't we boys? Come and meet Dan, you're in."

I stand up and offer my hand; I receive a firm handshake, "Jeff."

"Norm," is next with another vice like handshake.

Finally, Westy, "Pete mentioned you used to run with the Blades boys."

"Many years ago when I was a kid, what are you drinking boys?"

"Four bottles of Holsten cheers Dan," Pete orders for them all, I nod to Jane to get the bottles.

"Doubles up as a weapon," I smile, "I see old habits die hard."

Before we can get any further the door flies open, we all tense up expecting trouble, then relax as Janet comes in and shouts, "Oi fat prick you've got the car keys."

"See I told you she loves me," laughs John, "Come and sit down my little pumpkin and I'll get you a drink."

"Less of the pumpkin and get me a large bloody gin," she retorts still seething.

"Never a dull moment," Pete starts to laugh and we all join in.

An hour and several more bottles later, we've reminisced over past battles with different firms and I've outlined the plan to them, we've exchanged phone numbers.

"Sounds like it's gonna be a blast," laughs Norm.

"Just let us know when it is," interrupts Westy.

"Come on then boys let's get back to Bristol," says Pete then turning to me, "See you soon Dan you're a good bloke and we'll be with you all the way." We shake hands and they file out just as Rob and Allun are arriving.

"Who are they?" Rob asks taking a seat at the side of me.

"Don't you remember Pete from our day out?"

Rob looks confused but then the penny drops, "The ex-football hooligan."

"Well the other three Jeff, Norm and Westy are his mates who are also ex-hooligans and they are all coming to play when the MC arrive in the village."

"Awesome," announces Rob, "Do you know what, I think we've got this," I smile and nod in agreement.

"So have you heard from Lentil?" Allun asks.

"Funny you should ask he sent me a text while I was talking to the Bristol boys here I'll show you." I pull out my phone and place it on the bar so they can both read it. Rob reads it out loud.

"Date is set they are here I'll ring as soon as they have gone." As soon as he has finished my phone vibrates and lights up then starts to ring, 'Lentil' shows on the screen so I pick it up and answer it, "Ey up bro how's it going?"

"I've got a date for you, how does Halloween at lunchtime sound?"

"They're not in a hurry then it's a couple of weeks away yet."

"How's preparations your end?"

"Pretty much there, I've just put the last pieces in place and now we have a date I can get everything confirmed."

"Great, I'm meeting the MC at Hopwood Services I'll ring you when we've met up so you can tell me where the deal is being done if you see what I mean?"

"Gotcha we'll get everything ready here and Lentil."

"What Dan?"

"Thanks for this bro I really owe you now."

"No worries you two are good guys and I'm glad to help," he hangs up.

I turn to Rob and Allun, "I take it you guys heard that," they both nod and smile.

"Let the fun begin," chortles Allun.

"When are those bloody Hells Angels coming?" John shouts from the corner.

"Halloween," I shout back.

"Well that's them fucked then," we all look at him puzzled not making a connection.

"When they see 'er," he nods at Janet, "dressed as a witch they'll run a bloody mile!" He continues now laughing out loud.

"Cheeky old bugger," retorts Janet then she continues, "I'll bloody smack them one with my broomstick!" Then she turns to John, "Take me home and shag me you big stud." With that they both get up and leave.

"Only in Hanley," Allun shakes his head while Rob stares open mouthed at what has just happened.

Molly comes down from the flat and sits next to me at the bar, "Where are Lucy and Sally?" She asks.

"Lucy was just preparing dinner then she's coming over," replies Allun.

"Sally's at home with Callum," answers Rob.

"Well ring her and tell them both to come round, there's an x-box upstairs Callum can play on that, we don't want Sally missing out on the fun," Molly says as she heads off to the jukebox to put on her eighties playlist.

Lucy walks in just as the Human League are belting out there classic 'Don't You Want Me Baby'. The bar is getting a little crowded so we all adjourn to the table in the alcove. Rob is just winding up his air guitar to the strains of Def Leppard's 'Animal', when Sally and Callum arrive.

"My god it looks like I've got some catching up to do," she laughs as Callum leaps around with Rob, "Large gin and tonic please Jane." When the song has finished Molly stands up and speaks to Callum, "Come on I'll show you the x-box it's set up in the spare room," then turning to Sally, "He can stay tonight if you like it's not as if he's got school tomorrow.

"Yay go on mum it's been ages since I've stayed with Molly," then pleadingly, "Pleeeeease!"

"OK, go on then but you'd better not be any trouble."

"I won't I promise," as he skips off upstairs with Molly.

We pass a pleasant evening reliving our younger days through the music, the drinks flowing freely and there are lots of "Do you remember when?" And "Oh my god I haven't heard this in years." When Rob comes back from the toilet smiling mischievously to himself, no one seems to notice until the opening bars of the next song, then I stand beside him and we both start to dance.

"Oh my God," declares Molly finally recognising the song, "Surely they aren't going to, in here!"

We both start to lift our t-shirts as the rest of the group recognise 'You Can Leave Your Hat On' the Tom Jones rendition of 'The Full Monty' theme tune.

Molly and Sally start to squirm in their seats as we remove our t-shirts and throw them in their direction. Allun spots the chance of some fun and quickly removes his t-shirt and joins us. The three of us gyrate as we slowly slide our belts out of our jeans and wave them above our heads. The trainers never seem to come off sexily so we all just kick them off. Next we slowly unbutton our jeans, except for Allun who has a zip which he slides up and down instead. We turn around wiggling our bums as the jeans slowly come down.

"Oh my god they're not going to are they?" Squeals Sally.

"God I hope not I'll kill him," adds Molly while Lucy is clapping along seemingly enjoying the show.

We start to inch our boxer shorts down then back up again, each time getting lower and lower until pubic hair is on display. Then the song finally comes to a close so we all pull up our boxer shorts and stride off to the bar to order more drinks.

"That was fantastic," shouts Jane from behind the bar, "Can I book you for my birthday party?" She is roaring with laughter as she pours our drinks. I sheepishly return to the table to retrieve my jeans and therefore my wallet so I can pay for the drinks.

Molly smiles, "I'm glad you didn't do the Full Monty baby, save that for me."

"I'm disappointed," chuckles Lucy.

"Well I'm going to ask for a rerun when we get home," laughs Sally.

CHAPTER TWENTY FIVE

I'm washing the dishes after breakfast, musing, as Molly seems very quiet. I suspect it's the stress of the upcoming showdown, as I know it's affecting me.

"Molly, can I ask you something?"

"Mmmm," she answers distractedly.

"Molly," I repeat as she shakes herself out of her thoughts.

"Sorry darling I was miles away."

"I know you're worried about what will happen when the MC comes down, but it's a way off yet. So can you get cover for the pub this weekend and I'll take you away somewhere?"

"Ooh that sounds romantic, where are we going, let me get my phone and sort out cover," all without pausing for breath. She rummages around in her bag to fish out her phone and starts to make some calls.

I pull out my phone and start to browse through hotels, not even sure where I'm going to take her. I mouth 'cuppa?' to her and she nods back making a T sign with her fingers while she's still chatting away on her phone. I flick on the kettle, as well as setting the Rocket chugging away. I put Molly's mug in front of her and sit down as she puts her phone down and smiles at me, "All sorted darling, Jess is doing Friday and Sunday lunchtime and Jack and Jane are going to cover Saturday. So I'm all yours from Friday lunchtime until Sunday afternoon so where are you taking me?"

"Well I haven't booked anything yet as I needed to check whether you could get cover first," I stall as I still have no idea where to take her.

"You must know where you want to take me, even if you haven't booked it yet," she replies.

"OK babe we are going to Stratford upon Avon the home of Shakespeare," I blurt out with no idea why.

"Ooh that's fantastic I've never been before but I've always wanted to go, have you been there before?"

"No I haven't, I'm just going to get my laptop to book a hotel as my phones too small," I get up and head towards the spare room to go and get my laptop.

"Bring it in here baby," Molly shouts after me, "We can have a look together, after all you've chosen a romantic destination so let's choose a nice hotel together." I come back and put the laptop on the kitchen table to let the search begin. After an hour of searching, and much toing and froing, we finally settle on the Mercure Shakespeare Hotel, a seventeenth century black and white building right in the centre of town. I grab my wallet to get my card to pay. Molly kisses me "Oh darling, thank you this is exactly what I need."

"I think we'll take the car, so I'll book parking as well, then it doesn't matter about the weather."

"Oh this is so exciting," she says getting up, "I'm going to start packing."

"Er, Molly, it's only Tuesday and we're not going away until Friday."

"Well you know, I've got to sort clothes for every eventuality and I will also need to go shopping for some new things," and with that she flounces off.

Friday lunchtime and Molly is chatting to Jess with instructions for the weekend. I go and pull my Jag out of the garage and park it outside the front door. I pick up my overnight bag which I've left on the passenger seat and move it into the boot before I go back inside to find Molly.

"And if there's anything else at all just call me OK," I catch her saying as I walk in.

"Are you ready babe? Where's your bag and I'll put it in the car?"

"It's just over there darling by the door to the flat." I walk around the bar expecting a small overnight bag but I'm greeted by the most enormous purple suitcase you've ever seen!

"Jesus babe we are going away for a weekend not bloody emigrating!"

"Well I've got clothes for day time, clothes for night time, clothes in case it rains, clothes in case it's sunny, shoes, sandals, boots, hairdryer, hair straighteners, then the essentials like make up, tooth brush and tea bags!"

"Tea bags? We're staying in Stratford upon Avon, not deepest darkest Africa, I'm sure they have tea bags!"

"Well maybe they do," she says in a huff "but they never give you enough." I admit defeat and drag the huge suitcase through the pub and out towards the car. I move my overnight bag from the boot onto the back seat of the car.

I'm just hefting Molly's suitcase into the boot when Janet and John pull up, "Are you leaving?" Janet laughs.

"No, just taking Molly away for the weekend can you believe the size of this?"

"Actually I can," laughs John, "I took her to the airport the last time she went on holiday for a week and she took two that size," they drive off both chuckling to themselves.

Molly gets into the passenger seat and she makes herself comfortable as we set off.

"Ooh this is exciting baby are you OK?"

"Apart from a sore back I'm fine."

"Oh no, what have you done to your back?"

"It was putting that bloody suitcase of yours into the boot!"

"Well if you're happy to walk around with a skanky girlfriend all weekend, I can take a smaller bag," she says huffily.

"Its fine I'm joking." We both smile then laugh, "Come on let's make this the start of a fantastic weekend."

I manage to park on double yellow lines right outside the hotel entrance and put on the hazard lights. "Come on we'll go inside and I'll ask about the car park."

We approach the front desk, "Good afternoon can I help you?" Her name tag informs me her name is Sheryl.

"Afternoon Sheryl we have a reservation, it's Sampson."

"Thank you," she taps away on her keyboard, "Here it is."

"I'm parked outside on double yellow's so can I put it in the car park?"

"Yes of course sir it's round the back, you have to go up the street a little," she points in the direction my car is facing, "take the first left then turn left into the alleyway and the car park is behind the hotel there are signs from the car park leading you back to reception."

"Thanks, I'll leave Molly to fill the forms in and I'll be back in a few minutes to pay."

"That's absolutely fine Mr Sampson."

Five minutes later I'm back in reception having squeezed the Jag into the small car park.

"All done babe?"

"Yes you just need to pay."

I hand my card over to Sheryl who processes the payment.

"You are in the Hamlet suite on the first floor at the front I will take you up, do you want to collect your bags first?"

"No it's OK I'll come back down for them after we've seen the room."

Sheryl leads us upstairs and along a short corridor then stops and puts a key into the lock. She pushes open the door and holds out the keys, "This is your room key and the silver one is for the front door which is locked after midnight, enjoy your stay."

"Wow this is awesome darling," exclaims Molly as we look around the room taking in the four poster bed and the chaise lounge.

I push open a door to reveal the en-suite, tastefully decorated with dark grey slate tiles and a powerful looking shower in the corner.

"Come and look at the en-suite babe it's a wet room." Molly ducks under my arm and takes it all in then kisses me, "Its perfect darling."

"I'll go and get the bags then we can go out and explore."

"OK baby, I'm putting the kettle on, do you want a coffee?"

"No thanks babe."

I struggle up the stairs with Molly's suitcase cursing as I go, how much stuff can one woman need for two days? I let myself into our room still fighting with the suitcase.

"Are you OK darling?"

"No, I've got a right bloody sweat on carrying this bloody thing upstairs. Come on let's go for a wander round I need a pint or two."

"Ah baby, but I'm worth it," she smiles at me alluringly.

We walk through reception holding hands, and then out into the October sunshine.

"Which way do we go?"

"I've never been here before either let's try right." I smile at her feeling content as we stroll gently down the street. We wander along without a care in the world eventually coming across a large white pub called the 'White Swan, "Let's go in for a pint," I gesture towards the door. We go inside and head to the bar, "What do you want babe?"

"I'll have a Kronenbourg please."

I look along the bar at the pumps they only have two beers neither of which I fancy, the barman approaches, "A Kronenbourg and a Guinness please," then turning to Molly, "Go and sit down I'll bring them over."

"That will be thirteen pounds sixty please," the barman says as he puts the two pints onto the bar.

"I'm sorry? That can't be right, it's just the two pints."

"Yes sir, thirteen pounds sixty please, that is correct," he says stuffily.

"Jesus I only want to buy a couple of pints not shares in the bloody place," I mutter as I hand over a twenty pound note. I take the drinks over to Molly who has chosen a table by the window.

"Thirteen pounds bloody sixty for two pints," I'm still fuming.

"That's outrageous, they are making a fortune! That would only be six pounds ninety in my pub."

"Well we're not having another one here we'll find somewhere else."

"Look at these," Molly says changing the subject, "There are lots of quotes from Shakespeare painted on the walls." I look up and start to read a few.

"I know parking is a nightmare around here now but it must have been bad even in Shakespeare's day. Look parking is such sweet sorrow." I can't help myself, I just burst out laughing loudly while Molly looks at me perplexed.

"What?" She glares when I eventually manage to stop laughing.

"It says PARTING is such a sweet sorrow it's a quote from 'Romeo and Juliet'," at that we both burst into laughter as Molly reddens.

"Come on let's find another pub," I say as we empty our glasses, "and I'm leaving the bloody glasses on the table, let him earn his thirteen pounds bloody sixty."

"Come on then Mr grumpy," she says as she links her arm through mine and leads me out of the door.

We wander down the street window shopping, at the bottom of the hill I spot another pub, "Let's try the Pen and Parchment it's got to be cheaper than that last place," I say still grumbling.

This place is a lot busier so I say to Molly, "Go and find somewhere to sit and I'll get some drinks." I wait my turn at the bar then when I catch the barmaids eye I order, "An Abbot and a Kronenbourg please."

"Six pounds eighty please," says the barmaid.

"Thank you very much," I hand over the correct change and head off to find Molly. I spot her sitting at a table just outside of the door, "This is much better, they've got Abbot and it's only six eighty for two pints," I grin cheerily.

After a boozy afternoon and early evening we decide to grab a couple of kebabs before we head back to the hotel for an early night of passion.

After demolishing a huge full English breakfast including homemade black pudding, we are sitting finishing our tea and coffee respectively when Molly asks, "What do you have planned for today?"

"Pub," I grin cheekily.

"That's a bit too much like a busman's holiday for me spending all day in a pub again."

"I am joking," I laugh, "I am planning on hiring a boat to sail up and down the river and maybe stop somewhere for lunch. Then perhaps a bit of shopping in the afternoon, then the pub."

"That sounds perfect come on let's go."

We roam along the river bank and find a place called 'Avon Boat Hire' where I can hire a motorboat for a very reasonable forty pounds an hour, so I book one for three hours. We walk down and find the right boat, I help Molly aboard then I jump on after her.

"I hope you know how to drive this thing," she queries looking worried.

"Not a problem I was a sea cadet as a kid I'm qualified to sail anything."

"A proper dark horse aren't you," Molly smiles looking happier.

We sail the river Avon quite happily watching the world go by when I spot a place called the 'Riverside Restaurant', "Do you fancy some lunch?"

"Ooh yes, is there anywhere to park?"

"Or is it sweet sorrow?" Molly reddens. Then I add "Actually it's mooring a boat not parking." I get a punch in the chest for my cheek.

We have a very enjoyable lunch of lobster followed by strawberries and cream and a bottle of white wine. We then board the boat and wend our way back down the river and back to the boat hire shop. We spend the rest of the afternoon shopping, finishing off the day with a few pints before heading back to the hotel for another night of passion.

After another enormous breakfast I struggle down stairs with Molly's suitcase, "Will you go and check out please babe while I load the car up and I'll meet you out the front?"

She kisses me passionately, "Thank you for a perfect weekend darling I've loved every minute of it," then she heads off towards reception. I pull up outside the front of the hotel as Molly is coming out, she climbs in the passenger seat and I check my watch.

"Let's take the back roads home as we have plenty of time," she nods in agreement as I lower the roof. We set off back towards Hanley enjoying a perfect end to a perfect weekend.

CHAPTER TWENTY SIX

I'm sitting, quietly contemplating in the kitchen when Molly comes in. She flicks on the kettle then asks, "Do you want coffee darling?"
"Mm yeah, sure, sorry I'm just going over the plan for Friday in my head."
"Is everything OK?"
"Yeah its fine they will send a crew in first, but with the boys we have we'll have no problem with them."
"And then?"
"And then Hatch and Zeb will arrive later and it's how they react, that's the unknown."
"Are you worried baby?"
"No I've got the cash ready so as long as Lentil plays his part then it will be fine."
"Why don't you have a meeting with everyone on Wednesday so they all know what to do?"
"That's a good idea I've spoken to everyone already but this way they'll know what to expect from everyone else."
"That's it then I'll ring some people but you'll have to ring the Bristol boys as I don't have their numbers."
We both pick up our phones and start to arrange the meeting to organise the downfall of the Steel Riders MC in Hanley. With everyone organised for the meeting my phone rings again, it's Allun I wonder what he's forgotten.
"Alright boyo I've just been talking to Rob and we are going for a spin on the bikes do you fancy it?"
Molly has obviously heard him as she says, "Go and have fun, it will do you good and I've got plenty to do here."
"OK what time and where?"
"Pub car park in an hour is that OK?"
"Great, see you soon."

An hour later the three of us are standing in the car park chatting and smoking, letting the bikes warm up.
"New leathers I see Allun," I notice.
"Yeah I thought I would treat myself," he answers, "Dainese one piece."

"It's a bit gay having red, white and blue leathers to match your bike," mocks Rob, "let's see if they make you any faster." He starts to put his helmet on and Allun and I follow suit.

"Where are we heading today?" I ask.

"What about the Cotswolds?" Rob suggests.

"Yeah there are some great roads round that way, come on I'll show you," with that we all mount up and follow Allun out of Hanley.

We find ourselves some nice twisty roads; Rob is sat right on Allun's tailpipe looking for any opportunity to get past him. I'm happy to sit behind them both, leaving a gap so I can concentrate on my own lines. I'll show off later but for now I'm happy seeing how far I can lean it on the road as opposed to the track. We are cracking on, Allun and Rob are almost on the corner in front, as they hit the apex, I'm just entering the bend when I see their brake lights come on and they both sit up braking hard. I brake as hard as I can while leant over, dragging my back brake all the way to the apex, when I see the problem. I sit up and brake hard to avoid a broken down car just beyond the bend. I flash my lights but the others are already pulling into a layby beyond, so I follow and pull in behind them. We remove our helmets and walk up to the car to find a little old lady shaking and looking terrified in the driver's seat.

"Rob go around the corner and wave down anything that comes this way," I instruct so he trots off. I approach the car and tap on the window; she won't look up at me but opens her window a crack.

"Are you alright love?" She shakes her head so I add, "If we push are you alright to steer so we can get you away from this bend?" She nods gripping the steering wheel even tighter. We go around the back of the car, "Let the handbrake off will you love," says Allun. When she complies we start to push. We've only managed a couple of yards when two cars approach very slowly with hazards on. They stop blocking the road and six young lads get out and help us to push. We eventually get her into the layby behind the bikes, one of the young lads knocks on the driver's window and says, "Mrs Butler put the hand brake on now."

"Do you know her," I ask.

"Yes she lives next door but one to us, I'm going to ring my dad he owns a garage so he can come out with his breakdown truck."

"OK mate I'll let Rob know he can come back now and you guys might want to move your cars," I tell them as I set off back up the road. When we return Mrs Butler is out of her car surrounded by the lads.

"Thank you so very much," she says gratefully, "you have probably just saved my life I was absolutely terrified."

"It's not a problem we would have done the same for anyone," Rob smiles.

"Well, all the same thank you again and you bikers get a bad name but I'll be putting them straight from now on."

We say our goodbyes then mount up and set off again, this time Rob gets away first, so Allun is sitting behind him looking to pass. They manage to get by each other a few times while I sit back watching them. We potter through a village at thirty miles an hour and stop at a red light. The other two lift their visors and start chatting while I notice we are at the end of the village with a long straight in front of us. I leave my visor closed and my bike in gear waiting for the lights to change. As soon as they turn to amber I start revving the bike and feeding out the clutch, as soon as they turn green I launch my bike forward the front wheel rising gently. I work my way up through the gears into third hitting one hundred miles an hour while still on the back wheel, the other two are way behind. The front wheel starts to gently come down as I hit fourth gear and one hundred and twenty miles an hour, then I brake and tip it in to a long sweeping left hander. After passing a few cars I manage to open up a sizeable gap, I spot a layby so I pull in and quickly remove my helmet and light a cigarette. They pull into the layby as I'm puffing away, "What kept you girls?" I laugh, "That's why I've been sitting behind you both, cause you can't keep up when I lead."

"You cheeky fu...," Rob splutters, then starts to laugh as he realises I'm just winding them up. We all chuckle together while we have a cigarette, comparing tales of our ride. When we've finished I say, "Come on then let's head for home."

We arrive back at the Red Lion without further incident; I get off my bike, "Are you coming in for a pint?"

"I'm gonna take the bike home and come back," says Rob.

"Same here," adds Allun, "See you in a bit."

Wednesday evening and the pub is starting to fill up. I'm sat in my usual place with Molly sitting beside me. Rob and Allun are in the alcove with Steve, Jake and Joe, talking bikes. Janet and John are in the other corner as usual and the back bar is starting to fill with the youngsters. I have a look through the door and count Benny, Ash, Luke, Charlie, Jack, James, Kev, Matt, Sam and Josh ten in total. The front door opens and PJ comes in accompanied by Bill and Jack, "Alright mucker," he greets me then heads to the bar.

Next in is Pete followed by the Bristol boys Jeff, Norm and Westy. I wait until everyone has got a drink then poke my head through into the back bar, "Lads can you all come through." They all file past shaking my hand as they go, once they have settled I begin.

"Right guys thank you all for coming and thanks for offering to help me and my brother."

"You're both locals now and we all stick together," chimes in John.

"And you've helped out plenty round here," adds Janet.

"And you're both bloody nice fellers," adds PJ to a general chorus of approval.

"Thanks guys that means a lot," Rob joins in.

"It does indeed but these Hells Angels are no walk over so if any of you guys want to back out it's fine and no one will think badly of you," I look around but I'm met with steely stares and a stony silence.

"Right then I've spoken to you all about the plan but I thought it would be good to get together especially with the people who will be beside you," a murmur of agreement goes around the room.

"Right then let's get you sorted into groups, John, Janet your with Bill, Jack and PJ OK?" They nod and get together in the corner of the bar.

"Pete, Jeff, Norm and Westy you guys take the younger boys Ash, Benny, Luke, Charlie, Kev, James and Jack," they all move off together.

"Matt, Sam and Josh with me and Rob," they grin as they come over to join us.

"Allun, Steve, Jake and Joe you guys know what you have to do," they nod and carry on chattering between themselves. Matt, Sam and Josh look a little overawed as Sam asks, "So what do we have to do?"

"OK boys they will roll in on their Harley's."

Josh interrupts, "Cool," Matt punches him on the arm and he grimaces.

Rob continues, "As I said, they will roll in trying to intimidate everyone, when they've parked up they will be looking for me and Dan" the three lads are enthralled.

I take over. "Donk, a big ugly fucker will be directing things, he will send three or four younger ones up against us so you three and Rob can take them down and I'll deal with Donk."

"And after that?" asks matt wide eyed.

"It will be a general free for all," says Rob.

"The Bristol boys and the rest of the youngsters will be coming out of the close behind them," I add "and once it's all kicking off properly the rest will come out of the pub."

"Cool it's gonna be like a film," enthuses Josh.

"It won't be when you get punched," laughs Sam.

"No worse than playing rugby," Josh adds and they all agree.

"So what time is this all happening?" Matt asks.

"Well we are opening the pub from nine o'clock and serving everyone a full English breakfast," I answer.

"Brilliant I can't fight on an empty stomach," he grins.

"We expect them to arrive somewhere between twelve and one," I finish.

"Are you guys OK?" Rob asks.

"I can't wait it's gonna be awesome," Josh announces.

"We'll see," Rob says, "As long as you're not expecting an easy ride."

"Dan, Rob, we've seen you two in action and while we're not in your league we can scrap and we never back down," Matt finishes.

I shake their hands, "See you for breakfast on Friday boys." They shake hands with Rob as they leave.

The bar gradually starts to empty, with everyone leaving in good spirits, there seems to be a sense of everyone coming together as a community.

I smile at Rob and can tell he feels the same, he puts his hand on my shoulder, "This is home now and we couldn't have chosen anywhere better."

I clap him on the back and as I hug him I whisper in his ear, "We're gonna be fine."

CHAPTER TWENTY SEVEN

Its nine o'clock in the morning and the pub is already a hive of activity, whereas it doesn't normally open until twelve o'clock. Molly and Janet are up in the flat cooking multiple full English breakfasts to feed the starving hordes, with Sally and Lucy ferrying full plates downstairs and returning with empty ones. There is a general buzz of excitement around the bar. I'm looking for Rob I eventually spot him in the back bar chatting to Matt and Sam. As I pick my way through I stop to watch PJ and Norm comparing knuckle dusters.

"Nice boys," I smile at them.

"We're gonna show the buggers," laughs PJ as he starts shadow boxing.

Josh catches up with me as I get to the door of the back bar, "Dan do you think they'll have weapons?" he asks nervously.

"It's possible, in my day the answer would have been no unless we were up against someone we knew would be armed but I don't know the kids who are in now, let's go and ask Rob."

"Alright bruv?" I ask Rob as we approach, I nudge Josh to ask his question.

"Rob do you think they will have weapons?"

"I doubt any of them will be carrying anything but the youngsters in the car will have a boot full."

"Should we get some then?" Asks Josh with nervous excitement.

"Look, I know these boys and if we produce them they will grab anything and use it but if we fight with fists their pride won't let them use anything," Josh looks a little disappointed.

"If you boys want to collect some," I interrupt, "they stay in the pub but nothing lethal just coshes and sticks Ok?" The three of them go off to find the other youngsters to collect some weapons.

"It gives them something to focus on," I say to Rob, "too much nervous energy too early isn't good do you remember your first time?"

"Yeah scrapping at the Bulldog Bash," he laughs at the memory "but your right that just kicked off and I was buzzing for hours afterwards."

"Any chance of a pint?" PJ shouts from the front bar, so I wander through.

"When everyone has eaten and all the dishes are back upstairs and washed we'll open the bar," to loud cheers all round, "The drinks are on me but not too many mind we've got a fight coming." The cheers are even louder this time, then everyone starts collecting dishes and heading up to the flat.

Josh comes through with a two foot piece of iron bar, "Is this any good?"

"Its fine but it all stays in the pub unless I say otherwise," he grins and heads off to find the others.

Janet comes down and joins everyone else milling around in the bar so I head up to flat to find Molly. As I walk into the kitchen she's putting the dishes away, "OK darling how's it going down there?"

"It's fine they are all a little nervous and a few of them want a drink so can I open the bar? The drinks are on me."

"Of course darling I'm coming down now," she says as she puts the last of the plates into the rack, "God knows I could do with one myself."

I walk behind the bar with Molly and she announces, "Right you horrible lot free drinks," there is a buzz of excitement and a surge towards the bar.

"Take it easy everyone will get served," then I add "And it's only three drinks each no more than that."

"Spoilsport," shouts PJ.

"Now come on I don't mind a bit of Dutch courage but I don't want you all so pissed you forget the plan."

Molly and I are furiously serving drinks so Jack comes behind the bar to help out. When everyone has a drink I pour myself a large brandy, I put my arm around Molly's waist as she's making herself a large gin and tonic.

"Are you OK babe?"

She looks up at me and smiles, "I'm too busy to worry at the moment but yes I am, things are always OK when you're around" and she kisses me.

"You're good for me as well babe," I kiss her back just as my phone starts to ring.

"Quiet!" I shout and a hush descends over the bar. It's Lentil.

"Alright bro."

"Yeah I'm at Hopwood the MC are just leaving on masse, I'm following behind and you were right they're planning to shake you up a bit first, then do the deal, it seems your figure of a million is too much to resist."

"No worries bro we're all set here how many of them?"

"Twenty on bikes, including Hatch and Zeb and a car with four youngsters in it."

"That's great we outnumber them and our plan is good."

"You guys will have to deal with the soldiers I'm planning to arrive just after Hatch and Zeb to make sure things are completed without a hitch so I'll see you later bro."

"No worries catch you soon ," I hang up then turn to the rest of the pub, "Right people they are on their way and looking for trouble!"

"Bring it on they've definitely got trouble," shouts Westy bouncing on his toes.

"We've got an hour until they get here so one more drink each then into our positions."

I'm standing by the door as I shake hands with Steve, Jake and Joe as they leave, "Good luck boys."

I hug Allun and clap him on the back, "I love you mate, take care of yourself out there."

"Will do mucker and you take care as well," and he follows the others out.

"My lot to me!" PJ marshals his group.

"I shake his hand, "Are you Ok?"

"All good feller come on you lot," I shake each and every hand as they all file out. Rob is talking quietly to Matt, Sam and Josh.

"Come on boys we hit them first and hit them hard," the others nod, "if they don't go down hit them again, if they do go down put the boot in and watch each other's backs."

We all gather in a group hug, "Let's do this," I snarl "and remember Donk's mine.

"You guys know what to do," says Rob to be greeted by nods, "Good luck and I'll see you back here when it's all over."

We head out into the car park to wait in the weak autumn sun. We are not waiting long when Joe roars up on his bike, he flips up his visor, "They're on the A38, five minutes away, twenty bikes and a car." I nod my thanks and he roars off again.

I start to bounce on my toes, swinging my arms to loosen my shoulders, Rob is shadow boxing, the three youngsters look nervous.

"Right boys this is it are you ready?" They nod and follow me out into the street. The distant sound of rolling thunder, signalling their arrival is getting louder. I nod to Rob beside me and he gives me a wink in return. I can see them approaching, they start to fan out across the road, one of them mounts the opposite pavement and rides along it. They slow as they approach us, I turn to Rob without taking my eyes off of them, "if any of them come at us with their bike take them down."

"No worries bruv I've got it."

The lead biker comes to a halt the others stop and spread out behind him. He revs his bike loudly then kills the engine with the others following suit. I count sixteen bikes in the eerie silence which surrounds us, there are five of us no wonder they are all grinning as they get off their bikes. Donk is at the front he immediately recognises me.

"Dan you wanker this has been a long time coming."

"Still all talk and no brains," I shoot back.

He points to the Hells Angels either side of him and urges them forward. The five of them walk towards us menacingly, grinning manically. I hold out my hand to steady the boys behind me. I'm breathing shallowly, gently clenching and unclenching my fists as they get closer.

When they get to ten yards away I give Rob a nod and we all start forward. My focus is entirely on Donk but out of the corner of my eye I see Rob sprint forward and launch himself at one of them. He grabs him by both arms and head butt's him putting him down before anyone else can react. I charge at Donk while catching a glimpse of Rob sitting astride his opponent landing more blows. Donk grins swinging wildly as I near him, I slow waiting for my chance, he swings wildly with his right fist so I duck it and step in. I head butt his nose causing blood to gush from it and pummel his kidneys with my fists. He staggers back grunting and puts his hands on his knees trying to catch his breath. He raises his arm and waves the others into battle; just as they are starting forward a huge roar comes from behind them. The Bristol boys and the youngsters emerge from the Close.

Pete is first amongst them he punches two and kicks one to the floor. Jeff, Norm and Westy wade in and all hell breaks loose. I run at Donk and launch a two footed flying kick into the middle of his chest putting him down. Quick as a flash I'm on top of him pinning both his arms to the floor with my knees as I pummel my fists into his face. A body flies past my left hand side closely followed by Matt. We have the upper hand now as a tractor approaches from behind. I hit Donk one more time to make sure he stays unconscious and stand up.

Bill is driving his tractor with a horse box behind. It opens and PJ, Jack and John emerge carrying old fashioned stocks. PJ picks up a biker from the floor and throws him into the back of the horsebox, others soon follow his lead.

John comes over to me and points at Donk, "Is this the feller?" I nod and PJ helps to drag him away, my attention turns to the sound of a car approaching at high speed.

A red car roars up and slides to halt sideways behind the Harley's. It's that bloody Honda again! Four youths get out brandishing baseball bats, Rob appears at my side, "Shall I let the youngsters loose with their iron bars?"

"Ok but back them up and take PJ with you."

He rounds them up and they run into the pub returning moments later all armed. The youth's approach them swinging the baseball bats but before they get very far the Bristol boys are amongst them fists and boots flying. One of them jumps forward and swings his bat catching Sam across the forehead, he goes down, I set off running towards them. Before I have covered half the distance Matt punches him in the side of the head, he starts to turn when Josh unleashes his iron bar putting him down. Rob is on him as I arrive punching him incessantly, I pull him off, and once again it's all over. As the youths are dragged towards the horsebox, I turn to see Janet and Jack throwing eggs and rotten tomatoes at Donk who has been put in the stocks. Then John approaches riding a huge black stallion, he brings it to a halt beside the stocks and pats it on the neck. The horse then starts to urinate all over Donk's hanging head.

"See I told you I'd get a horse to piss on them," laughs John, "Bring back National Service!"

I hear more bikes approaching expecting Allun, Steve, Jake and Joe to be escorting Lentil into the village, but our celebrations are brought to a brutal close by the sound of a gunshot. I turn to see Hatch, flanked by Zeb and two others, pointing a gun at me.

"It's been a long time Dan," then surveying the scene, "I see that useless twat Donk has fucked up then."

Everyone's focus is on Hatch and the gun, when I hear Bill shout from the tractor, "Not so fast fellers." I turn to see him brandishing his shotgun in the direction of the Hells Angels.

"Easy Bill I've got this."

"Well I ain't putting mine down till he does!"

"Easy Hatch I'm just going to get the money."

He watches me intently as I walk towards the pub door and lean inside to grab a black holdall, then I start to walk slowly towards them.

The sound of bikes approaching at speed disturbs the proceedings. Allun, Steve, Jake and Joe pull up and dismount. Zeb pulls out a gun of his own and points it at them. Allun removes his helmet and shakes his head at me. Shit! That means they haven't found Lentil, this thing is going downhill very rapidly indeed.

"Not so clever now," Hatch gives me a crooked grin and urges me to walk towards him, "I think that bag is mine." I walk slowly forward, fearful of the potential outcome and drop the bag at his feet.

"Pick it up," he sneers at me, I bend down to pick up the bag and feel a huge blow to the side of my temple. He's pistol whipped me, my head spins and my vision starts to blur. I'm fighting to remain conscious, hearing strange noises as I push myself up to my knees, my head is still spinning wildly. The thumping noise in my head is getting louder and louder, I close my eyes and shake my head trying to clear it. When I open them the sound is even louder, my vision gradually returns and I slowly manage to focus. A helicopter is hovering twenty feet away and moving closer, hanging out of the doors on both sides are men armed with semi-automatic machine guns.

"Drop your weapons," a tinny voice comes from the helicopter, no one moves.

"DROP THEM NOW! PUT YOUR HANDS ON YOUR HEADS!" Hatch and Zeb both comply as the helicopter lands. The two gunmen disembark; guns trained on the Hells Angels at all times, then out of the helicopter comes Lentil! I breathe a sigh of relief, then tense again as I watch Hatch visibly relax, I wonder whose side he's really on.

Lentil walks over to the Hells Angels, flanked by the two gunmen; he puts his hand into the pocket of his jeans and pulls out a wallet. He lets it fall open so they can see it then announces, "Charles Moseley MI5, it's over boys."

They stare at him in dismay then Hatch starts to stutter, "L, L, Lentil what the fuck?"

"It's Agent Moseley you dumb shit," then to the gunmen, "Cuff them and call it in, get me uniform and we will need a few vans to take them all away."

I am as stunned as anyone as he bends and helps me to my feet before picking up the holdall and handing it to me, "I believe this belongs to you we wouldn't want it to go missing so I suggest you take it inside before uniform arrives."

CHAPTER TWENTY EIGHT

There are police cars and vans everywhere, all with lights flashing, Lentil is chatting to the officer who appears to be in charge. He shakes his hand and walks over to me, "Come on let's go and get a drink it looks like I've got some explaining to do."

As we walk into the pub a huge cheer goes up, Molly rushes over and hugs me, "You did it baby is it all over now?"

"It's over," says Lentil or Agent Charles Moseley as it appears he actually is.

"Thank god," Molly kisses me then turning to Charles, "And thank you, if you hadn't arrived I dread to think what would have happened."

"I was just having a rest, then I was going to kick their arses," shouts PJ and everyone descends into fits of laughter.

"I could have got him on the back of the horse then pushed him off on top off them," more laughter as John joins in.

Rob comes over, "Abbot," he hands me a pint, "and what are you having Lentil er Charles?"

"Scotch on the rocks please," he answers, "Shall we sit down?" We sit at the table in the alcove Rob returns with his drink and sits down, Molly is straight in before anyone else can speak.

"So were you undercover or something?"

"Yes I was for the last fifteen years, I was tasked with first infiltrating then later influencing the Hells Angels."

"Well you did a good job of convincing everybody me included," Rob says.

"Yeah you had me fooled but what I don't understand is why did you help us?" I enquire.

"Well when you got out and before Rob took over the finances the MC asked me to check things over, I spotted your scam and after a bit of digging I realised it was a means to escape. Then when Rob followed suit I thought maybe there was more depth to you two, so I helped out to see how things turned out."

"But you blew your cover, why?" Asks Molly pertinently.

"The truth is, my time is up, I'm moving onto MI6 to set up a task force in six months, so it was basically now or never."

"But why us?" Rob asks.

"Because I worked out that at heart you are both basically good guys who took a wrong turn. Look around and see what you have achieved today," he gestures around the bar, "Not only have you beaten the Hells Angels you have brought this whole village together as a team that was with you one hundred percent of the way." I look around our rag-tag team all enjoying their victory and realise he is right.

"I need guys like you on my team if you're interested?"

"What us, become spies?" Rob asks incredulously.

"Not exactly spies per se but each mission will need people with a certain skill set and the skill set you both possess will be required."

"Go on," my interest is piqued.

"We will pay you a retainer of say thirty thousand per year, then pay for each mission we use you."

"Is it dangerous?" Molly asks.

"I'm not going to lie it can be but then taking on a gang of Hells Angels is hardly playing bridge," he can see the mixed emotions in my face. "Look I'm not expecting an answer straight away, think about it and I'll be in touch in a few weeks, in the meantime let's enjoy the party."

"That I can manage," announces Rob, "More drinks Lentil erm Charles?"

"Is there a hotel around here?" He asks.

"No but we have a spare room upstairs so stay with us," Molly smiles.

"Ok if you're sure."

"That's settled then, you're staying here, now we have a few people to thank," I insist.

Rob returns with some drinks, we all take one and head towards the bar.

"Excuse me everyone I would like to say a few words," I announce over the din.

"QUIET for the man," shouts PJ.

A hush descends upon the bar, expectant faces all turn in my direction.

"First I would like to thank each and every one of you for your part in today it has been a fantastic team effort ending in victory." I raise my fist in the air to loud cheers, once they subside I continue. "You have all found something within yourselves today and in doing so have helped your friends and neighbours in Hanley."

"What about Bristol?" Norm shouts.

"Well Bristol, what can I say, it's a nice place but you wouldn't want to live there," lots of laughter ensues. "Seriously though I would like

to thank our friends from Bristol, Jeff, Norm and Westy take a bow."
They step forward and bow to the crowd, "And Pete of course, he's
now a local, well done boys but thankfully we can send you home
now."

"Not so fast Dan," shouts PJ from the back, "I think I'm gonna adopt
them all."

"God help us," I mutter, "Has everyone got a glass?" I'm met by
nodding heads, "then I will ask you to raise them for a toast." They
all raise their glasses waiting expectantly for my toast.

"To the people of Hanley you are special one and all."

"The people of Hanley," the response comes back."

"Now let the party commence."

I look around for Molly and spot her chatting to Rob and Sally so I
walk over and slip my arm around her waist, "Are you Ok babe?"

"Yes darling are you," then without waiting for an answer, "I was just
chatting to Sally and Rob about Charles offer its exciting isn't it?"

"Yeah maybe let the dust settle on today first then I'll consider it."
Rob looks at me as though I'm mad, "but in the meantime I've been
thinking, as Lentil is no more I'm gonna ask Charles about all his
tuning machinery at the farmhouse in Shropshire, I'm thinking
maybe me and Rob can set up a tuning shop."

"That's not a bad idea it'll give us something to do when we're not
charging around the world playing at James Bond," he makes a gun
with his hand and strikes a pose and we all fall about laughing.
Charles is chatting to PJ so I wander over with Rob, PJ spots us
coming and with his arm draped around Charles shoulder says,
"These two fellers they're diamonds you couldn't ask for two nicer
fellers than these."

"I know, they've been friends of mine for the last fifteen years,"
Charles smiles wearily and rolls his eyes at me.

"Are you one of those bloody Hells Angels?" He makes a fist, "I'm
gonna knock you out!"

"I was an MI5 agent undercover as a Hells Angel and before that I
was in the SAS so may I suggest for your own safety you do not try
to punch me." We all start to chuckle as PJ reddens, obviously
flustered, he unfurls his fist and pats Charles on the chest.

"I was only joking actually you're a nice feller as well." We all laugh
loudly as PJ turns and heads back to the bar.

"Are you two Ok?" Charles asks.

"Yeah we've been thinking, whether we take you up on your offer or not we need something to do, so we were wondering about all the tuning kit you've got at the farm."

"What about it?" He grins knowingly.

"Well you aren't going to be using it, so we were wondering how much you want for it?"

"Well considering it was all payed for by the Hells Angels so the government has no claim on it I would suggest you make a trip up with a couple of vans and I'll call it a thank you for your help."

"Really? You are joking right," exclaims Rob.

"Robert when it comes to my work I rarely joke, so it's all yours," he rummages in his pocket and produces a key, "That's for the workshop, go and help yourselves."

"Thanks mate that's another one I owe you," I say, "excuse me a sec I need to speak to Bill about renting a barn from him."

I head off to find Bill in conversation with Jack, two gnarly old farmers together, drinking pints of rough cider.

"Excuse me boys another pint?"

"Don't mind if we do you young Dan," so I order them another pint each.

"Bill, me and my brother were wondering if we could rent a barn from you?"

"What do you want it for?"

"We want to set up a motorbike tuning shop and thought we would rent somewhere first and see how it goes."

"Ere they might be able to make that bloody tractor of yours go a bit faster," Jack quips.

"Well I've got the big one by the road doing nothing its got electricity you can use that if you like."

"Sounds perfect," says Rob, "How much?"

"Hmm as it's you two and as I haven't had as much fun in years as I did today, how about one hundred pounds a week is that fair?"

"That's more than fair Bill," I say shaking his hand, "if you're sure."

"Yah it's been empty for years might need a bit of fixing up but I'll leave that to you."

Rob shakes his hand as well then Bill adds, "Come round tomorrow and I'll give you the keys, not too early mind I'm planning on having a few more of these," he raises his glass to us.

We go back to Molly and Sally to give them the good news. The girls are both excited as we tell them the news. Rob finishes off with, "What a day we've kicked arse are becoming spies and now we're ace motorbike tuners as well!"

"Have you ever tuned a bike?" I try to bring his feet back down to earth.

"No why would I? Lentil always did mine."

"Exactly, so we'll have to learn how to use the kit first."

"Well you can fix stuff you were always building bikes when I was a kid," he shrugs.

"That was years ago, things change, come on let's enjoy the party." I take Molly's hand and lead her off to dance.

By the end of the night there are only a few very drunken people left in the bar. Molly has taken Charles up to the flat to show him his room, so I'm left with sorting out PJ, Pete, Jeff, Norm and Westy.

"Come on boys it's been a cracking day but it's time to go home."

"Just one more for me and me muckersh," PJ slurs.

"No PJ the bar closed half an hour ago."

"OK," he staggers to his feet and hugs me, "I love you, you're a nice feller," then promptly falls onto a stool. Pete seems to be the soberest of a drunken bunch, "Come on you lot back to my place, you too if you want PJ."

He shakes my hand, "Cracking day out Dan it brought back a few old memories."

"You boys did well it's a good job we're not hooligans anymore neither of us back down."

He laughs, "On the same team we can beat anybody."

"We can and thanks again."

We both help PJ up and I wave them off as they wobble up the street. Luckily they haven't got far to go. I watch as Pete ushers them through his front door, then I lock up, turn the lights out and go up to the flat. I climb into bed with Molly, "One hell of a day babe."

"Is it really all over?"

"Yes we can all sleep easier now."

"Thank god," she snuggles up, "And what about his offer?"

"I'll think about it, there's no rush it's not happening for six months."

"What are you thinking?"

"Six months ago I would have jumped at it but now I've got you I've got something to lose."

"Don't be silly I'm not going anywhere you go for it, Charles said it may only be once a year."

"Yeah you're right, I'll have a chat with Rob and we've got the tuning company to set up."

"Exciting isn't it?"

"Yeah," I smile at her, "lot's of changes and all for the better." I kiss her and we drift off to sleep in each other's arms exhausted by the day.

CHAPTER TWENTY NINE

I wake up with a throbbing headache, for a moment I think it's a hangover then I remember being pistol whipped. I climb out of bed take a couple of codeine and go into the bathroom to inspect the damage. The left side of my forehead is an angry mass of purple and black bruising spreading onto my upper eyelid. Oh well, it's not like it's going to spoil my looks! I go into the kitchen and turn on the Rocket, once it has finished chugging away I pour myself a large espresso then sit down and light a cigarette. Charles's offer is very tempting but my only problem is, how dirty will it get? He knows what Rob and I used to do so I'm sure he'll want us to, how did he put it, utilise our skill set. On the flip side we would be working for Queen and country. On to more pressing matters, I need to go and see Bill and get the barn organised before we bring the equipment down from Shropshire. My thoughts are interrupted by Charles coming onto the kitchen.
"Coffee?" I ask.
"Yes please."
"Espresso any good?"
"Mm yes make it a large one."
I get up and pour his drink thinking there's something different about him, then it hits me.
"Ah your ponytail has gone."
"Yes, it was part of the disguise," he touches the back of his head where it used to be, "I'm glad to get rid of it to be honest."
"Is that why you were late?" I joke.
"God no, five minutes with the clippers, I was waiting for clearance from GCHQ to take off with the bird. In the end I had to get my boss in London to stick a rocket up their collective arses," we both laugh.
"So have you thought any more about my offer?"
"Yeah I have, what sort of things will it entail?"
"Well I will be looking to utilise your skillset, urban warfare and the ability to handle fast motorbikes are the obvious two."
"So I'll be getting my hands dirty then?"
"Yes but this time legally you are also a natural leader with exceptional organisational skills."
"My only problem is I've left that life behind and I'm trying to start a normal life with Molly."

"I can see that but this wouldn't encroach too much, maybe two or three weeks once a year."

"That sounds doable I'll have a chat with Rob and let you know."

"Ok no pressure and here's my card, the old phone will be handed in later when I debrief, my personal number is on there."

"Cheers, do you want some breakfast?"

"No thanks Dan, I'm going to make a call and get a car to collect me."

"How the other half lives."

"It could be you just say the word. I'll tell them the tuning equipment is yours, but if I were you I'd get there as soon as possible, as once they start crawling all over the place it will be locked down for months."

"Will do, I just need to organise the barn with Bill later today."

He glances at his phone, "my car is on the A38 so I'm going to go down and meet it."

I look at him quizzically, he smiles and adds, "My phone shows tracking for all kinds of things."

"Ah very James Bond," I smile as I get up to show him out. At the front door we shake hands. "I'll give you both a call in a couple of weeks but think seriously about it."

"I will do, I'm going to see Rob later so we'll have a chat then."

"See you soon Dan," he smiles as he walks towards a completely blacked out Range Rover Sport V8.

I head back upstairs to find Molly coming out of the bedroom yawning, "Was that Charles leaving?"

"Yes he had to get back, work to do."

"That's a shame I would have liked to have said goodbye."

"Look why don't we go out on the bike later maybe even stay over somewhere the bars covered isn't it?"

"Yes darling that would be nice I can get dressed and we can go soon."

"No rush babe I've got to go and see Bill to sort out the barn first we'll leave about two."

"That's fine then but where will I put all my things if we're staying over?"

"Not in that bloody suitcase that's for sure, I'll get my throw over panniers and tank bag out and you can fill those."

"Ok darling I'll look for somewhere to stay while you're out," and with that she goes back into the bedroom with her tea.

I get the luggage from the spare room for her to fill. I put my wash bag, trainers, jeans and a T shirt in the tank bag and tell her, "Here you go, you can fill the rest."

"Cheeky sod I'm not taking that much with me just some nice underwear," she smiles flirtatiously. My phone pings with a text, its Rob telling me he's up and ready.

"I'm off then babe," I kiss her, "I'm gonna pick Rob up and go and see Bill we'll have a chat about the offer while we're out."

I pull up outside in my van and Rob comes out and climbs in the passenger seat.

"Have you thought anymore about becoming a spy?" He grins.

"Stop saying bloody spy will you and yes I have, I think it's worth exploring."

"Cool because I think the same."

"Charles is going to ring in a couple of weeks but I can let him know earlier if you want?"

"Yeah go for it bruv."

We drive down to the farm and as I pull in Bill is already coming out to meet us.

"Morning boys," he says cheerily, "I've got the keys here, come and have a look."

We walk across the gravel path to the big barn by the road, Bill unlocks two padlocks then puts a big key into the main lock, "It's safe as houses but if you want to make it more secure crack on," he opens the door, turns on the light and lets us in. It's a vast space with a concrete floor and a high vaulted ceiling but there are only two fluorescent lights for the whole place and everything is covered in a thick layer of dust. Rob sets off to have a look around while I ask Bill, "The electrics how many amps has it got?"

"Whatever you need, I've got a three phase supply and this runs off one phase so whatever you need."

"Perfect," I answer, "we'll take it." I pull out my wallet and count out a thousand pounds in twenty pound notes then hand it to Bill.

"What's all this for?"

"Call it two months' rent and a deposit deal?" We shake hands to settle the deal.

"While I'm here do you have a trailer I could borrow?"

"Yeah there's a twin axle Ifor Williams round the back and if you need more space you can borrow my Transit and the horsebox."

"That's great can we take them on Tuesday?"

"No problem, just give me a knock when you get here and early as you like I'm up at five."

"Thanks Bill you're a star," he heads off back to the farmhouse while I go inside to find Rob.

"What do you think?" He asks.

"I've given him two months' rent already and he's lending us trailer and his van and horsebox on Tuesday."

"Blimey you don't hang around."

"No point, we'll need to get the electrics sorted and some heating in but we'll get all the equipment in first and go from there."

"No worries what are you up to later?"

"I'm taking Molly away on the bike why?"

"Nothing I'll call in the pub later and get a few of the boys to come with us on Tuesday Ok."

"Sounds good," as we close the barn and lock it behind us.

Later that afternoon I'm trying to load my panniers onto my bike but it's not going well, the Tuono is built for going fast not carrying luggage. I'm about to call it a day and get the car out when I have an idea, I pull out my phone and call Gareth. Two rings later and he answers, "Castle Motorcycles can I help you?"

"Gareth mate, its Dan."

"Hi Dan what's up?"

"Have you still got that red Triumph Sprint with the panniers in the shop?"

"Yes mate it's a tidy bike that who's it for?"

"Me mate I'm trying to take Molly away and I can't get the bloody panniers on the Tuono."

"They're hardly made for touring," he laughs.

"Get the Triumph ready I'll be there in half an hour."

"No probs see you in a bit mate."

I go back inside to get my helmet and jacket.

"I'm not ready yet," says Molly.

"I can't get the panniers on the bike," she looks disappointed, "Don't worry I'll be back in an hour is that enough time?"

"Perfect darling," she kisses me. I head back outside and jump into my van and drive up to Gloucester. As I'm pulling into the car park Gareth is giving the Triumph a last wipe over so it's gleaming in the sun.

"Is that OK for you?" He asks as I get out of the van, "I've had the boys do the fluids and filters so it's all set."

"Perfect mate let me pay and I'll be off, oh and take my van keys in case you need to move it otherwise I'll pick it up on Monday."
"No worries come into the office."

Its half past three and I'm back in the Red Lion car park, Molly comes out to see me.
"Ooh that's nice who's is it?"
"Mine, I've just bought it, the Aprilia isn't really up to taking a pillion so I've got this as well."
"Wow thank you, do I need to unpack everything?"
"No babe my throw overs will fit inside the panniers and I'll just move everything from the tank bag to the top box did you manage to book somewhere?"
"Oh yes come inside and see," she says excitedly.
We go up to the flat and sit at the table, she opens the laptop and shows me the screen, "What do you think of that?" It's a small cottage with its own hot tub on a farm in the middle of Devon, "Lush isn't it?"
"Yes it looks perfect what about food?"
"They bring it to us and champagne as well."
"What are you waiting for get your gear on and let's go," I note down the address for the sat nav.
I've loaded all the luggage and I'm just programming the destination into the sat nav when Molly comes out dressed in new leathers.
They are all Alpinestars black trousers and a bright pink jacket, carrying a fluorescent pink and black helmet.
"Wow when did you get those?"
"Us girls went shopping at that big bike shop in Bristol last week so I got these I thought I would surprise you what do you think?" She performs a twirl.
"You look fantastic," I kiss her, "Come on put your helmet on and we'll get going.
We climb on the bike and I set off at a steady pace, enjoying the freedom motorcycle travel affords. I take the A roads to avoid the monotony of the motorway. Following a pleasant two hour journey we arrive at our destination. The owner comes out to meet us, a homely looking woman in her sixties.
"Hi I'm Sandra we don't get many motorbikes here but there's a car port round the side of the farmhouse if you want to park it in there."
"Thanks that's great, we'll check in and unload then I'll move it."
She produces a key and ushers us towards a small cottage then opens the door. There is one room downstairs with comfortable

sofas and a large TV on the wall, the back half is tiled with a fridge a small worktop with a sink and patio doors. She shows us towards the patio doors and pushes a hidden door in the wall, it opens to reveal a spiral staircase and an open door beyond containing a wet room. We climb the staircase to find a huge king sized bed in the eaves with a large window overlooking the fields beyond. I open the window and look down onto a large private decked area with a hot tub and table and chairs.

Once back in the living room Molly announces, "It's perfect I love it." Sandra smiles and asks what time would you like the food?"

"About eight," answers Molly, "but can we have lots of champagne straight away?"

"It's already chilling in the fridge dear," smiles Sandra.

"Ooh, thank you," and she dives to the fridge to check.

"Right then I'll leave you to it and I'll see you at eight and don't worry I'll knock first," Sandra winks.

I go out to the bike and take off the top box and panniers carrying them inside in turn, and then I take the bike over to the car port and walk back crunching across the gravel in my boots.

When I get back Molly is dressed in a little black bikini holding two glasses of champagne, "Come on get out of those leathers and let's get in the hot tub." I climb the staircase, strip off my leathers and put on a pair of shorts. Molly is sat at the table outside with a towel around her shoulders, "Come on hurry up it's a bit chilly." I push the hot tub lid back, check the controls, then turn on the lights and bubbles and climb in.

"Mm this is good come on in you'll soon warm up," Molly hands me the glasses of champagne then joins me in the warm bubbling water. After ten minutes I announce, "I'm going to get my ipod and put some music on."

"Mm good idea," she says, "And more champagne."

I return with my ipod and dock put on an eighties genius mix on and refill our glasses. I put the remains of the bottle back in the fridge and join Molly in the hot tub.

"This is lush darling," she says sipping at her glass.

"It is," I smile, "Can I ask you something."

"Anything darling," she snuggles into my chest.

"Ok," I get up disturbing her and manoeuvre onto one knee, "Will you make me the happiest man in the world and become my wife?" I produce a huge ruby and diamond solitaire ring. For a moment she is speechless.

"Oh my god oh god yes, yes, yes," she kisses me and I slip the ring onto her finger.

"Oh it's beautiful, oh god I love you I've got to tell everyone."

"Later," I kiss her and unfasten her bikini, "Oh mmmm," and we make love in the bubbling warm water of the hot tub.

Later we are sat inside, Molly is ringing everyone in her phonebook and there is a knock at the door, so I get up to answer it.

Sandra presents me with a huge platter of ploughman's, "I see you've settled in," she smiles. Molly springs to her feet holding out her left hand to show off her ring, "He's proposed look," she exclaims excitedly.

"Congratulations, I'm sure you'll both be very happy," Sandra smiles, "and you can come back and visit us every anniversary."

"What a fabulous idea," enthuses Molly.

We spend a happy evening drinking, dancing and dipping in and out of the hot tub before retiring drunkenly to bed.

The next morning after a hearty breakfast in the farmhouse I load up the bike and Sandra comes out to wave us off. Molly hugs her, "It's been fantastic this place is so lush."

"You're welcome dear come back anytime you feel like it." We climb on the bike and wend our way back home to Hanley both beaming inside our helmets.

CHAPTER THIRTY

I pull up outside the Red Lion in my van towing Bill's trailer behind, Rob pulls in after me towing the horsebox. Allun is waiting outside with Matt, Sam and Josh. Allun opens the door, "Morning boyo all set?"

"Yeah get in," Josh gets in followed by Allun. Matt and Sam jump in the van behind with Rob and we set off on the journey to the farmhouse in Much Wenlock. Two hours later we are pulling up outside the large barn. I climb out of the van and unlock the door. We all go inside, I reach for the light switch but the electricity is off. "I'll get a couple of torches from the van, start bringing out what you can." When I get back all five of them are carrying out the dyno. "Put it in the trailer it'll be easier," I offer in advice. The two roll cabs full of tools and the bike lifts come next. Right at the back of the barn are a pile of boxes partly covered by a tarpauling. I pull the tarp off to reveal the back wheel of a motorbike hidden amongst the boxes. "Come over here and give me a hand moving these boxes," I shout to the others.

The boxes are heavy, so after moving the first two Allun says, "Bloody hell what's in these?"

"Dunno," answers Rob, "let's open one and have a look."

I go outside and get a couple of pry bars from one of the roll cabs to force the lid open. With a bit of brute force it eventually pops off and we all stare open mouthed. It is full of AK47 assault rifles!

"Fuck are they real?" Sam asks going ashen.

I pick one up and turn it over in my hands, "Yep it's real I better call Charles about these."

After a long discussion with him, it turns out the boxes belong to the Devils and we are to leave the rest of them unopened as they will become evidence against them. On the plus side the bike is some sort of Norton. He can't remember which one, but I can have it. We move the boxes of guns just enough to get the bike out, the brakes are seized so we have to carry it outside.

"What do you want that old nail for?" Allun asks.

"It'll be even worse than a bloody Harley," adds Rob.

"It'll be fine once I tidy it up," I run my hands over it taking in the lines I recognise it as a nineteen fifty four Manx Norton. A bike I had a poster of, on my bedroom wall as a kid.

"Come on let's get it loaded up." They all grumble but move it into the back of my van.

The last bits out are the two work benches, once they are secure in the horsebox I turn to Rob. "You set off I'm just gonna lock the barn and put the keys through the letterbox."

With the barn secure again I walk over to the farmhouse and post the keys as Charles asked. I'm just turning to leave when I hear a faint 'mewing' sound coming from near the door. I listen carefully and follow the sound until I reach a cardboard box by the side of the porch. I open it carefully to reveal two very frightened kittens inside.

"Quick come over here," I shout to Allun

"What's up mate?" He asks strolling over.

"Look at these," I answer as he approaches, "They have just been abandoned here in this box."

"Cute but what are we gonna do with them?"

"We can't leave them here," I glare at him as I pick up the box, "I'm taking them home."

We get back to the van and I hand the box to Josh before we both climb back into the van.

"I thought we had everything," says Josh.

"Have a look inside," I answer.

He opens the box and goes all gooey. "Aww kittens they're cute," he strokes the little black one and picks it up. "This one's a boy," he puts it back in the box and does the same with the black and white one, "and this one's a girl, are you keeping them?"

"I dunno," I answer truthfully, "but we can't leave them here, anyway how do you know so much about cats?"

"I'm studying animal management at college I'd love one but I'm away at college too much."

"Well," I say picking up the black one, "I suppose I could keep them I'll tell Molly they are a present."

"Good luck with that," Allun laughs.

"You'll be OK no one can resist kittens," smiles Josh as we pull out of the farm and head for home.

We have just pulled onto the M5 when Josh announces "we are gonna have to stop."

"I thought you said you were fine for a pee before we left." I glare at him.

"It's not me, the little black kitten has escaped, he's under the seat and I can't reach him.

"Some bloody emergency." Laughs Allun.

I scour for signs for the services until I eventually spot one. "Four miles, OK."

"Brill, just be careful where you put your feet until then."

I pull off the motorway and into the caravan park reasoning it will be safer there with the trailer on the back. The moment I stop Josh has his seat belt off and is fishing about under the seat trying to catch the errant kitten.

"I can't reach him have a go Dan."

I sigh as I unbuckle my seat belt and get on my knees to help. Allun starts to laugh. "I told you cats are trouble."

I reach under the seat and stroke his head until he moves enough so I can grab him. He mews as I pull him out, then he snuggles into my chest and starts to purr.

"He likes you," smiles Josh.

I spend the rest of the drive back to Hanley stroking the little black kitten in the box while Josh pets the other one.

I park in front of the pub and say, "I'm gonna take these two inside why don't you two take the van and I'll follow you down."

"Any excuse to get out of the heavy lifting," laughs Allun.

"Can I drive," asks Josh.

"Sure, I won't be long." I answer as I close the box and pick it up.

Jess is behind the bar as I walk in to the bar, "Is Molly in?"

"She's upstairs what's in the box?"

"A present," I answer as I head up to the flat.

"Hi darling how was it?" Molly asks.

"Fine until we were about to leave then I found this box."

"Ooh what is it?" Molly asks inquisitively then, "Oh kittens how gorgeous who's are they?"

"Well they were abandoned so I was thinking maybe ours."

"Ooh you cutie," she picks up the black and white one, "Do you mean it?"

"Yeah I pick up the black one, we'll have to get food and stuff but why not?"

"We have to think of names," she kisses me, "And take them to the vets."

"That one is a girl," I point to the one she's holding, "and this little bundle of trouble is a boy, I thought I would call him Diavel it's Italian for devil."

"Ooh an expert on cats as well, is there no end to your talents?" she grins.

"No Josh told me he's doing some animal course at college."
Well I'm going to call her Princess," as she cuddles the little black and white kitten who promptly starts purring.
"Can I leave them with you for an hour while I unload the vans then when I get back we can go and get the stuff they need."
"Ok darling but Princess needs a sparkly collar with a little bell on it."
I hand her Diavel and start to leave, I turn and smile as I watch her mothering the two kittens.
I jog down to the farm. When I get there the only things left to unload are the dyno and the bike. The others are inside moving things into their positions.
"You turned up in the end then," laughs Rob, "Allun told us about the kittens you soft sod."
"Well I couldn't just leave them, come on let's get the dyno unloaded leave the bike I'll free off the brakes before I get it out of the van."
After some huffing and puffing and a little bit of swearing, the dyno is in pride of place at the back of the barn. "Thanks boys, I'll just drop off Bill's trailer then I'll take you all for a few beers."
We are back in the bar and Allun announces, "That was thirsty work," as he winks at me.
"Pints all round please Jess," I pull out forty pounds and hand it over, "That should cover a couple each."
"Are you not having one bruv?"
"No, I've got to go out with Molly to get some stuff for the kittens," they all laugh.
"See I told you he was going soft," smirks Allun.
Molly comes into the bar and grabs my arm, "Are you ready baby?"
She kisses me then adds, "Have you seen the cute kittens he brought me? They are called Princess and Diavel isn't he sweet."
She leads me out of the door and I glance back to see Allun mouthing 'soft' at me.

CHAPTER THIRTY ONE

"Hi Charles it's Dan, I've spoken to Rob and we are both interested, we have got the tuning kit and the bike back down here and we left the guns alone give me a call when you get a chance."
I'm never sure about voicemail but I suppose he's got a lot on his plate right now. Molly kisses me as she puts a plate of poached eggs on toast in front of me.
"No answer darling?"
"No it went straight to voicemail."
"What are you up to today? I'm going to the cash and carry this morning and running the bar this afternoon."
"I'm waiting for Rob we are going to start getting the barn organised," just then my phone rings.
"Ey up Rob," I answer without looking.
"Good morning Dan I've just listened to your message," Charles cuts me off.
"Sorry I was expecting Rob how's things?"
"All good I'm very busy trying to wrap things up here, it's great news that you're interested," he pauses then continues, "I'll need you both for a week in April to get you both signed up and to do some training is that going to be Ok?"
"Sure that'll be fine, shall I let Rob know?"
"No I'll call him myself now, shall I tell him you're waiting for him?"
"Yeah that'll be great."
"OK and one more thing we haven't managed to round up the leaders of the Devils so far so be careful," he hangs up.
Five minutes later my phone pings with a text message, 'Spoke to Charles I'll be there in ten'.
"Right darling I'm off."
"Have a good day baby," Molly kisses me.
"You too see you later."

I unlock the barn and let us in turning the light on as I pass.
"I'm gonna find the fuse box and start measuring for cable why don't you have a sweep round and see where we need sockets just mark the wall." I hand Rob a stick of chalk and a broom.
"I get all the best jobs," he grins, "but first the most important thing," he produces a site radio and turns it on tuning it to a rock station.

We work in silence for the next hour nodding our heads in time to the music.

"Cuppa," announces Rob producing a small espresso machine.

"My hero," I reply.

We sit down on a couple of old crates drinking coffee and comparing notes on electrical requirements.

"I think we should have an office here," Rob paces out an area, "we can have a couple of computer terminals and phones, then on the other side of the door is plumbing, so we can have a toilet and kitchen area."

"It's a lot of work I think we need to get some help in or it's gonna take us months."

"Funny you should say that, Steve's a builder and asked if we needed anything doing, shall I give him a call?"

Around four we pack up for the day, Steve has been and quoted us for the work and added a few more ideas including a suspended ceiling to give us better lighting. It's been a very productive day all in all.

"We should be able to open in a couple of weeks," Rob smiles, "I'll get started on a web site for us but we need a name."

"Yeah I know."

"I was thinking Rob and Dan's Tuning Shack."

"How did I guess your name would be first," I laugh, "I prefer Sampson Tuning."

"Yeah I like it Sampson tuning it is then."

We lock up and both head home happy.

Molly is behind the bar when I walk in, "Can I have a pint please babe?"

"Have you had a good day?" She smiles as she pours my pint.

"It's been productive I've ordered the electrics so that gives us something to be getting on with and Steve has been round and quoted us for an office kitchen and toilet as well as a new ceiling."

"You have been a busy boy."

"Oh and we've decided on a name we are now known as Sampson Tuning."

"Mm I like it."

"Rob's gonna build a website and I'm gonna order some business cards so hopefully in a few weeks we should be open."

"Wow that's quick, come here baby," I lean over the bar and she kisses me, "Jane will be here soon then I'll come round and we can celebrate."

When Jane arrives, Molly hands over to her then pours us both a drink and comes around the bar to sit beside me.

"I've been thinking about our wedding."

"Oh have you now and what have you been thinking?"

"Well first of all how about June?"

"Yeah why not, but not the beginning cause that's when the TT is on."

"Great that's settled then but it's only just over seven months away so we need to start getting things organised."

"Do you know where you want to get married?"

"Well that's the other thing I don't really want a normal wedding it's not really me."

"OK," I'm not sure where this is going so I just nod.

"Well you know when we watched Grease the other night?"

"What you want me to dress up like John Travolta?" I start to laugh.

"No baby but at the end when they are all in the fairground I'd like that, a fairground wedding." I'm not sure what to say so I just listen.

"Then we can invite everyone we know and we can feed them burgers and hot dogs and candy floss and doughnuts," she is in full flow now.

"You boys can arrive on motorbikes and we can have the ceremony on the steps of the Waltzer Oh darling can we? It'll be fantastic."

"If that's what you want I'll make it happen," I kiss her and she throws her arms around me.

"Oh darling I love you, come on let's go upstairs and start looking at fairground rides."

Two weeks later Steve rings to say the work in the barn is finished and can I meet him there. I pick up my phone and call Rob, "Ey up the barns done, do you want me to pick you up to go and have a look?"

"Nah I'll see you there, I'm already on my way down, the guys with the signs have turned up."

"Great I'll see you there."

I load up the old Norton into the van and strap it down before gently setting off. It may be old but in its day it was a race winner and I plan to restore it and use it as a centre piece in the tuning shop. I shake the thoughts out of my head as I approach the farm to see two guys erecting a large sign pronouncing 'SAMPSON TUNING'.

"Looking good," I say to Rob as I pull up.

"This one's going by the door," he shows me another sign resting against the wall.

"Come on let's get inside," I get out of the van and we go in together.

"Afternoon boys what do you think?" Steve asks. I look around we have a kitchen area with a fridge and a microwave with a toilet beyond. On the other side of the door is a glass office with a long counter and two computer terminals. The ceiling has been lowered with multiple lights, the walls are now gleaming white, giving the whole place an almost surgically clean look. Steve shows me to a metal staircase off to one side, I go up to find it has lighting and flooring and the walls are lined with racks for storage. I come back down beaming. "Excellent job mate, come into my office and I'll settle up," we both laugh.

Rob is already sat at one of the terminals browsing the internet, so I take the other, "Cash or bank transfer?"

"Either way mate I'm not fussed."

"I'll transfer it now I haven't got that much cash laying around, have you got your account details?" He hands me his company bank card as I log in to my account and pay his bill.

"All done and thanks again you've done a fantastic job mate."

"No worries any time," he shakes my hand before leaving.

The two guys with the signs come in the door, "All done chaps do you want to come and have a look?"

We follow them outside to admire their work, "Nice work fellers," Rob thanks them as he counts off a bundle of twenty pound notes from his wallet.

"Right come on give me a hand," I say to Rob.

"What with?"

"I've got the Norton in the van."

"We don't need that piece of old junk in here," he retorts.

"Go inside and google nineteen fifty four Manx Norton," we head inside and he taps away at the keyboard.

"Wow is that what that thing is?"

"Yes, a proper old school race bike, I'm gonna restore it and use it as a working centre piece."

"Now I've seen the pictures of it that's a great idea."

"You can learn to twirl spanners on it we'll call it your apprenticeship," we both laugh.

"Talking of apprenticeships get the coffee on will you."

He scowls at me, then answers, "After we get the bike inside."

We unload the bike from the van and Rob asks, "So what are these bikes like then?"

"Well in its day it was a proper race bike, they were raced in GP's and at the TT hence the Manx name. It's a five hundred cc double overhead cam single and it's good for one hundred and forty miles an hour and the featherbed frame handles like a dream," I give him a brief history lesson.

"A hundred and forty! Back in the fifties, Jesus that's still quick today!"

"I know, now can you see why I want it as a centre piece, just imagine being able to fire it up in here!"

"So what's the plan with it?"

"Strip it completely, send the frame, bodywork and wheels off for refurbishment while we get the engine and suspension on the bench and start from there."

"Come on then let's get on with it," he says grabbing a set of sockets from the roll cab.

CHAPTER THIRTY TWO

The Manx Norton project is coming along nicely, the frame, tank, seat and wheels have been dispatched to various specialist restorers. The rest of the parts have been through the blast cabinet and are ready to be re-assembled. Rob is next to me at the work bench patiently assembling the forks with new springs, bushes and seals. I am making a start on the engine, which is in surprisingly good condition. I am using new bearings and seals throughout, the bore just needed honing with new rings on the piston. Straight cut gears will replace the worn originals, everything else will be refurbished and go back into the engine.

"Cuppa?" I ask.

"Yeah great, I'm enjoying this, I don't know why I've never done it before it's quite therapeutic."

"We'll make a mechanic out of you yet," I throw over my shoulder as I head into the kitchen to make espressos.

While I'm waiting for the machine to finish chugging away I hear my phone ringing, I pop my head out of the door, "Get that will you, I'll only be a minute." The machine finishes and I pour the hot liquid into two cups.

"Dan you need to get over here now!"

I rush back into the workshop, "What's on fire?"

Rob points to my phone which he has put on loudspeaker, "Listen."

"Dan are you there?" It's Molly sounding worried.

"Yes babe what's up?"

"It's, erm, erm, it's the Devils, they're here and they are looking for you two."

"Ok babe calm down, how many are there?"

"Five of them but Dan they've got guns!"

"Try to stay calm and don't do anything to upset them if they ask, tell them you'll get us there OK."

"Yes but I'm scared."

"It's gonna be OK, I just need to make a few phone calls then we'll be there and don't worry I've got this."

"Ok darling just be careful."

"You too babe I love you," I hang up then turning to Rob, "Bastards I'm gonna fucking kill them!"

"Ok Dan calm down and let's think this through."

"Yeah you're right," I take a deep breath, "I'll ring Charles to see what help he can get us, you ring round and see if you can round up any of the boys."

We both start to dial numbers and walk away from each other so our conversations don't clash.

"Charles its Dan, the Devils are in the pub and they've got Molly can you get some muscle here ASAP."

"I'm on it Dan but it's going to take me a little while do you know the scene?"

"Five of them apparently all armed, Molly is in there I don't know if there's anyone else."

"I take it they are after you two?"

"Yeah, Rob's rounding up a few boys now, we'll see if we can take them down, just get your lot here as soon as possible."

"I'll get some uniform out but I'll make them stay back and hold the perimeter until we arrive and Dan don't try to be a hero just wait for my backup."

"I'll try mate but if they hurt Molly I'm going in."

"OK but try and stay calm I'm on top of it this end," he hangs up.

"Pete and Allun are on their way and they are picking up Matt, Sam and Josh it's the best I can do, what did Charles have to say?"

"He's sending backup but it will take a while and uniform are coming to surround the village," my phone rings again it's Molly, I answer it and put it on speaker so Rob can listen.

"Now then Dan," a gruff voice comes through, "You owe us big time."

"What for big man?" I answer Brad, the leader of the Devils.

"I've got a long list but the latest is the shipment of AK47's you've just lost us," he snarls menacingly.

"Nowt to do with me."

"I beg to differ, you've got half an hour to front up with a million quid or I start cutting up your pretty little girlfriend here," I hear Molly squeal in the background.

"You touch her and I'll rip you apart with my bare hands," I threaten.

"I'd like to see you try, now I suggest you get a move on, you've got twenty seven minutes," a click and the phone goes dead.

"Bastard I'm gonna .."

"Come with me," Rob interrupts me and I look at him quizzically.

"Bill has a shotgun at the farmhouse let's go and see him," I follow his train of thought and quickly follow him over to the farmhouse.

Rob knocks at the door and we wait.

"How do what's up boys?" Bill answers the door.

"More trouble from the Hells Angels," I answer, "They've got Molly in the pub and they are armed can we borrow your shotgun?"

"Well now that is trouble, you'd better come in," we follow him inside and he leads us out to the back to his gun cabinet,

"I've got a few in here it sounds like you're gonna need em," he unlocks the cabinet and starts to pass out guns.

"There are two shotguns and a couple of high powered air rifles I use for hunting," he passes them out to Rob and I.

"This might come in handy, I kept it from the war," he hands me a Browning handgun.

"Have you got ammo for all of these?"

"Yup next cabinet," he says moving along and unlocking it.

"Bloody hell," splutters Rob, "God help anyone who tries to break in here."

Bill grins as he hands us two boxes of shotgun cartridges followed by a box of 22 pellets.

"Any for the Browning?" I ask.

"You know your guns then," he says as he hands me a box of 40 shells for the Browning.

"Hello are you in there?" Allun's voice shouts from outside.

"Come on in" shouts Bill and in troop Allun, Pete, Matt and Sam.

"Josh couldn't make it," explains Sam.

"Allun told us what's happening what's the plan?" Matt asks.

"They are in the pub with Molly; you guys take the shotguns and air rifles and go outside the front of the pub."

"What about you?" Rob asks.

"I'm taking the Browning and I'm gonna get inside."

"How?" Pete asks.

"Let me worry about that. When I'm in I'll send you a text and you guys create a diversion, hopefully some of them will come out and I can grab Molly."

"Not much of a plan but it could work," Rob looks sternly at me, "Just be bloody careful."

"Always, now come on let's go."

I leave the others before we get to the pub and head up a garden path. I jump a couple of fences and finally arrive at the top of the car park unseen from the pub. I take the gun from my pocket, check the safety is on and slip it into the waistband at the back of my jeans. I can see our bedroom window is slightly open, so I climb carefully up onto the roof of the garage. I edge slowly across until I reach the drainpipe on the side of the pub. Thankfully it's an old cast iron one so I'm praying it will take my weight. I test it and it seems firm enough so I inch up it precariously, a few minutes later I'm level with the window. I reach across and slowly ease it open thankful that it makes no noise. I inch up a few more feet then carefully put my foot on the window sill and step across. I pause a moment to catch my breath then silently slip inside.

I walk gently across the flat then inch slowly down the stairs, missing the fourth step down as I know it creaks. I crack open the door into the pub an inch and listen carefully.

"What the fuck are those twats up to out there?" I hear one of them say.

"Who is it?" Brad's voice is clear.

"That bastard Rob is there with a few others and it looks like they've got bloody air rifles," he laughs.

"Any sign of Dan?" Brad asks.

"Not yet, hopefully he's getting our money then we can fuck off to Spain," I recognise the voice, its Sonny the second in command.

I hear them moving, it sounds like they are heading towards the windows so I pull my phone out and hit send on a pre typed text which simply reads, 'Make some noise'.

I wait a couple of minutes then the sound of shotguns fills the air. "What the fuck?" I hear from in the bar then the sound of shattering glass as a window is shot out, time to move. I ease the door open and head into the pub amidst a cacophony of noise. I survey the scene, there are four of them flanking the windows and the door, Brad is standing behind the bar with Molly cowering at his feet. One of the Devils squeals as he is hit by an air rifle pellet.

"Enough, lets finish this," Brad reaches down and grabs Molly by the hair.

I'm seething as I draw the Browning from my waistband and take aim. I loose off a round hitting him squarely in the shoulder. He spins dropping his gun his face distorted in agony. Sonny starts to turn but I've already got him in my sights, I let another round loose and watch as his elbow shatters. Molly grabs Brad's gun from the floor and stands up, she takes aim and shoots the Devil by the door in his left thigh and he falls to the floor clutching his leg. Three down, reality dawns on the last two and they drop their guns as the sound of sirens fills the air. I rush to Molly and hug her as she sobs in my arms.

"Bloody good shot babe."

"My dad taught me to shoot when I was a girl," she manages between sobs.

Rob bursts through the front door brandishing a shotgun closely followed by Allun and Pete. Pete turns to the Devil closest to him and punches him square in the jaw dropping him instantly to the floor. Moments later a gaggle of flashing blue lights arrive outside followed by the unmistakeable sound of an approaching helicopter. I take Molly around the bar and sit her down Rob passes going the other way and approaches Brad who is curled up on the floor, he swings his boot kicking him in the face and shattering his teeth.

"Bastard, don't mess with the Sampson's cause we'll always fuck you up!"

The police remain outside waiting for the chopper to land. Charles climbs out followed by two armed soldiers and walks into the pub.

"I hope you haven't killed anyone," he grins.

"No mate a couple of flesh wounds and a few bruises," I grin back.

"Where did the bloody arsenal come from?"

"Bill the farmer and it's all legal," I lie slipping the Browning into my waistband and pulling my t-shirt over it.

"Bloody good job boys," then turning to the soldiers, "Get uniform in here and get an ambulance to patch these buggers up."

An hour later we are all sat with a drink to calm our frayed nerves. The street outside has returned to normality. Steve comes in having boarded up the shattered window.

"That'll do for now, I'll fit a new window as soon as I can get hold of one."

"Cheers mate what are you drinking?"

"Thatcher's Dan cheers." I get up and pull him a pint of cider before returning to sit by Molly.

"How are you doing babe?"

"I'm shaken but you were awesome how the hell did you get in?"

"I climbed through the bedroom window these boys knew what to do, I was just praying I could get to you first."

"And you did," she kisses me, "I'll always be safe with you around.

"Not sure you need me, that was one hell of a shot," I smile lovingly.

"Not really I was aiming for his balls," and we all descend into raucous laughter.

CHAPTER THIRTY THREE

It promises to be a landmark day at Sampson Tuning; our first customer is due today. He's from Walton and has a Yamaha MT-10 which he wants upgrading and apparently he has more money than sense, this could prove to be quite fruitful. The other landmark is the Manx Norton is all back together and ready to fire up for the first time. It is sat on its paddock stand looking menacing, resplendent in its alloy tank, new suede covered seat and finished off with number boards bearing the legend '#1 SAMPSON TUNING'. The boards are bright red with silver lettering, exactly matching our signs outside.

"Let me start it," Rob asks.

"OK do you know how to?"

"Hmm I presume it's not as easy as just pressing a button."

"No," I laugh, "first you need to find top dead centre." I put pressure on the kick start rotating the engine until I feel the pressure build.

"Then pull the decompressor," I show him the lever, "Give it a couple of handfuls of throttle then jump on the kick starter and hope it doesn't kick back."

"Sounds complicated isn't there an easier way?"

"Yeah, I can build an electric roller which bump starts it but we haven't got one so get on with it."

"OK let's give it a go," he pulls the decompressor and primes the carb, "all set." He leaps on the kick start and the bike splutters but doesn't quite start.

"Just one handful this time otherwise you'll flood it."

"Alright," Rob concentrates as he finds top dead centre, pulls the decompressor and gives it a handful of throttle. An almighty leap on the kick start sees the bike burble then roar into life.

"Give it a bit of throttle until it warms up," I shout above the cacophony of noise from the open megaphone exhaust.

"Wow what a noise," Rob is grinning broadly as he keeps blipping the throttle until it warms up and settles to a lumpy tick over.

"Nice sound that's what I'm after," I hear a voice from the doorway.

"Oh hi, sorry I didn't see you there, I'm Dan," I offer my hand and receive a firm handshake.

"And I'm Rob," he follows suit.

"Richard nice to meet you guys," he says in return.

"Have you got your bike with you?" I ask.

"Yeah it's parked outside."

"I'll open the main door bring it in then we'll have a look at it."

He goes outside to get his bike as I open the big barn door allowing him access. He rides it in and parks it next to the Norton, which is still burbling away, and dismounts.

"Turn that off," I gesture Rob towards the Norton then turning to Richard, "Come into the office mate do you want a coffee?"

"Cheers milk one sugar."

"Rob do the honours will you."

We sit at the desk in front of the computer and I grab my pad and pen.

"What exactly are you after?"

"Well for a start I want a noise like that one," he smiles at the Norton, "and I want to make it handle better."

"Why didn't you buy the SP?" I ask, "That comes with Ohlins suspension."

"I didn't like the colour and I wanted fluo wheels."

"OK I'll price up Ohlins front and back any ideas on an exhaust?"

"Yeah I've been on Youtube I want the Austin Racing can and de-cat pipe it sounds amazing."

"No worries we can do that but I'll need to flash your ECU or it'll run lean and we can set up your suspension to suit you how does that sound?"

"Exactly what I'm looking for erm who's is that Tuono?"

"Oh that's mine did you not fancy one?"

"I thought about it but I love the way the MT-10 looks it's like a transformer," he grins.

"Why don't you take it for a spin I need to take yours out so we've got a starting point before we upgrade it."

"Do you mind?"

"Not at all," Rob arrives with the coffees, "We'll drink these then go for a spin."

"I hope that's not porn you're all looking at," Molly pokes her head into the office.

"I've got Sally for that," laughs Rob.

"What's up babe?"

"You forgot your lunch and I wanted a nosy it's nice in here but it's missing something," she grins.

"Like what?"

"Oh I don't know maybe pictures of naked men on motorbikes," she tosses her hair as she strides out.

We don our helmets and climb aboard each other's bikes; I follow Richard out onto the road where he promptly gives it a big handful and wheelies off. I spend the ride assessing every aspect of his bike so I can give him my opinion on where best to spend his money. We arrive back in the workshop and he removes his helmet to reveal a massive grin.

"Wow that's awesome."

"I might be in danger of losing custom," I smile at him, "but why don't you trade yours in and get one?"

"It's tempting but I prefer the look of mine," we sit back at the desk.

"Right first thing I need to know is what's your budget?"

"Whatever it costs," he flashes me a perfect smile, "and I want the same brakes as that Tuono as well."

"That's some shopping list," I beckon Rob over, "Why don't you two get it on the dyno to get some baseline figures while I price it all up," they head off into the workshop chatting amiably, while I set to work tapping away on the keyboard.

They eventually return still chatting, Rob sits at his terminal.

"I think you had better sit down," I tell Richard.

"Ouch that bad," he takes a chair.

"OK we've got Austin Racing carbon can and de-cat pipe, Ohlins TTX shock, Ohlins forks Brembo brake calipers and master cylinder, an ECU flash and bolts gaskets etc. is there anything else?"

"Not that I can think of."

"That lot comes in at six thousand two hundred quid plus labour."

"That sounds fine when can you do it?"

"It'll take a week to get all the parts in," I'm amazed at the amount he's spending on a bike which only cost him eleven and a half grand, "then two days to fit it all and set it up do you want a price for the labour?"

"Nah just charge by the hour I might have more stuff done," he gets out his wallet and hands me his card. "Take for the parts now I can leave the bike and get a taxi home."

"Pay for it when we've finished," I dismiss his card, "and Rob will run you home."

"Wow fantastic service already."

"I'll give you a call when it's done then you'll need to come back in and ride it so we can make any minor adjustments to the suspension that may be necessary," I shake his hand again and he follows Rob outside while I get on with ordering all the parts I need.

Ten days later Richard is back and we are sitting at the desk comparing before and after dyno charts.

"You've got an extra eighteen BHP at peak," I point to the graph, "but you can see you've got a lot more at the bottom end and in the midrange."

"That's great what does it ride like?"

"It's a lot meatier all the way through and we've got rid of the snatchy on-off throttle."

"Wow that's amazing and the brakes?"

"One finger has the back wheel waving in the air and the suspension is a massive improvement."

"I can't wait to try it."

"I need you to take it out and test it, I've set up the suspension fairly stiff but it's still compliant, let me know how it feels when you get back." He puts on his helmet and sets off on his test ride" "They were right he's definitely got more money than sense you want to see the size of his house," says Rob. On his return he is grinning broadly as he comes into the office and sits down.

"That's not the same bike it's phenomenal."

"I can assure you it is and it's costing you enough, anything you want to change?"

"No it's perfect but I wouldn't mind a few carbon fibre bits if you can get them for me," as he gets his wallet out to pay he glances at the office walls, "I see you put up pictures then."

"Yeah," laughs Rob, "and not a naked man in sight."

"Can I ask how you heard of us?" I ask as I put his card in our machine.

"Sure my brother's a civil servant and his boss recommended you guys highly." I hand his card back and wave off our first very happy customer recommended I suspect by Charles.

CHAPTER THIRTY FOUR

I'm busy packing for my week long training and induction course with Charles and his new team.

"I'm gonna miss you darling," Molly cuddles me, "Ring me every day."

"I will babe and don't be having lots of wild parties while I'm away."

"Some chance," she laughs

I finish packing and text Rob to let him know I'm on my way. Molly comes out to the car with me, I put my bag in the boot and give her a big hug, I kiss her then get into my car and set off to collect Rob, waving as I leave. Rob is waiting outside, when I arrive, he throws his bag into the boot and climbs into the passenger seat.

"What do you reckon we are gonna have to do?"

"I've no idea but I suspect we'll have to sign some stuff and probably loads of physical exercise."

"I'll put some tunes on, let's go," he pulls out his ipod and connects it to the stereo as I set off towards the SAS training base in Hereford.

I pull up at the barrier and lower my window.

"Dan and Rob Sampson we're expected," the soldier in the booth looks down his list then raises the barrier.

"Follow the road around to the left, when you get to the car park on the right stop there and stay by your car, someone will come out to meet you."

We are standing by my Jag when a tall figure in black combats comes out of the building and heads straight towards us. He offers his hand and introduces himself.

"I'm Matt Grey I'm in charge of the unit, Charles speaks highly of you both, follow me," he turns and heads back towards the building. We are shown into the barracks, a large room with eight bed spaces.

"The two at the end on the right are yours, unpack and get changed I'll be back shortly," he turns on his heel and leaves.

"Bloody hell we've joined the army," Rob grumbles.

"It's only a week how bad can it be?"

"Come on, I'll introduce you to the others," Matt says on his return. We follow him down the corridor to the door at the end and he holds it open while we enter.

"Take a seat," he walks to the front of the room to join Charles.

"Good morning people my name is Charles Mosely I'm responsible for setting up this task force," everyone in the room stares intently at him.

"This is Commander Matt Grey he will be in charge on the ground, you will follow his every order," he steps back taking a seat and let's Matt take over.

"You have been specially chosen for your individual skillsets there will be others joining as and when necessary depending on each mission's requirements, two of whom are at the back, so we'll start the introductions with them," he points at me.

"Hi guys I'm Dan Sampson."

"And I'm Rob Sampson, his brother."

"Shaun West, computer specialist."

"Craig Foster, navy."

"Charlie Foreman, SAS."

"Stubbs, just Stubbs, army."

"I'm Fiona Eve, assassin," we all turn to stare at the slight woman with the short blonde bob.

"Thank you people, in front of you is all the necessary paperwork. Please fill it all out and when you get to the last page raise your hand and either Charles or I will come and witness you signing the Official Secrets Act."

I work my way through the paperwork, the first is a form listing contact details, next of kin, bank details etc. The next is a contract stating payment details and a maximum of four weeks a year. There are three different types of disclaimer, the gist of which being, if I fuck up it's on my head not the governments, no 007 license to kill here. Finally the Official Secrets act, I raise my hand and Charles comes over.

"Are you happy with everything?" I nod as I sign it then Charles signs as a witness. "Welcome aboard Dan," and he moves off towards Rob.

The morning passes with boring monotony as Matt discusses each of the items of paperwork in depth before announcing, "Right then its lunchtime anyone that doesn't know where to go just follow Charlie," and we all file out.

"That was fun," moans Rob.

"If you want fun I can fry your testicles with a red hot poker," deadpans Fiona.

"You're not getting anywhere near my balls," blusters Stubbs.

"Come on girls keep up," shouts Charlie from a way down the corridor.

"Ooh wouldn't want to keep mother waiting now would we," quips Craig.

"This looks like it's gonna be fun after all," I wink at Rob.

The afternoon passes with more monotony with both Charles and Matt stressing the fact that any mistakes we make are our own fault and nothing to do with the government. At five o'clock Matt announces, "OK that's it for today, tomorrow we are on the range to see how you handle various weapons. The bar is open tonight so you can have a few drinks, relax and get to know each other, I'll see you all at O eight hundred tomorrow."

"Come on, I need a pint," says Rob.

"I'm with you feller," adds Stubbs.

"I just need to ring Molly and I'm with you," I add.

"Is that your cat or your mother," Fiona deadpans again.

"Nope neither but mine are all alive what did you do with yours kill and eat them?" I shoot back. She walks up to me smiling sweetly like butter wouldn't melt and whispers in my ear, "Don't fuck with me boy or I'll hurt you."

"Only if you bring your mother little girl," I whisper back.

"Pack it in you two," Matt says from behind me, "Play nicely." We glare at each other as we head off to find the bar.

"Get me a pint," I say to Rob, "I'll be in soon."

"Ok what do you want?"

"Whatever beer they've got, in fact just get me the same as you," I wander off to call Molly.

"Hi babe how's it going?"

"Aww you called, I'm great, how is it up there?"

"Boring today, it was all paperwork, tomorrow should be better we're on the shooting range ."

"Ooh that sounds more like it what are you doing tonight?"

"We've met the rest of the team so we're all going for a few pints to get to know each other."

"What are they like?"

"They seem Ok, I'll let you know when I get to know them better."

"Ok darling enjoy yourself, I love you."

"I love you too, speak tomorrow," I hang up and head inside.

"I've got you Butty Bach it seems Ok," says Rob as he hands me a pint.

"The Fuggles is a decent pint," says Stubbs as he wanders over to join us.

"I'll try that next," I answer.

"So what's the deal with you two?" he asks.

"We knew Charles when he was undercover and we seem to keep helping each other out," I answer.

"The others are all military so they are a bit suspicious."

"That explains a lot, come on, let's get this sorted out now," I say to Rob. I walk over and stand in the middle of the group receiving a lot of glares and a look of bemusement from Charlie.

"I hear you're not sure of me and Rob because we aren't military," a few nods of agreement.

"Well let's get this straight, we are here because of Charles, we helped him out when he was undercover. We aren't permanent, we've been asked to help you guys out when we are needed, so does anyone have a problem with that?"

"You've got some balls," Shaun smiles, "you'll do for me."

As long as you don't run at the first sign of trouble sweet cheeks," Fiona is still looking for a fight.

"When you get to know us you'll find we stand our ground and never back down," Rob joins in.

"Ah you must be the ones that helped Charles take down the Hells Angels," Craig pipes up, "from what I've heard you boys did well."

"You've been at them twice now," adds Shaun, "from the intel I've seen."

"Hells Angels are just a bunch of schoolgirls on motorbikes," snarls Fiona, "I'll reserve judgement until I've seen you two in action."

"Fair enough," I smile, "we're all gonna have to trust each other at some point. Now let's have some fun, where's the jukebox?"

"I'll go, what does everybody like?" Shaun says.

"Rock for me," I go first.

"Rock," adds Rob.

"Gotta be rock," from Stubbs.

"Rock, although I like a bit of Oasis and they're not really rock," Craig adds.

"Well I like classical music but it looks like I'm outvoted," Fiona smiles for the first time.

During the course of the evening I discover that Craig is married with two kids, Charlie is mad about rugby and would have played professionally if he hadn't joined the army, Shaun was a hacker and was recruited by MI5 and Fiona hasn't eaten her mother in fact she lives with her.

I'm aiming at my target with a rifle while in the next bay Stubbs is peppering his target with an assault rifle. I put three shots in the head but they are all spread down the right hand side. Fiona walks up, "Not bad have you used one of those before?"

"Nope, first time."

"You need to adjust the sight for the wind," she shows me how. "Now try."

I put three shots in the centre of the head, then move down and put three more through the centre of the body.

"Thanks," I smile.

"Not bad for an amateur," I watch as she picks up a Glock 17 handgun and sights the target and shoots three rounds all to the centre of the head.

"Wow nice shooting."

"I was born with a gun in my hand," she smirks as she wanders off. At the end of a fun week of shooting, fighting and various assault courses we are called to the classroom where it all began.

"People can I have some quiet please," says Charles above the general din of our chatter. He waits until we all fall silent.

"Thank you for all your hard work this week I hope you have all started to bond." There are a few smiles exchanged as we recall the trials and tribulations of our week together.

"The next stage for all of you, except Dan and Rob is Argentina."

"Are we not going?" I interrupt.

"Not on this one I only need a small team so if you would both like to leave I can brief the rest of the team on their mission."

Rob and I get up and exchange handshakes with the rest of the team.

"See you soon sweet cheeks," Fiona smiles.

"OK guys I'll see you all soon," says Rob.

"It's been fun I can't wait to meet you all in the field," I add. We finish our goodbyes and as we leave I close the door behind us.

"OK bruv ready for home?"

"You bet I can't wait to see Sally and Callum."

CHAPTER THIRTY FIVE

The Hanley fete is a yearly event and the whole village comes together to make it an affair which attracts visitors from the surrounding villages and beyond. It is held in Bill's large meadow, putting our workshop in a prime position right at the entrance. We have agreed to have a motorbike display in our workshop and Rob and I are going to be giving beginner lessons on our trail bikes. Bill has spent the whole day organizing the arrival and erection of the many marquees required for the event. When I wander across to see him he is organising the erection of the last marquee, a particularly large one.

"What's going on in that one," I ask.

"Beer tent the most important one."

"Ah shall I let Molly know it's almost ready?"

"Nah its OK she's coming tomorrow to get it all set up, how are you boys getting on with the bikes?"

"We've got eight bikes spread around the workshop and two more outside for people to learn how to ride."

"Do you fancy another bike in there?"

"Sure the more the merrier who's is it?"

"Ah, it's mine I haven't used it in years."

"Wow I didn't know you were a biker!"

"In my youth, I was a proper rocker one of the ton up boys."

"This place never ceases to amaze me, what bike have you got?"

"Well after the Triumphs of my youth I needed to get something sensible when I got married so I bought a Sunbeam S8, though it still managed eighty five," he grins.

"You are a dark horse I'd love to have it on display where is it?"

"Ah it's in my dining room, one of the joys of being widowed."

"How long is it now?"

"Nine years now and I still miss Bella every day, cracking woman she was, though you've got yourself a good 'un."

"I know Bill best decision I've ever made moving down here."

"Right you lot that's finished," he says to the lads erecting the marquee, "I'll see you in the morning hay bales to move tomorrow."

I follow Bill back to his farmhouse where he leads me through the kitchen and into the dining room.

"There she is," he points to his beautiful Sunbeam S8 resplendent in grey with black tank pads and a peashooter silencer.

"Does she start?"

"Probably not, it's been a couple of years now."

"I'll tell you what, when the fete has finished I'll give it a service and get her running for you."

"Hmm how much is that gonna cost?"

"Nothing, call it a present from me."

"Humph I'll let you do it but I want to pay for the parts deal?"

"OK deal I'll price it up and let you know, have you got the keys?"

"In the ignition do you need a hand?"

"Its fine I'll manage, though if you wouldn't mind getting the door."

"No problem Dan."

I push the bike out into the daylight for the first time in years and across to the workshop. I manoeuvre it around and park it between my Manx Norton and Allun's BMW. Then I lock up and head home to see Molly.

The day of the fete dawns bright I help Molly load up my van with the last of the drinks needed for the day. Molly puts the chalkboard outside the pub reading 'Closed today, at the fete come and join us', and then she joins me in the van.

There are people milling around everywhere getting their final preparations in before the gates open at nine o'clock. I help Molly unload the van, give her a kiss and leave her to it. I drive the van back to the workshop to see how Rob is getting on.

"Ey up all done here."

"Nice one, I'll get the coffee on before the mad rush starts, Janet and John are manning the gates but Bill asked if we could do it later on this afternoon."

"Makes sense as we'll be here anyway."

By eleven o'clock the rush has died down, we've had a steady stream of people through the workshop admiring the bikes and four people have had a go at learning to ride.

"We're going to go and have a wander round," I say to Janet and John, "We'll be about an hour, then when we get back we'll take over from you."

"Thanks Dan that'll be lovely," answers Janet.

As we wander around there seems to be a bit of a fracas going on at the beer tent.

"Let's go and see what that's all about," suggests Rob. As we approach we see what's happening.

"You're trying to fucking short change me," a large red faced man is shouting at Jess in a broad Irish accent.

"No I'm not," says Jess standing her ground, "you gave me a ten pound note and I gave you six pounds eighty change."

"I gave you a bloody fifty pound note you stupid bitch," and he pushes her hard. Rob sprints over to help, so I stand back and let him get on with it. He places himself between them both.

"Calm down feller, don't be throwing your weight around with a girl."

"Who the fuck are you?" He whistles loudly and is soon joined by six burly fairground lads. I spot Allun standing with Pete and beckon them over to join Rob.

As we near, Molly comes out of the beer tent, "We haven't even got a fifty pound note in the till so you must have made a mistake."

"Don't you fucking start Bitch," he sets off forward with his hand raised in a fist. Rob is too quick for him he grabs his arm and turns it up his back, spins him round and shoves him firmly into the fairground hands. One of them charges straight at Rob fists raised but he is ready. He sidesteps and kicks him hard at the back of his knee making his leg buckle. He then lets loose with a barrage of punches to his head. I begin to sprint as the others start forward.

"Hold it there boys you really don't want to get involved," I shout as Allun and Pete join me.

"Fuck off prick," one of them shouts as all five of them start forward. Pete launches himself into the middle of them landing punches everywhere. I catch the one closest to me square on the jaw and he goes down spark out, that evens things up a little. Allun charges forward and rugby tackles the big loud bloke who started it all. One of them grabs Pete from behind by the arms while another steps up to punch him, before he gets a chance Pete kicks him hard between the legs and he goes down clutching his groin. I punch the one holding his arms forcing him to let go, Pete turns and launches a vicious attack landing a flurry of punches to his head and body. I launch an attack on one of them as he heads towards Molly and Jess. I land a two footed drop kick in the middle of his back; I'm up and on him before he can move. I slam his face into the solid earth causing his nose to shatter and pour with blood. I see Rob launch himself behind me then I feel a blow on my shoulder, I glance sideways to see Rob astride a man driving his fists into his face. I smash the man beneath me into the ground twice more, then get up to survey the scene. There are four of them unmoving on the ground, Pete is chasing one of them across the meadow, Rob is astride his victim while Allun has one held on a table while he head butts him. Looks like job done.

"Pete let him go mate," I shout as I help Rob to his feet.

"I think he might have had enough now," I shout to Allun as the sound of police sirens fills the air.

The police are soon moving amongst the crowd taking statements and handcuffing the seven fairground workers.

"From what I've been told you boys did a good job but in future wait for us to arrive," the sergeant says to me.

"I need you to call my boss and let him know about this," I say handing him a card with Charles's name and the legend 'MI6' on it. The officer promptly stiffens and makes the call.

"What's going on with the copper?" Rob asks as he comes over.

"I've asked him to call Charles and explain things."

"God I never thought of that do you reckon he's gonna give us a bollocking?"

"I don't know but I'm just covering our backs."

"Jesus I haven't scrapped this much in years," grins Pete as he joins us.

"Me neither, not since I gave up playing rugby," Allun laughs.

"Glad you're having fun boys, I'm gonna check on Molly and Jess."

"How are you doing babe?" I kiss her.

"I'm fine darling are you?"

"Yeah no worries what about you Jess?"

"I'm fine thanks Dan."

"So what was that all about?"

"He was trying it on reckoning he had given me a fifty pound note, he was pissed mind, I must have served him at least eight pints."

"OK no harm done, well not to us anyway, I'm just gonna check with the coppers then get back to the workshop what time are you closing?"

"I'm closing the bar at eight are you coming back?"

"Of course, I'm closing at five so I'll come back then, see you later gorgeous," I kiss her again and go and look for Rob.

"Have we missed all the bloody fun?" John asks as we get back to the workshop.

"Yeah we could have done with you John," laughs Rob, "and your bloody horse to teach those bloody pikeys a lesson."

"Ere Janet wants a go on one of those bikes any chance?"

Sure let me get the keys from the safe and a helmet." Once she's suitably attired I get Janet to sit astride the bike.

"Are you comfortable?" She nods, "Right the green light shows it's in neutral so press the starter," she does and the engine burbles into life.

"Pull in the clutch with your left hand and put it into first, that's down with your left foot OK," she nods while grinning broadly inside her helmet.

"When you're ready give it some gentle throttle and ease the clutch out slowly, once you're moving put your feet up on the pegs but be gentle with the throttle. She eases the bike forward and puts her feet up. Within minutes she's zipping around the car park changing up and down gears, before finally coming to a stop in front of us. I help her take off her helmet revealing a huge grin from ear to ear.

"Wow that's fantastic will you help me pass my test?"

"Yeah no problem, I take it you want a bike then?"

"Yup I've seen those little Harleys I want one of those will you help me find one?"

"Sure come into the office and we'll have a look," she follows me in and we both sit by the computer.

"Here we go what about this one?"

"Ooh I like that in blue and it's only four thousand where is it?"

"It's in Bristol."

"Right I'm gonna call them and put a deposit on it how soon can I take my test?"

"You'll be better off doing a week long course with your test at the end it's the quickest way, I'll look it up while you ring the bike shop." Fifteen minutes later and she has paid her deposit on the Harley Davidson 883 Sportster and booked her training course.

"Come on I'm gonna close up let's go for a pint to celebrate."

Its half past nine and we have just finished loading up the van.

"Well that was a strange day."

"You're not kidding," laughs Rob.

"Come on darling let's go home."

"Ok babe do you want a lift Rob?"

"Nah I'm gonna ride my bike home see you tomorrow."

CHAPTER THIRTY SIX

The wedding plans are coming along nicely except we can't actually get married outdoors in this country. To get around this we have booked a ceremony at the registry office in the morning to get the legalities done. Our proper wedding will be conducted by a celebrant and is scheduled to take place in the afternoon at five o'clock, followed by a huge party revolving around the fairground which I have booked. Obviously not the same one as the fete. Plans have been made for every minute detail, the only thing that could possibly go wrong is the weather. I constantly check the long range weather forecast which tells me we will be in the middle of a heatwave, but it doesn't stop me worrying. My other worry is the stag party, Rob and Allun have organised. They wanted to go abroad for a week long drinking session which I politely declined. They have eventually settled on hiring a coach and doing a tour of all the local villages, obviously the pubs, and in fancy dress. I can't say I'm looking forward to it but I'm sure we'll have some fun along the way.

Of more immediate concern, we are expecting a visit from a Somerset based bike racing team with a view to looking after their race bikes. The phone rings and Rob ignores it so I reach over to answer it and glare at him.

"Good morning Sampson Tuning can I help you?"

"Hi yes, its Andy Smith is that Dan?"

"Hi Andy, yeah it's me, what's up?"

"I'm just coming into Hanley from the A38 how do I find you?"

"Just stay on the road you're on, you will come to the Ship Inn, take the left there and just follow the road. You will pass the Red Lion on your right, go about three quarters of a mile further on and we are on the left, there's a big sign by the road you can't miss it."

"Cheers Dan I'll see you soon."

"As you couldn't be bothered to answer the phone you can make the coffee," I glare at Rob.

"Isn't that what your apprentice is for?" He salutes me and heads off to the kitchen laughing.

The sound of a car on the gravel outside heralds the arrival of Andy Smith the owner of Smith Racing. I get up and go to the door as he's getting out of his car and I offer my hand.

"Dan Sampson nice to meet you."

"Andy Smith," he shakes my hand firmly, "Likewise."

"Come on in," he follows me and as we pass the kitchen, "That's Rob my brother."

"Ey up mate, I'm making coffee do you want one?"

"Cheers, black no sugar."

"I'm doing us espresso if you fancy one."

"That's brill cheers," he follows me into the office and we both take a seat, Rob arrives with drinks and sits with us.

"What exactly can we do for you," I ask.

"Do you know anything about my team?"

"Only what's on google."

"Well we race BSB and Supersport we have two riders in each. We also have two riders who compete on the roads in Ireland and the Isle of Man."

"So where do we fit in?" Rob asks.

"Well, all the big tuners are either based up north or around London so our bikes spend a lot of time being ferried around the country in vans, whereas you guys are just up the road."

"So how did you hear of us, we haven't been open long."

"Ah you did a fantastic job on my business partner's bike," he notices my frown so he adds, "Richard Shaw MT-10."

"Now I see," realization dawns.

"Ok then," interrupts Rob, "How many bikes do you need looking after and what about mechanics at the track."

"There are eight bikes in total, four six hundreds and four thousands. This year we've got Yamahas R1's and R6's."

"So what's the deal with us?" I ask.

"Basically the job you did on the MT-10 we need doing on all the bikes, then during the season if we blow one up or crash one they'll come back to you."

"So again, what about race meetings?" Rob asks.

"We have our own mechanics at the tracks but you guys are welcome to come to as many or as few races as you like."

"That's where I'm at," smiles Rob.

"And how much are you expecting to spend?" I ask.

"Whatever it costs within reason, we are in it to win, do you guys want to chat about it and get back to me?"

"Well," I look at Rob who nods and grins at me, "No we'll do it but when each bike is done I want your mechanics to come up so we can go over every detail with them."

"And we want Sampson Tuning stickers on all the bikes," Rob adds.

"That all sounds great," he shakes both our hands.

"When can we have the bikes?" I ask.

"We are taking delivery next week but I can get them shipped straight here."

"That's great, I also need a copy of the rule book to see if we can find an extra edge anywhere."

"That just reassures me I've made the right decision, Dan, Rob," he shakes both our hands, "it's been an absolute pleasure, call me when the bikes arrive and I'll come up."

"No worries." I see him out to his car, a brand new BMW M4 Bi Turbo, and wave him off. When I return Rob is chuckling to himself.

"Nice one Dan, not only do we get to go to the racing for free we get paid for it."

"I know but we have to make sure they are the best bikes on the grid it's not gonna be easy."

"But we can even go to the TT; I've not been in years."

"We've got our work cut out trying to get eight bikes ready before the season starts, so why don't we take on an apprentice?"

"Oi I thought that was me."

"Nah you've graduated, now we need another, even if it's only to make the coffee."

"I'll put an advert together you ask Molly to put the word out in the pub."

We have two lads to interview Sam, one of the lads from the village who we know well, and Tom a lad from Oxford, not the Oxford but a village about eight miles away. We really need to take one of them on as the Smith Racing bikes are arriving tomorrow. Tom is first and he's sat nervously in the waiting area.

"If you're ready I'll bring him in," I say to Rob.

"Go on let's put the poor bugger out of his misery he looks like he's gonna cry."

I put my head around the door, "Tom do you want to come in?" He gets up smiling nervously.

"Take a seat before we start do you want a drink?"

"No thanks."

"Right let's get on with it, why do you want to become our apprentice?"

"Well I'm mad about engines I've been messing about with them since I was a kid, I race karts and I've tuned my Focus myself, fast as fuck it is."

"So you're all about four wheels then?" Rob asks.

"Yeah of course," he smiles relaxing a little, "I'm a proper petrol head."

"Maybe, but you haven't done your research have you," I say sternly.

"What do you mean?" He stutters.

"We are bike tuners," says Rob, "So thanks but no thanks, I'll show you out."

Rob comes back in shaking his head, "That was a waste of time, bloody Ford Focus!"

"He might have been useful, he can obviously twirl spanners we could have taught him the rest," I shake my head, "What time's Sam due?"

"Speak of the devil," Rob nods as Sam walks in the workshop.

"Dan, Rob, how is it?"

"Come on in and sit down," says Rob.

"Before we start do you want a drink?" I ask.

"Erm no I'm OK but I bet you both do, I'll make some espressos before we start," he smiles and heads off to the kitchen.

"See better already," laughs Rob.

"Well it's not a bad start."

Sam comes back with two large espressos, "Here you go," then takes a seat.

Rob decides to start this time, "So what do you know about engines?"

"To be honest nothing about tuning them, that's why I'm here, I can strip and rebuild a lawnmower engine but I've never really worked on bikes."

"Have you even ridden one," I ask.

"Oh yeah I've got a YZF 125 and my test is next week."

"So what have you done to your own bike?"

"Nothing apart from maintenance there's no point in tuning it as when I pass my test I'll get a bigger one and I'll get a better trade in if it's standard."

"Do you know anything about suspension set up?" I ask.

"Not really, the only adjustment on mine is rear pre-load which I've wound right up."

"Why did you do that?"

"Well it raises the back end so it quickens the steering and gives me more ground clearance."

"Where did you learn that?"

"Erm nowhere it just seemed obvious to me is it wrong?"

"No that's perfectly correct, now just take a seat outside will you while we have a chat," I ask.

"What do think," asks Rob.

"He's got potential, he's got the right ideas and seems keen to learn, what about we offer him a month's trial?"

"Ok that sounds fair and he does make a decent cuppa I'll get him back in," he stands up and beckons Sam through the window. He comes back into the office and takes a seat.

"Ok Sam are you working at the moment?"

"Only a few days here and there in the Co-Op while I look for something, my mum works there."

"Ok we would like to take you on a month's trial, after three weeks we'll have another chat and see how we all feel, how does that sound?"

"Fantastic I won't let you down."

"If after a month we decide to keep you on we'll enrol you in college one day a week the rest you'll learn in the workshop."

"That sounds brilliant when can I start?"

"We've got eight race bikes arriving tomorrow so what about eight in the morning?"

"Awesome, I'll be here what do I need to bring?"

"Yourself and a sandwich, we'll sort the rest out and Sam."

"Yes boss," he beams.

"Welcome aboard," I shake his hand.

"Welcome to the team mate," adds Rob.

He gets up to leave beaming from ear to ear then turns back to us and his face drops, "Erm I'm really sorry to ask but can I have some time off next Tuesday morning as it's my bike test, I'll stay late to make it up."

"Take the morning off, just make sure you pass or you won't be able to road test anything," I smile.

"Yes boss will do," his beam returns and he almost skips out of the workshop.

CHAPTER THIRTY SEVEN

I'm at the workbench with Sam teaching him how to use a torque wrench and how to use it for getting a feel for bolt tightness.

"I want you to use the torque wrench for everything until you get the feel Ok."

"Yes that's fine," he smiles as he sets about torqueing down a cylinder head as he's been instructed.

"Morning, who's this?" Andy Smith says as he walks in.

"Sam our new apprentice the bikes aren't here yet."

"I know I've just passed them on the A38 shall I make some drinks?"

"I'll do it," Sam leaps up.

"No you finish the job you're doing, never leave anything half done," I scold.

"No worries I've got it, where's Rob?" Andy replies.

"Picking up our engine and fork oil order he'll be back soon,"

Andy heads off to the kitchen to make the drinks then shouts back, "Do you want one Sam?"

"No thanks mister, I drink water."

"No worries and its Andy."

Rob arrives back followed by two large vans, "Bikes are here, they asked me for directions so they followed me in."

An hour later Andy has waved off the van drivers and Sam is drooling over the bikes.

"Cor, they're just like mine but bigger how fast do these go?" He points at the R1's.

"By the time we've finished, over two hundred miles an hour. Do you reckon you can hold on at that speed?" Rob mocks.

"Really, the fastest mine will do is seventy five."

"I'll get them all dynoed first to get some baseline figures then we're gonna strip them down completely and start work."

"Blimey that's thorough," says Andy.

"Fine tolerances can make a big difference."

"And suspension?"

"Ohlins arriving today for both ends on all the bikes, I'll do the initial set up but we're gonna need some track time to finalise it."

"Not a problem. When do you want my mechanics here?"

"I'll need them for a day next week, I want them to help rebuilding the bikes, once I've sorted the tolerances, so they have a feel for them, they only need to be here for one of each."

"Let me know when and I'll send them up."

"Let's say Wednesday and what about exhausts?"

"Yes, I've got a deal with Scorpion, they should be here tomorrow, full titanium systems you'll like them."

"Who's doing the bodywork?"

"Dream Machine, it's already there we'll drop that off when it's done."

"I'll box up the original parts and you can collect them when you're passing."

"Keep them, they are no use to me, our bikes never go back on the road."

"Ok mate I'll store them upstairs," then turning to Sam, "Make a start on that R1, take off all the bodywork and lights and don't break anything."

"I'll treat it like it's my own," he grins and gets to work.

"How's he doing?" Andy asks.

"First day, but he's like a sponge, can he come to the track with you?"

"If you can spare him at the weekends, he can come to every race."

"He'd love that but I'll tell him later, I don't want him getting too excited while he's got work to do."

"Oh hi, I'm Molly, ooh they're pretty,"

"Andy Smith, I take it your Dan's other half."

"Sorry yes, I've just called in to remind him to pay for the wedding cars."

"Already done babe."

"I'm off I'll leave you to it," says Andy.

"I'll go too it looks like you've got your hands full, see you later darling," and she leaves chatting to Andy as she goes.

I hear the tinny noise of Sam's bike arriving, Rob and I leave the bike we are working on and rush outside to see if he has passed. "He's still got the 'L' plates on," I say dejectedly. He climbs off and removes his helmet revealing a sad face.

"Never mind you can take it again," Rob consoles.

"Ha I've passed," he breaks into a huge grin and rushes up to hug me.

"You little bastard," Rob punches his arm, "Well done mate."

"I don't want to put a damper on things but Rob you tell him."

"We've been watching you work these last ten days," says Rob with a stern face.

"What, I've been doing what you tell me," Sam looks worried.

"And we've made a decision, I'm sorry," he pauses, "we are gonna have to ask you," he pauses again and Sam's face goes from elation to dejection, "to come on board permanently got you back you little bastard."

"What really? This is the best day of my life, I've got to ring my mum, I haven't told her I've passed yet, I came straight here," he rushes into the office to make an excited phone call home.

"Dan, phone for you," Sam shouts from the office so I go in to take it.

"Hello Dan Sampson."

"It's me, darling I'm just checking you've paid the man for the fairground,"

"It's all under control babe stop worrying it's gonna be a fantastic day I love you."

"Ok I love you too, I'll see you later darling," she hangs up and the phone immediately rings again.

"Good morning Sampson Tuning."

"Hi Dan its Janet, I've just passed my bike test."

"Wow two in one day, Sam our apprentice has just passed as well."

"That's fantastic but I'm after a favour, I was gonna ask if someone will ride my bike back from Bristol for me. I don't fancy getting used to it on roads I don't know."

"When do you need it by?"

"Whenever Dan, there's no rush."

"Ok, tell them Saturday and one of us will get it for you."

"Thanks Dan you're a darling." I hang up and ring our insurance company to let them know Sam has passed so they can update our policy. I go out into the workshop where Sam is talking animatedly with Rob.

"Sam, on Saturday I need you to pick up a bike from Bristol OK."

"But I can't drive the van."

"No but I've sorted our insurance so you can ride it back."

"Wow really, that's fantastic."

"Don't get too excited though it's only a Harley 883 Sportster, probably no faster than your 125 I laugh."

"Still that's brill, thanks a lot I love working here."

"Just get on with those bikes and we'll take you for a beer after work to celebrate."

He puffs out his chest in pride then goes back to concentrating on the R6 he's working on.

CHAPTER THIRTY EIGHT

The Smith Racing bikes are back with the team and the workshop has returned to normality. Rob and Sam are finishing off a Honda Fireblade for collection tomorrow and I'm in the office reading through emails when my mobile rings.

"Dan its Charles, I need you and Rob to go to France tomorrow."

"What's the deal?"

"The team are having a problem with a local bike gang; I need you to either get them onside or removed."

"Ok, we'll need bikes out there."

"It's all sorted, you fly from Bristol to Paris at eight o'clock in the morning. Collect the tickets from the BA desk, you'll be met at Charles De Gaul airport with two Ducati Panigales are they suitable?"

"I'm sure we can make them work, Rob's here with me so I'll let him know."

"That's fine you'll be given an address when you meet Commander Grey to collect the bikes. Ride there and get it done quickly," he hangs up. Well this is it our first mission, I go out into the workshop.

"Rob come into the office I need a word."

"What have I done now," he laughs as he hands his spanner to Sam.

"Charles just called we have to go to Paris tomorrow."

"Wow what are we doing?"

"The team are having trouble with a local bike gang and they want us to try and get them onside or they will have to be taken out."

"Cool we need to take bikes then."

"Nope, we fly from Bristol and we are being met at the airport in Paris with two Panigales."

"Nice I like this job already."

"Give Sam your keys and tell him to look after the place, I'm going home to see Molly I'll pick you up at five in the morning, OK."

"Ok bruv let's do this."

I kiss Molly goodbye and pick up my bag with my bike gear in it.

"See you soon babe."

"Be careful darling I love you."

"I love you too, don't worry I'll be back soon," she kisses me again and I head out to the car.

I put my bag into the boot and drive round to pick up Rob. After a few moments he comes out, puts his bag in the boot and climbs in.

"All set, any more idea what we're facing?"

"None at all, we'll find out when we meet Matt in a few hours."

The flight passes quickly; we collect our bags and walk out into the Paris sunshine. I'm busy scanning the causeway looking for bikes when a Frenchwoman takes my arm, "Follow me."

We head away from the terminal towards an office block, she is walking quickly and purposefully as we struggle behind with our bags. As we approach the building she heads down a ramp into an underground car park and leads us towards a black Renault Traffic van in the far corner. As we approach, Matt Grey gets out of the van and walks towards us.

"I hope you've had a pleasant trip, now for business."

"All good mate," answers Rob.

"What's the deal?" I ask.

"We are chasing a terrorist cell who are now holed up on the outskirts of Paris. Unfortunately their hideout is on the route a local bike gang use for their nightly street races."

"And you want us to stop them," interrupts Rob.

"Charles does, he wants you to get them onside. He thinks they might be useful later, Fiona and Stubbs just want to kill them."

"And you?" I ask.

"I just follow orders," he shrugs.

"How long have we got?"

"Two days, then we're going to have to move on them."

"Give us the bikes and a hotel and tell us where we can find them and let us get on with it then."

"Bikes are behind the van, you are staying at the Hotel Campanile in Saint Denis, take this envelope it has a map showing the route and photographs of the main players. You can contact me on the number inside. Good luck and remember you only have two days."

He gets back into the van with the French woman joining him and drives off, revealing two bright red Ducati 1299 Panigale's.

"Looks like we're changing in the car park," laughs Rob, "come on."

I unzip my bag and pull out my leathers, boots, helmet and a Kreiga rucksack. I kick off my trainers and jeans and climb into my leathers before packing everything back into my rucksack making sure the envelope is safe, Rob follows suit.

The bikes both have the keys in them so we fire them up and let them gently warm as we put on our helmets and gloves. Once we are both ready we ease out of the garage into the Paris traffic in search of our hotel. As we ride towards Saint Denis the general demeanour is less and less salubrious. We cross an area that can only be described as rough, then cross a junction and our hotel appears on the right. We park directly outside and dismount.

"Stay with the bikes, I'll check in and see if they have somewhere to park them," I say to Rob.

"Great idea I'm shit at French," Rob laughs.

I enter a standard looking hotel lobby and approach reception, a dark haired girl with the name tag 'Chloe' is sitting behind the desk.

"Bonjour erm un reservation?" I struggle with my schoolboy French.

"Yes Mr Sampson and Mr Sampson we've been expecting you," she answers in perfect English.

"You speak English well," I smile.

"It is one of seven languages I am fluent in I was told you have motorcycles, yes?"

"Yeah they are right outside."

"If you turn right and right again you will get to the underground garage at the back of the hotel," she produces some key cards, "This is for the garage and these are for your room. It is a twin room, number one hundred and twenty seven, is that OK?"

"Thank you very much, how do we get back from the garage?"

"There is a lift, you need to go to floor one. Is there anything else I can help you with?"

"No that's fine."

"Have a pleasant stay Mr Sampson," she smiles before returning to her computer screen.

I return outside to find Rob sitting on his bike smoking.

"Garage is round the back, come on finish that," I say as I put my helmet back on.

After parking the bikes we find our room, it contains two beds and a wardrobe and has an en-suite shower and toilet.

"It'll do for a couple of nights," says Rob as he throws his rucksack on the bed.

"We've slept in much worse places," I laugh as I pull the envelope out of my bag and spread the contents on the bed.

There are photographs of eight young Frenchmen, two of which have names on them, 'Pierre' and 'Francois'. There is a map which shows our hotel and a route a little further north marked in red, through some back streets. Lastly is a hand written note from Matt, which reads, 'We need them to co-operate with us tomorrow night so we can take down the terrorist cell who are holed up on Rue

Emile Cannay. If not we will take them out, you will find them in the car park of KFC just off Rue Gabriel Péri good luck'.

"Come on then I'm starving, I could go for a KFC," says Rob.

"Might as well I suppose, I've never been to KFC in France, I wonder if they have gravy."

We hear the sound of bikes revving before we even see the car park, I indicate left and pull in, Rob follows close behind. I park to the side of the lads revving their bikes and Rob pulls in beside me. A few of them come over to check out our bikes, they notice the English number plates and wait for us to take off our helmets.

"You English?"

"Yeah mate, are you French?" Rob smiles making them laugh.

"Nice bikes are they fast?"

"Faster than those heaps of shit," I gesture to their bikes in challenge.

"Ooh do you want to race?"

"Yeah why not but I need food first," smiles Rob.

"No, no, not now later, we will race later, we race every night come inside and eat," he claps Rob on the back and leads us inside. Rob emboldened by his new friends goes up to the counter and stares at the menu.

"Ey up love, I'll have a bucket of chicken and have you got any gravy?"

The young girl looks perplexed and answers, "Um gravy, non," with a shrug.

Rob looks back to the guy next to him a little lost now, "Sorry mate I didn't catch your name."

"I'm Pierre."

"Don't they have any gravy round here?"

"Ah gravy, it's a sauce no?"

"Ah sauce," the girl behind the counter says, "Barbecue, ketchup or curry?"

"No bloody gravy," Rob mutters, "Barbecue then."

"Frites?"

"Mm, oh you mean chips; yeah I'll have some of those and a coke."

She takes his order to the back and returns for mine.

"Un Box Master BBQ avec frites s'il vous plait."

"Bloody show off," mutters Rob, while the girl smiles.

"Parlez vous Francais?" Pierre asks.

"Un peu, a little," I answer, "But your English is better than my French."

"Non c'est bon," interrupts his friend offering his hand, "Francois."
"Dan," I reply taking it with a firm grip.
"Do you speak English mate?" Rob asks.
"But of course," he offers his hand to Rob, "Pleased to meet you."
"Cheers mate I'm Rob."
We collect our food and take a seat by the window; Pierre and Francois join us sipping at cokes while we eat.
"Are you alone or with a gang?" Francois asks.
"We're alone," I answer, "We're Hells Angels but the police took our chapter down so it's just us now." One of the other boys has wandered around to stand by our table.
"Ooh Hells Angels big scary bikers," and turns to his friends laughing. Quick as a flash Rob is off his seat and grabs him by the throat.
"Don't be taking the piss out of me boy or I'll fucking do you!" I see some of the others producing knives so I kick back my chair and stand up.
"Come on just a little fun," Francois raises his hands smiling.
"Tell your boys to put the knives away or we'll take you all down."
"That's big talk," says Pierre standing up.
"No, it's a warning get them to back off and Rob will let him go," Francois waves them to back away, Rob let's his victim go and sits down to finish his food.
"You really are not scared," Francois stares at us intently.
"No mate we've beaten bigger and better," says Rob between mouthfuls of food.
"Now tell us about this racing," I stare back.
"You really want to race us?"
"Yeah why not," I answer.
"Ok tonight, here at six o'clock, and its five hundred euro each," he sits back smiling.
"And what are you boys putting up?"
"We'll match it between us, winner takes all."
"You're on," smiles Rob, "bring the money with you."
"You think you are going to win?" Pierre asks.
"No, I know it," laughs Rob.
We'll see later," he smiles, "Come on boys let's ride." They all go outside and get on their bikes.
"Nice move," I grin at Rob, "that certainly broke the ice."
"Cheeky French twat," Rob retorts.

"You need to calm down, we're trying to get them onside."
"It'll be fine when we spank them later, come on let's find out if these bikes are any good."
We put on our helmets, mount up and head north out of Paris in search of some decent roads.
As we clear the outer reaches of the city we find some quieter roads, eventually leading to open countryside. In front Rob guns his bike, so I wind mine on in pursuit. The road ahead sweeps gently right so I pin the throttle, kicking through the gears using the quickshifter, watching the speed rise. I see the speedo hit one hundred and seventy five before braking hard for a left hander then I wind it on again, revelling in the sound of the Termigoni exhausts. It certainly has the power we just need some twisty stuff to see how it handles. That question is soon answered as we hit a series of switchbacks as tight as any race track hairpin. I scythe through, kneesliders kissing the tarmac with nothing else touching down. The French boys are going to have to be very good riders to beat us.
Rob indicates and pulls into a layby ahead so I follow. We park up and both light cigarettes.
"What do you reckon?" Rob asks.
"Nice mate, it's just a question of whether you can keep up and come second," I laugh.
"You couldn't bloody keep up then so you've no chance later. As for the French boys, they're toast."
"We'll see later, come on let's get back," we get back on the bikes and head back to the hotel.

CHAPTER THIRTY NINE

As we arrive back at the KFC car park at exactly six o'clock, someone is performing a huge burn out on a Ducati Diavel, shredding its monstrous rear tyre. I spot Francois and Pierre and park next to them with Rob pulling up beside me.

"All ready to race? I hope you've brought your money," says Pierre. I pull out a wad of notes from my leathers, wave them at him, then put them back in the inside pocket of my leathers.

"You won't be seeing that again," I laugh.

"Cocksure, hmm?"

"Nah I'll be taking it home have you got yours?" Rob smiles.

"Indeed," he pulls a wad of notes out of his own leathers.

"Come on we'll show you the route we don't want you crying an unfair advantage." He dons his helmet and climbs aboard a Kawasaki ZX10 R, which he definitely didn't have this afternoon. As we put our own helmets on I see Francois climb aboard a Yamaha YZF R1 which he also didn't have earlier. We head out of the car park and turn right, we turn right at the lights then almost immediately right again, half way up the street we stop.

"This is where we start, follow us, we won't be going fast, too much traffic now, just get a feel for it." We turn left at the end of the road then left again we follow the road across an intersection all the way to the end, a kink, a sharp left then a straight past the Art History museum. Two more sharp lefts are followed by a short straight; a sharp right precedes another straight then a sharp left and a switchback left. A left hand kink and a sharp right brings us back to the beginning, they stop and take off their helmets so we follow suit.

"Any questions?" Pierre asks.

"Yeah do you close the side roads?" I ask.

"As much as we can, but we can't stop everyone, there will be the odd car but most people know to stay away."

"And if someone crashes?" Rob asks.

"We clear out and call an ambulance," Francois shrugs, "We are all experienced riders none of us have crashed in over a year, so try not to hurt yourself English boy."

"Oh don't worry about me, you boys will have to go faster than you've ever been to beat me," Rob retorts.

"Enough," I step in, "let's do our talking in the race what time are we starting?"

"Around eight o'clock, the girls will be manning the junctions by then."

"Right let's get a decent coffee somewhere the stuff in KFC is shit," I laugh.

"That's true, come with us, there is a good coffee shop near the Art Museum," answers Pierre. We mount up and head off in search of espresso. We park up outside a little place called 'Chez Rochette' and find a table outside. The waitress comes out to take our orders and looks to Rob first; this amuses Francois and Pierre so I step in.

"Deaux espresso s'il vous plait," and raise my eyebrows at Pierre.

"Deaux cappuccino," he says gruffly.

"Excusez-moi grande s'il vous plait," I ask for large ones.

"Your French isn't too bad, you should learn more," smiles Francois.

"Schoolboy stuff and a few holidays, I can get by," I answer.

"Why don't you all speak bloody English," Rob grumbles.

"We do," laughs Pierre, "I just like to see you struggle."

"Bastard," mutters Rob.

"That's cannard in French," he laughs.

"Cannard," repeats Rob.

"Look he speaks French now," jokes Francois as the waitress arrives with our drinks.

"So do you boys just race and party?" I ask as I sip my drink.

"Mostly," Francois smiles, "but like your Hells Angels we deal drugs and other things."

"Do you deal guns?"

"Sometimes," he smiles.

"To terrorists?"

"No never, I would kill those bastards with my bare hands," he spits, "and you?"

"Nothing anymore, we got out, most of our lot are now in prison so we made our move at the right time," Rob answers.

"Pourquoi, sorry why?"

"We'd had enough," I take over, "Twenty years is a long time so we decided to live a normal life."

"What do you do now?"

"We run a motorbike tuning shop."

"Cool, did you tune your Ducati's?"

"Not yet they are new for this trip."

"Where are you heading?"

"Not sure yet, we'll see how much money we have after the race," I laugh.

"Come, it's time to race," we finish our drinks and get back on our bikes, and follow them back to the start. I notice them nodding to people in cars at every junction and notice a distinct lack of traffic on the roads. When we arrive there are about twenty bikes there and many more people milling around.

"Bloody hell," exclaims Rob, "How many are we racing?"

"Ah tonight," says Pierre, "just the four of us France against England."

"Do you want your bikes lining up or do you want to do it yourself?" Francois asks with a cigarette dangling from the corner of his mouth and a pretty girl draped on his arm.

"Carry on," I smile, lighting my own cigarette.

"It's going to be two laps," says Francois pointing to the line painted across the road, "First to cross the line on the second pass wins Ok."

"No worries," I turn to Rob, "Alright bruv?"

"Yeah all good, let's do this," he puts on his helmet and I do the same and we walk up to the bikes.

The French boys are bumping fists and laughing as they approach theirs. Rob climbs on his bike and fires it up then spins the back tyre creating a cloud of smoke. I close my eyes and zone out my surroundings, running through the course in my head, picturing where I can overtake if necessary. I open my eyes and climb on my bike, the last to do so. I start it up, knock it into gear and wait for the flag to drop.

The young girl holding the flag drops it with a flourish and four engines scream as we head for the first corner. We all brake hard, the other three spin up their back wheels and back their bikes in. I take a wider line, treating it as a double apex corner and trying to get the better drive onto the straight. Francois is first into the corner followed by Rob while I bring up the rear. At the second corner the others do the same while I cut a late apex and fire past them while they are still struggling for grip. I pull clear keeping the throttle wide open and feeding it gears as fast as I can. Soon I'm braking hard for the left hand bend. A right then a left and I'm passing the museum. A left and a right interspersed by two straights and I'm approaching the tight left-right-left section. I risk a quick glance behind to see Rob out dragging Francois with Pierre a few bike lengths further back. I flip-flop through the twisty section then a sharp right takes me back to the start. Lap two follows in much the same way, I can hear the other bikes close behind so I can't relax. As I take the left hander before the Museum I see a truck at the entrance and hope it will stop. It doesn't, I hit the brakes and slew around it losing precious seconds. Rob and Francois blast past before I'm back in control. I hit the next two bends in the wheel tracks of Francois who is stalking Rob. We fly through the tight left-right-left leaving only one corner left to make a move. Francois pulls to the inside of Rob and brakes late trying to out brake him, I hold off the brakes even longer and lunge up the inside of Francois. Three abreast we all slide the back wheels millimetres apart. I'm sliding across the front of Francois blocking his line. I pick up the bike and power it forward crossing the line in front. I glance back and see Rob pip Francois for second. I haul on the brakes and do a huge burnout in celebration, to the applause of the crowd. I park up and walk back to the others, Francois comes towards me his face like thunder. As he gets to me he breaks into a broad grin, hugs me and claps me on the back.

"You've got some balls man," he grins, "You didn't slide your bike the whole way round, you're quick but without that slide at the end I would have won what happened?"

"I know mate, whatever it takes to win," and I clap him on the back.

"These English boys are alright, now everyone back to my place for a party," Francois shouts to loud cheers.

"Where do you live?" I ask as we head back towards our bikes.

"Just around the corner, we park in the haulage yard across the road, they are on our payroll so it's safe for our bikes there."

We all get on our bikes and ride around the corner. As we park in the yard I notice a black Renault Traffic van which looks remarkably like the one Matt Grey was in earlier, but this time it's empty. As we cross the road I notice the street name and realise this is where the terrorists are holed up.

We go inside and sit down, Francois offers Rob and I a joint which we both take.

"You know," he sits back inhaling deeply, "that's the first time I've ever lost and you both beat me."

"I did warn you," laughs Rob, "I'm just pissed off you blocked me so I couldn't beat my brother!"

"You are brothers?" He asks, "You don't look alike."

"Nah," I jump in, "I got the looks and the brains," we all laugh while Rob scowls.

"Anyway this is yours," he pulls a wad of notes out of his pocket, "you won it fairly."

"Nah keep it but do me a favour instead," I ask.

"What do you want?" He sits forward his interest piqued.

"Some friends of ours are part of a Special Forces team hunting a terrorist cell."

"So how can I help?"

"They are holed up two houses away."

"Bastards, I will kill them myself," he leaps to his feet and picks up a gun.

"No they need them alive; they want you not to race tomorrow so they can get them out without casualties."

"Hmm," he muses for a moment, "I have a better plan get them to come and join the party, they can go through my attic. I escaped the police that way years ago before they were on our payroll." I pull out my phone and dial the number Matt left me earlier.

"Matt, what's happening Dan?"

"They are onside, in fact Francois will show you a way in through his attic, he wants you to come and join the party."

"We'll be there in a minute."

"I thought that was your van"

"You are as sharp as Charles says," and he hangs up.

A minute later Matt Grey works his way through the crowd outside followed by Fiona and Charlie.

"Dan, Rob," he nods at us then offers his hand to Francois, "I'm Matt Grey."

"Francois," he shakes his hand, "If I'd known there were terrorists I would have killed the bastards myself but Dan says you want them alive."

"We do, Dan says you can get us in through the roof what about the back?"

"No problem, shall we do it now?"

"I don't want any casualties so I don't want all these people around."

"Then we'll run another race, less suspicious that way."

"I like that idea, show me the back then call it."

"Ok," he leads Matt through the kitchen into a back yard, there are only low walls between the houses, we go back inside.

"People we are going to run another race," Francois announces to cheers from the crowd, "And no English boys this time," to much laughter.

"Vincente, Davide you will race with Pierre, five hundred euros to the winner," more loud cheers from the crowd.

Matt beckons Rob and I to follow him, so we do.

In the back of the van Shaun is monitoring a bank of screens in front of him. Stubbs and Craig are playing cards in the corner.

"Any movement?" Matt asks.

"None, all four of them are upstairs."

"Great, Craig come with me we are going in through the roof. Charlie and Fiona are taking the back. Stubbs, arm Dan and Rob, you three take the front and no movement until my signal." Craig gets out and Rob and I get in closing the door behind us.

"How have you boys been?" Stubbs asks as he hands us both guns.

"Great, we've been chilling at home," answers Rob, "how about you?"

"Argentina, Bolivia then here, if we take these bastards down we get some R and R."

We hear the sound of bikes roaring past then a crackling followed by Matts voice through the comms, "To the front now."

I pick up the Glock and follow Stubbs out. We sprint across the road as we hear a loud bang followed by a flash appearing at the upstairs window. Stubbs shoulders the front door and it splinters open on its hinges.

"All still upstairs proceed with caution," Shaun's voice comes over the comms.

"Don't fucking move," I hear Matt shout from upstairs as we check the downstairs is clear, Charlie comes out of the kitchen and nods to show it's clear, so we take the stairs two at a time.

"Where's Fiona?" Stubbs grunts.

"Went up the drainpipe daft bitch," is Charlie's response. By the time we get upstairs there are four figures lying face down, hands and feet bound by cable ties.

"Got the bastards," Francois grins.

"Cannards," says Rob and the three of us burst out laughing.

"What's this French shite," grumbles Stubbs.

"You wouldn't understand," I manage between laughs.

"How's it hanging sweet cheeks," Fiona appears.

"Is this your girl?" Francois looks bemused.

"He wishes," she shoots back.

"No, this lunatic is part of the team."

"I've called it in," says Matt, "Vans on its way. Dan, Rob, go back with Francois and wait until it's time to debrief."

"Ok mate," answers Rob as we all leave.

We are sitting in Francois's living room and he is looking a little confused.

"I thought you guys were ex Hells Angels and you run a tuning shop?"

"We are," I respond, "but we help these guys out when we're needed."

"How did that happen?"

"We knew the boss when he was undercover and he recruited us," my comms buzzes on the table so I pick it up and listen.

"Guys come over to the van and bring Francois."

"Come on debrief time and they want you to come," I nod to Francois.

As we cross the road there are two black vans surrounded by armed soldiers outside the other house.

We cross the street and I knock on the van and the door opens. Charles greets us as Francois stares in awe at the array of screens.

"Come on in and sit down," as we do I make the introductions.

"Charles, Francois."

"I know of you but I'm pleased to meet you."

"How do you know of me?"

"We know about most illegal activity but if you are prepared to help us from time to time we can overlook most things."

"Then I have no choice, but can I say I did it because I like these two, but also because I love France."

"Thank you," Charles smiles, "I'm sure both they and I will come and see you shortly but if you could leave us for now," he climbs out of the van and closes the door.

"Well done team a successful mission completed, Dan, Rob, you weren't involved throughout but you performed well when necessary. The rest of you, well done take some time off."

"You keep saying team," pipes up Charlie, "but we ought to have a name."

"Funny you should mention it but upstairs have named us already."

"What is it?" Matt asks.

"Tactical Warfare Anti-Terrorist Section."

"You are fucking joking?" Stubbs bursts out laughing, "Have you worked out the acronym?"

"TWATS," Rob guffaws, "what about Tactical Intelligence Terrorist Squad?"

"Or Advanced Search Squad," I join in.

"Hmm, maybe not then, any suggestions?" Charles asks.

"What about United Nations Intelligence Team," Matt suggests.

"UNIT I like it," Stubbs agrees.

"I'll take it upstairs but once they realise their original cock up I'm sure they'll approve it. Now disappear for a few weeks you deserve it."

"Charles, how are we getting back, the plane tickets were only one way," I ask.

"Ah yes," he reaches into his pocket, "Here are the log books, keep the bikes and ride them home."

"Bollocks I'd have been more careful with it if I knew I was keeping it," laughs Rob.

"Come on, let's go and see Francois then get back to the hotel, we've got a long ride tomorrow."

I knock on Francois's door, he opens it and we follow him inside, Pierre is already there.

"So are you heading home now?"

"Yes mate we've got lives to get back to."

"It's been our pleasure to meet you, we will visit you soon if that's OK?"

"Of course it is, I'm getting married soon. Why don't you both come over for the wedding?"

"That would be cool but we would like you to tune our bikes."

"Rob can do them just as well as me so come anytime," I hand them both a card, shake their hands and bid them both goodnight. Rob and I mount up and set off into the cool Parisian night.

CHAPTER FORTY

The two Ducati's are booming as we ride back into Hanley, it's now six o'clock in the evening and it's been a long day. Rob waves as he turns off for home; I carry on to the Red Lion and pull into the car park. As I get off I can see faces at the window wondering who it is, so I leave my helmet on and walk in.

Molly shrieks as I remove my helmet, "Oh baby you're back," and rushes over to kiss me.

"Where did that bike come from?" She asks still hugging me tightly.

"Perks of the job, Rob's got one as well."

"How did it go?"

"All good, mission accomplished."

"Wow that was quick."

"Well when you have the best," I manage before she slaps me.

"No one likes a show off."

"You do," and I receive another slap for my trouble.

"Watch it, I'm glad you're home I've missed you."

"I'm just gonna put the bike away then get out of my leathers it's been a long ride."

As I turn I see Sam sitting in the corner, "How's it been?"

"All good boss, I got the Fireblade out, I've made a start on the ZX 10 R, a bloke called about a Harley I've taken his number and I'm going to pick up Janet's bike tomorrow."

"Well done Sam, you've done a good job," he beams with pride, "How are you getting to Bristol tomorrow?"

"Janet is driving me."

"What time?"

"Ten o'clock is that OK?" Janet says from the bar.

"That's fine, I'll grab a lift if that's OK, my car is still at the airport."

"No problem Dan."

"Oh and Andy Smith called, he's booked a day at Castle Combe next week, I said you guys would be in touch," Sam smiles.

"I'll ring him in the morning and speak to him, did he speak to you about racing?"

"No why?"

"He's offered you the chance to work with the race mechanics on race weekends."

"Wow really which race?"

"All of them, if you want."

"That's awesome," then his face drops, "But what about my job with you?"

"It's fine, I've spoken to him about it and if we need you, you'll have to stay. Other than that I think it'll be good for your education but if you decide to go to the Isle of Man for TT fortnight it will have to be holiday OK."

"What I can go to the TT?"

"Yeah but don't get too excited you'll be working a lot."

"It doesn't matter that's fantastic," he grins and rushes off to tell his mum.

Molly and I are lying in bed and she's probing me about the mission.

"I can't go into details but let's just say there's one terrorist cell less in the world."

"Ok darling but why did they need you?"

"They were having trouble with a French bike gang."

"Ha and you and Rob turned up and beat them up!"

"Nah we raced them then made friends with them, I've invited two of them to the wedding."

"Is that allowed?"

"What inviting them to the wedding?"

"You know what I mean, making friends with them."

"Yeah that's why we were there, they're good guys, they helped us out in the end and the team may even use them again."

"What are they called?"

"Francois and Pierre."

"Ooh proper French men what are they like?"

"French blokes with bikes," I get another slap, before we snuggle up and go to sleep.

Janet is singing along to the radio as we head down the M5 towards Bristol, nodding her head along to Bon Jovi's 'Living on a Prayer'.

"Do you mind if I look at a bike while we're there," Sam asks from the back seat.

"I'll help you choose," smiles Janet, they've got a nice purple Harley in."

"I was thinking of getting something smaller," Sam answers taking her seriously.

"What are you fancying?" I ask.

"I really want an R1 after working on them but I can't afford the insurance and it would have to be restricted so I want to look at the Ninja 250."

"Tell you what, I'll come with you I can pick up my car afterwards." Janet goes off to sort out all the paperwork for her new bike so Sam and I have a look around the showroom.

"How much are you looking to spend?"

"Depends on what they offer me for trade in."

"Let's find a salesman," I attract the attention of a young lad wearing a name tag revealing his name is Brad.

"Hi Brad, Sam here is interested in a Ninja 250 but wants to know what you'll give him in part-ex."

"Come over to my desk and we'll have a look."

After fifteen minutes of keyboard tapping and negotiation on my part, we come to a deal, Sam's bike in trade in and twelve hundred pounds.

"How much will that be on finance?" Sam asks.

"Forget that mate," I say to Brad.

"But I can't afford to do it any other way," Sam protests.

"Yes you can," I pull out my card and hand it to Brad then say to Sam, "Fifty pounds a month for the next two years out of your wages."

"You're the best boss ever," he stands up and hugs me.

"So am I processing this?" Brad looks miffed at the loss of commission on the finance.

"Yes mate put it through."

Rob and I are waiting for Sam to arrive; we gave him the morning off to collect his new bike. It's a Kawasaki Ninja 250 in bright green. He's been like a kid waiting for Christmas the last couple of days. The sound of a bike outside heralds his arrival, he pulls into the workshop, parks up and take's off his helmet beaming broadly.

"You like it then?" Rob asks.

"Yeah it's fantastic I was sat on the M5 and opened it up and it got to ninety and it was still pulling!"

"Ooh fast then," mocks Rob.

"Yeah I'll be able to come out with you lot now," he says triumphantly.

"I'll go out with you," I say feeling sorry for him.

"I bloody corner at ninety!" Rob is still mocking.

"Well I love it," Sam proclaims as he heads off to his toolbox.

CHAPTER FORTY ONE

I'm in the kitchen with Molly having my pre stag party breakfast. I've got scrambled eggs on toast, to line my stomach for the oncoming alcoholic onslaught.

"Do you know where you are going?"

"No idea, I've kept out of it all I know is it involves a coach, beer and some sort of fancy dress, which I'm being presented with this morning."

"Oh Jesus god help you darling," she laughs.

"On a serious note I've been thinking."

"This sounds ominous," she half laughs.

"No, I think we ought to buy a house, maybe let one of the barmaids rent the flat."

"Hmm let me think about it. Have you seen somewhere?"

"The old Rectory is up for sale."

"But that's gonna be expensive."

"It's not as though I'm short of a few quid, the business is going well and I've got an income from the team as well."

"I suppose darling, let me think about how it would work with the pub."

"Ask one of the barmaids to be manager and let them have the flat as payment and take a step back. We're looking at taking someone else on so we can have some time off."

"What would I do?"

"Holidays, talking of which I've booked the honeymoon."

"Ooh where are we going?"

"It's a surprise but it'll be warm."

"That's no help, as we've got a heatwave at the moment. I'll tell you what, I'll book a viewing on the Rectory and we can think about it after the wedding."

"Ok babe," my phone pings with a text, "Wish me luck babe they are outside."

"I'm coming down I've got to see this."

I open the front door of the pub to be greeted by Allun and Rob dressed as 'Fatman and Blobbin' sort of like Batman and Robin in sumo suits.

"Come in," I laugh.

"This is yours," laughs Rob holding out a bag.

"I'm scared to look."

"Come upstairs darling let's get you ready."

"You know what it is?"

"Oh yes."

Rob and Allun are waiting patiently when Molly returns to the bar, "Come on it's not that bad," she giggles. I wander into the bar sulkily, I'm dressed in pink tights and a pink tutu and sporting a long curly pink wig. Molly has applied bright pink lipstick and eyeshadow to my face and made me wear one of her bras stuffed with socks.

"Ooh darling do you fancy a drink?" Allun quips.

"Get together, I need a picture," Molly demands. We shuffle together then just as Molly is ready with the camera Allun grabs my bum and I yelp in surprise.

"Oh that's priceless," laughs Molly showing us the picture, "I've got to have that behind the bar."

A horn honks, the coach has arrived, and so we troop outside and climb aboard.

"Give us a kiss darling," PJ puckers up as I pass.

"Where have you got your wallet?" Steve asks.

"Oh bugger I forgot it."

"Typical woman, no money," quips Pete.

"If I'd known I would have got you to iron my shirt," John joins in.

"Bugger off you lot, let's find some beer."

"Sit down then we've got an hour to go," shouts John.

"Why where the bloody hell are we going?" I ask.

"Weston Super Mare," Allun answers.

"We're meeting the Smith's racing boys," adds Sam.

The coach pulls up on the seafront and we all file off. PJ, dressed as Elvis, is in front of me.

"Come on boys let's have a good drink today weyhay," followed by, "Ey John what have you come as, a bloody tramp?"

"No you daft bastard, I'm John Wayne."

"You best get over there with Fatman then, cause he's Bruce Wayne," to many groans.

"Right then where to first?"

"Follow me, I know this place like the back of my hand," shouts PJ then pointing at the floor, "Look there's a mole."

"That's not a mole it's a hedgehog," responds Jack, dressed as Dracula. Somehow I think this is going to be a long day.

We settle into the Crown a couple of streets back from the seafront and as the beer flows the banter continues.

"What are you having darling, Babycham?" Jack shouts from the bar.

"No you old bugger I'll have a gin and tonic," I shout back entering the spirit, "I'm a classy bird."

"Ooh get you," shouts Pete.

"I'm going outside for a minute, the Smith's boys have arrived I'm going to meet them," Sam has come as a sheikh; he's wearing a bed sheet with a tea towel on his head.

He arrives back with Andy Smith and his mechanics Dave, Fred and Simon. They are all wearing matching football kits.

"We've come as a five-a-side team," Andy announces.

"There's only four of you, stupid bastard," shouts John.

"Slow down mate we've got another one," he opens the door and I immediately recognise the newcomer.

"Who are you the sub?" Pete shouts.

"Shut up," I get up and walk over to shake his hand, "This lad is Ian Crookes, winner of this year's Senior TT." A reverent hush falls around the bar. Ian shakes my hand then breaks the silence.

"Get me a pint Fred I'm spitting bloody feathers." With a loud cheer he has instantly been accepted by the group.

By mid-afternoon it's been decided that we need to get some food so we head for the seafront in search of fish and chips. We drift into smaller groups as people decide on different food.

"Remember Barmouth?" Allun walks up giggling, "Shall we?"

"Let's get everyone and we'll all go on together."

We eventually round everyone up and join the queue for the rollercoaster. As we near the front PJ shouts, "How many does it hold mate?"

"Four in a car how many of you are there?"

"One, two, three," he does a quick headcount, "Nineteen."

"Yeah no worries, that's five cars mate."

We soon draw a crowd especially when Elvis starts serenading us, with Dracula and John Wayne joining in the chorus.

We adjourn to another pub, The Bell this time. As we settle in, Dave one of the mechanics comes over to me.

"Sorry to talk shop on your stag do but have you got a minute?"

"Yeah what's up?"

"Andy mentioned you might be looking for another mechanic."

"Why do you know someone?"

"I'm interested, the commute would be a bit further but I'm having to quit the race team as my wife is pregnant."

"Ok what are you earning now?"

"Twenty six grand."

"Look I've seen you work, let me have a chat with Rob and I'll let you know," I wander over to Rob who is sat with Sam.

"Dave wants to come and work for us what do you guys think?"

"Yeah he's a good guy," says Rob but what about all the time he spends with the race team?"

"He's quitting his wife is pregnant."

"In that case, go for it."

"What do you think Sam?"

"Whoa, do I get a say?"

"Of course we're a team."

"Thanks and yeah I like him, obviously I'll have to teach him a few things though," he laughs.

"Ok I'll tell him, are you happy for me to negotiate wages?" I ask Rob.

"Crack on bruv."

"I've spoken to the guys," I say to Dave, "and yeah we'll take you on, what time scale are we looking at?"

"I've got a week's notice at work and we are already training my replacement on the race team so is two weeks ok?"

"Sounds good," and as I shake his hand, "Welcome aboard."

"Thanks," he smiles, "Sorry to ask but I presume you'll match my wages."

"Well I thought given the commute and with the baby on the way, I can offer you thirty grand and four weeks holiday?"

"That's awesome, thanks Dan," he shakes my hand, "I've got to ring my wife she'll be chuffed to bits."

"No worries," I smile, "When you've called her go and a have a chat with Rob and Sam."

"Of course and thank you so much," he beams.

Andy Smith comes over as Dave rushes outside to call his wife.

"I take it you've offered him a job then."

"Yeah thanks for the recommendation."

"He's a good guy and I hate losing him but at least this way he's still involved."

"We'll let you have Sam every race weekend now we've got Dave."

"What the fuck are you looking at knobhead?" PJ breaks the drunken calm. I look round to see three young lads squaring up to him.

"I'll knock the lot of you out," PJ takes up a boxer's stance.

"I don't know what's going on boys," I say as I walk over, "but look around the pub every single one of us is with this fine drunken gentleman. So as it's my stag do I suggest you either calm down and have a drink with us or fuck off before you get hurt." They eye me suspiciously, and then burst out laughing.

"I can't believe we've just been threatened by a pink fairy, fair play mate we'll have a drink with you," then turning to PJ, "Sorry man."

"OK, but he's a ballerina," PJ grins and the calmness returns.

"Drink up boys the coach is here," shouts Pete.

I say goodbye to Ian Crookes and all the Smith's boys then file out with the rest to board the coach. Matt and Josh get on carrying a horrible looking drink in a plastic glass.

"We've got you a special pint for you to drink we can't have you going home sober."

"Down in one, down in one," the entire coach starts to chant.

I take the glass and chug it down until it's finished, loud cheers erupt around the coach.

We arrive back at the Red Lion and I'm feeling very much worse for wear. I stagger off the coach and wobble towards the entrance, listing at a forty five degree angle and almost bent double, trying not to fall over.

"Come on chief let me give you a hand," Allun straightens me up and helps me inside. Molly and her friends are sat around the bar.

"Oh my god what have you done to him?" Molly yells.

"Nothing to do with me, they gave him a dirty pint so he drank it."

"Of course he did, bloody idiot!"

"Do you want a hand putting him to bed?"

"Thanks that would be great."

I drift off into blackness with my head spinning wildly.

CHAPTER FORTY TWO

The day of my wedding and the Gloucestershire sun is already blazing, it looks like the weather is going to be kind to us. I spent the night at Allun's while Lucy stayed with Molly. To continue the tradition of not seeing the bride before the wedding, I'm taking Sally to the registry office while Molly is riding pillion with Rob.

"Nervous mucker?" Allun asks.

"I'm fine mate what could possibly go wrong."

"Here get that down you," he passes me some toast.

"Beicars am byth," he says to me as I eat my toast.

"What the fuck does that mean?" I ask.

"Bikers for life!"

"Beicars am byth" I repeat, "Look I've spoken to Rob about this and I want you to be my best man this afternoon as Rob and Sally are being witnesses this morning."

"Really?" he gives me a hug, "That means a lot Dan, I love you mate."

We park the bikes in the car park in the centre of Gloucester and make the short walk to the registry office. I go inside to check in then return outside smoking and pacing while waiting for Molly. She finally appears looking radiant as she laughs and jokes with Rob, she hugs me and gives me a kiss.

"Ok darling?"

"Yeah babe, are you?"

"God yeah, this is not the real wedding, I'll be nervous later though," as we go inside.

"Dan Sampson and Molly Hopkins," the receptionist calls, so the six of us get up and follow her into an ante room. The registrar gets up and introduces himself.

"Daniel Freeman nice to meet you is this everyone?"

"Yes we're having a big wedding in a fairground this afternoon this is just the legal bit," says Molly.

"In that case let's get on with it then."

Within half an hour we are all gathered outside, legalities over.

"Rob, can you hang on a bit I need a lipstick," Molly asks.

"And I need eyeshadow," says Lucy.

"I'll drop Sally off then I need to go to the workshop," I say, "I'll catch you boys in a while."

I let myself into the workshop as we are closed today, come to think of it so is most of Hanley. I make a drink and get out the polish to give the Manx Norton another clean, as it's going to be my wedding transport. As I polish I let my mind wander and reflect on the changes in my life over the last couple of years. I've gone from the brink of self-destruction to a happy place. I'm stirred from my reverie by the sound of my mobile ringing, I glance at the screen it's my mum.

"Ey up Mother what's up?"

"Where are you? We are sat outside the Red Lion pub but there's no one there."

"I'm in the workshop down the road come on down, just follow your nose and it's on the left."

I hear a car arrive so I go outside to meet them; my dad has brought his old Mercedes SL 500 convertible down. My mother gets out first and kisses me on the cheek.

"How are you Son?" She asks, "and how's your brother?"

"We're both fine and settling into normal lives."

"It's about time you boys grew up, you always worried me."

"Alright son," my dad shakes my hand.

"Yes Dad I see you've brought the old Merc out."

"I thought you might need a wedding car."

"Thanks, but the boys are arriving on motorbikes, come inside and I'll show you mine," but at that moment the trucks carrying the fairground rides start to arrive.

"Go into the office, I'll be a minute while I get these organised." I go up to the lead truck and speak to the driver.

"Past the farmhouse mate and into the meadow everything needs to revolve around the Waltzer."

"What time's the wedding?"

"Five o'clock but I need it all running by half three at the latest."

"No problem mate we'll be done well before then."

I go into the workshop to find my dad admiring the Manx Norton, "Is this yours?"

"Yeah, I restored it."

"Nice job, I had one of these when I met your mother but she made me get rid of it and buy a car."

"I never knew that."

"Oh god, I was a right tearaway as a kid your mum always says that's where you boys get it from."

"Well bloody hell Dad."

"Where are we staying?" Mum interrupts.

"With my mate Allun you'll like him."

A crunching on the drive heralds more arrivals. Rob and Allun come through the door.

"Ey up Mum, Dad, I see you've got the old wreck out."

"Cheeky bugger," my dad shakes his hand while my mum offers her cheek for a kiss.

"Mrs Sampson," Allun steps in and kisses her cheek, "It's a pleasure to meet you."

"Oh you're a nice polite boy," my mother flushes as she affects her best accent.

"You're staying with me, shall I take you to my house and show you your room."

"That would be lovely thank you," then turning to Dad, "Come on Roger I need to freshen up."

I'm standing in Allun's living room dressed in a baby pink shirt, black drainpipe jeans and black boots.

"Looking good mucker," Allun is similarly attired except for a white shirt, "You ready?"

"Yeah come on let's go," we don our Brando style leather jackets and open faced helmets and go out to the bikes. Rob arrives on a 1968 Triumph Bonneville he has hired for the occasion. Allun has borrowed Bill's Sunbeam S8 for the day. We ride slowly through the middle of Hanley. Many of the people making their way to the wedding wave as we trundle past. As we pass the farmhouse Bill comes out in his old army uniform.

"I thought I'd make an effort is this ok?"

"That's awesome Bill," I wave to him as we ride towards the waltzer and park the bikes by it. A crowd soon forms around us as I glance at my watch, quarter past four so I go up to Sam.

"Get Matt and Josh and clear a path so Molly and the girls can come through when they arrive get everyone behind the hay bales."

He goes off happily to help when the buzz of cheery chatter is broken by the sound of approaching Harley's. I squint against the sun to see who is coming.

Twelve Harley's enter the meadow and fan out before parking up. As they get off their bikes I realise it's the Edinburgh Rats, this doesn't look good.

"We heard you Sampson boys were having a party so we thought we'd come and play," grins Bonzo, their leader.

"Invite only dickhead," shoots Rob bunching his fists, "So fuck off before I come over."

"Still talking bollocks I see," Bonzo pulls out a pistol and fires it in the air causing the crowd to duck and scream.

"Look boys you fucked with the Angels now you're gonna pay," more weapons are produced as they start forward menacingly. I step forward, Allun and Rob joining me. Suddenly Pete, PJ, Sam, Matt and Josh are with us, I look around.

"Thanks boys this might get nasty!"

A roar of engines can suddenly be heard approaching and moments later two black Range Rovers slew through the entrance to the meadow. The doors fly open and the members of the UNIT team emerge, spreading out behind the Hells Angels.

"Hello boys," grins Fiona almost flirtatiously.

"Who the fuck are you bitch?" Bonzo snarls.

"Your worst nightmare lover," she fires back.

He raises his gun pointing it in their direction, "I suggest you leave before you get hurt darling it's the Sampson boys we're after."

"Oh ok," Fiona ducks back inside the Range Rover re-appearing moments later holding a flame thrower.

"Come and play with mama," as she fires a flame in their direction, "I like my sweetbreads cooked."

Stubbs, Charlie and Craig produce AK 47's and take aim at the Hells Angels.

"I suggest you boys get on your bikes and ride up the road to the nice police officers who are waiting to arrest you," Matt suggests firmly.

"And leave your weapons behind;" demands Charlie, "We don't want you giving uniform any trouble. They take the hint and trudge forward dropping their weapons in front of the Range Rovers. Fiona looks around mischievously and points her flamethrower at the last Harley, she lets the flame play over it causing it to crackle and pop then explode!

"Oops," she grins, "It looks like one of you girls is riding side saddle."

As the Hells Angels leave I walk over to the team, "Thanks guys, I thought they were going to ruin my wedding."

"Not on our watch," Stubbs shakes my hand.

"Looking good sweet cheeks," mocks Fiona, "Where's the lucky lady?"

"Good question," I look at my watch, "She was due fifteen minutes ago."

"If she's anything like the lady I am she'll make a grand entrance."

"You're no lady," banters Stubbs.

"You should see me in a dress lover, you'll be drooling," she retorts.

The distant sound of approaching cars heralds Molly's arrival.

"Come on guys let's get into place," I shout.

Charles is performing the celebrant duties as his status as a Naval Commander entitles him. He joins Allun and I on the steps of the waltzer as a white Rolls Royce Silver Cloud convertible approaches, followed by two white BMW X5's. Molly's dad, dressed in teddy boy drapes, gets out and helps Molly from the rear of the car. She looks stunning dressed in a white 1950's dress, with a cinched waist and flowing petticoat underneath. The two X5's disgorge a gaggle of bridesmaids, they vary in ages but are all wearing matching 50's dresses in a pale purple. Molly's dad hands her a bouquet and the bridesmaids line up behind.

The band starts to play 'You're the Best Thing' by the Style Council as they make their way towards the waltzer. Allun steps down and helps everyone to climb the steps. Once we are all assembled Charles raise his hand to quell the chatter. Calm eventually ensues as I gaze into Molly's eyes and we both smile.

"Thank you all for coming today to witness the joining together of Dan and Molly in Matrimony."

"Yey," a voice comes from the crowd which is quickly silenced.

"I have known Dan for many years and you are lucky to have him as part of your community as he is lucky to be here," I nod in thanks as he continues.

"Molly is at the heart of Hanley, as you all know and I have found her to be a special person," he turns to Allun, "The rings please." Allun produces two rings from his inside pocket and hands them to each of us.

Charles places Molly's hand within mine then turns to me, "Dan please repeat after me. I solemnly promise."

"I solemnly promise."

"To love cherish and honour you."

"To love cherish and honour you," I repeat.

"I give you my body and soul today and in all eternity."

"I give you my body and soul today and in all eternity."

"I take you Molly as my wedded wife."

"I take you Molly as my wedded wife," I slip the ring onto her finger.

"Now Molly," he turns to face her, "repeat after me. I solemnly promise."

"I solemnly promise," she repeats.

"To love cherish and honour you."

"To love cherish and honour you."

"To remind you I am always right," a titter goes up from the crowd.

"To remind you I am always right," she smiles.

"I give you my body and soul today and in all eternity."

"I give you my body and soul today and in all eternity."

"I take you Dan as my wedded husband."

"I take you Dan as my wedded husband," and she slips a ring onto my finger.

"You may now kiss the bride." Which I promptly do to raucous cheering from the assembled crowd. I sweep Molly off her feet and place her into one of the waltzer cars as the band starts to play 'You're the One That I Want' from the film Grease.

Allun, Charles and the bridesmaids fill the remaining cars and the ride begins. Rob, PJ and Pete jump up and start to spin the cars wildly with every one cheering, dancing and singing along. When the ride comes to an end I help Molly off the ride and she raises her hands for quiet.

"I want to thank everyone for coming. The stalls have food, help yourselves. Now let's have a bloody good party."

The band strike up 'We Go Together' again from the film Grease, as everyone scatters towards the various rides and food stalls and of course the very large beer tent.

At midnight I announce we are leaving to get changed before we go to the airport for our honeymoon.

"Where are you off to?" Sally asks.

"I have no idea," Molly replies smiling dreamily, "but as long as I'm with my man it'll be perfect."

"We're going to St Lucia," I say to put her out of her misery as I help her into the Rolls. I climb in beside her and she snuggles into my chest.

"It's been a perfect day I love you."

"I love you too Mrs Sampson and this just the first day of the rest of our lives."

"It's been one hell of a ride so far," she smiles up at me.

"That's the story of my life," I laugh.

"You should write a book about it."

"One day maybe I will."

THE END

Printed in Great Britain
by Amazon